THE RELIC

Book 1 of The Labyrinth

BILL COULTON

REVISED EDITION, SEPTEMBER 2012

ISBN: 0615642640
ISBN 13: 9780615642642

Printed by CreateSpace, a part of Amazon.com Group of Companies.

Other books by Bill Coulton

The Sea Siren, Book 2 of The Labyrinth

The Minotaur, Book 3 of The Labyrinth

Escape to Lisbon

Stalker

Acknowledgements and Special Thanks

The author is indebted to mentors and colleagues at the Army Intelligence School, Ft. Riley, Kansas; to the team at 44th Strategic Intelligence Detachment (Pentagon) at Third Army Headquarters, Fort McPherson, Georgia; and, to all those fine men and women who served in overt and covert intelligence roles with the U.S. Army Security Agency, European Headquarters, Frankfurt, Germany. It was my privilege to be part of the intelligence-gathering enterprise at a critical time in the history of the United States. It enabled me to gain a perspective on the large and small events of our time and provided me with many of the skills required to succeed in life following my service in the United States Army and the United States Air Force Reserve. For these opportunities, I am eternally grateful. In particular, I wish to thank Colonel William Smith, Retired Commander, 44th SID, U.S. Army for his generous mentoring and friendship.

For Lucie

With appreciation and admiration for the person she is.

THE RELIC

A Novel

By

Bill Coulton

*"You never know what is enough unless you
know what is more than enough."*

From Plate 9, The Marriage of Heaven and Hell
by William Blake

Chapter 1

Fatherly Advice

Easy Ed Blakely smiled at his image in the mirror of the barrack room. New charcoal flannel pants with a buckle in back, new Oxford cloth button-down with black and red regimental tie, a vertical striped gray tweed jacket from Ely's, cordovan wingtip Florsheim shoes, and London Fog trench coat. "You are something else, tonight, man," he whispered at his image. "Lookout *frauleins!*"

He smoothed his blond hair and pulled in his stomach, extending his height to a full six one. "Yes, sir, Sergeant Blakely, you are looking sharp tonight."

He strode down the stairs two at a time and joined about twenty-five other new arrivals to Frankfurt for a briefing by First Sergeant Samuel Easterling in the lounge outside the Orderly Room at the *Gutleut Kaserne.* Easterling was already pacing back and forth, appearing to be building up a head of steam for his five-minute lecture. At six four, two hundred-fifty pounds, the old graybeard was still a formidable obstacle, if you tried to be cute with him. Thirty years of gold service stripes ran up the arm of his Ike jacket. His shiny pate belied his years. The left breast of his jacket was a mountain of ribbons capped by the blue and silver infantrymen's badge and silver paratrooper's badge.

He was what Blakely recognized as the last of a breed: a no-nonsense, tight-assed, usually divorced, career non-commissioned officer, who lived and breathed olive drab. One of the old school from before World War II. The kind who earned his stripes because he was the toughest but not necessarily the brightest guy in his out-fit. Cross him and you were mincemeat.

Easterling checked his clipboard. "Everyone here that's going out tonight?"

1

The men looked around and mumbled "Yes, Sergeant."

"Line up in front of the pool table. Let me see a straight line."

The men shuffled into a reasonable facsimile of a curved line.

"Okay, men, listen up. I realize this is your first night out in Germany. Many of you want some German nookie. As the NCO in charge of this barrack, I must advise you to stay the hell away from the whores. As a member of the United States Army and representing your country in a foreign land, those whores are not worthy of your consideration. By going to bed with one of 'em, you're disrespecting the uniform of the United States Army and your fellow soldiers. Do you understand that?"

The men mumbled "Yes, Sergeant."

"Besides that, you get into any trouble on my watch and you'll find yourselves in deep shit. So deep your career in this man's army is kaput. Is that clear?

The men mumbled "Yes, Sergeant."

"Unfortunately, many of you will ignore my advice. Some of you will get rolled tonight, lose all your money, get beat up. Others of you will get drunk, end up in fights, and find your asses in the city jail or the post stockade or in some damned hospital. A few of you will get the clap or worse… So, don't be crawlin' back to me, asking me to help you outta the mess you make. I won't do it. Count on it. You're on your own when you walk outta that door tonight. Is that understood?

The men mumbled "Yes, Sergeant."

Easterling paced back and forth, looking directly into the eyes of every man. The only way to avoid eye contact, Blakely figured, was to concentrate on the large wart on the right side of Sarge's face. It worked.

"Judging by the looks on your faces, my words don't mean a God damn thing to you. You're bent on raising some hell tonight, aren't you? Behaving very differently than you'd behave back in the old forty-eight. Isn't that right, men?"

The men mumbled admixtures of Yeses and Nos.

Easterling's voice softened.

"Well, gentlemen, let me give you some fatherly advice—same as I'd give my own son if he were in your shoes. Stay together, in groups of at least two. Don't go off by yourselves. Take no mor'n $30 in German *marks* with you. Don't use dollars in the bars or with the women. Why? You'll be missing your wallet before you can say shit. Know this: the American dollar is the most sought after currency in the world—and 'specially here, where basic items are still being rationed. Unless you didn't know it, our good ole American dollar is the currency of choice on the black market. So it is in your best interest to keep it outta the hands of the nationals. Is this understood?"

The men mumbled "Yes, Sergeant."

"If you are smart, you'll change your money into *marks* before you board the *strassenbahn*. Remember, thirty dollars equals 120 *marks*—four to the dollar. You are rich by German economy standards. I suggest you limit the mark denominations to small amounts. Ya don't want to flash a 100 *mark* note in a bar or when you're with a woman. Especially now, just three weeks before Christmas. They'd love to have some extra cash for the holidays."

"The safest places to find nookie are a few clubs on *Romer Platz*. They're all right together. You can't miss 'em. One of the best is the American Bar. The women there are clean, licensed, and checked by a doctor once a week. Nevertheless, it goes without saying that you should use a condom. You can obtain these at the Post Exchange. Otherwise, there's a good chance you'll get VD. Worse, you make the girl pregnant and have to deal with that. A pregnant *fraulein* will cost you plenty in money and heartache. And in case you are wondering, Frankfurt is surrounded by orphanages brimming over with GI-sired kids. You don't need to add babies to that population.

"The cost of a lay shouldn't exceed 80 *marks*—and that is high. Most go for between 40 and 60 *marks*. I can't stress enough: Don't mess with the prostitutes on the streets or in the parks—'specially *Rothschild Park*. The women there are full of diseases. Some are older than your mothers. They are old whores left over from the war. They're unlicensed. They like to take you to bed with the intention of robbing you, or worse. Is all this understood?"

The men mumbled "Yes, Sergeant."

"Do you have any questions?"

The men mumbled "No, Sergeant."

"Well, then, get the hell outta here and have a good time. But watch your step. Take care of each other. I sure as hell don't wanna hafta file any reports tomorrow morn'n on any of you."

The men hustled out the door into the cold, chuckling and talking in low tones. Blakely stayed back and followed Easterling into the Orderly Room.

"Sarge, I'm supposed to meet a friend of mine at *Meir's Bavarian Garten.* Can you tell me which *strassenbahn* I should take?"

Easterling turned and gazed into Blakely's face. "Be careful down there. You don't need a trolley. Walk out the gate, turn left, and keep going until you see the *Hauptbahnhof* on your left, the *Schumann* Building on the right. Turn right on *Fredrich-Ebert Strasse* and go half a block up the street. It's on your right."

"Thanks, Sarge. By the way, just out of curiosity, how do you meet regular women over here?"

Easterling scratched his bald head and grinned. "Ain't nobody ever asked me that one before. Certainly not in the bars and clubs. I guess it's just like in the states. Nice girls go to church or waitress or work in bakeries and the like. There's plenty of nice *frauleins.* You just hafta meet 'em in the daytime. Most of 'em would love to nail a GI for a husband. But go slow… Some of 'em just want a free ticket to the old forty-eight. Know what I mean?"

"Yes, sir."

"Same with their relatives. Before you can say 'I do', half the relatives want to come along under your sponsorship. Know what I mean?"

"Yes, sir. Thanks, Sarge."

Blakely nodded and headed out into the dark.

Chapter 2

Meir's Bavarian Garten

Blakely crossed the snow-covered cobbles of *Fredrich-Ebert Strasse*. The marquee above *Meir's Bavarian Garten* flashed in red and gold letters. A little neon man in green *lederhosen* blinked on and off atop the sign, hoisting a blue stein to his mouth. The muffled tones of an oompah band grew louder.

The double doors burst open. Two GIs in uniform with mechanized infantry patches on their sleeves came flying out, hitting the iced sidewalk with a crunch. They picked themselves up, swearing at the large bouncer who stood with hands on hips in the doorway.

"*Ungezogen Knaben!*" (Naughty boys!) "Go home. Get some sleep."

Blakely moved past the bouncer, a stereotypical *Third Reich* "superman" with a Charles Atlas physique that tested the seams of his gabardine jacket. The din of *Meir's* was unbelievable. The hall was filled with old men singing at the tops of their voices, *Nach Hause Gehen Ver Nicht!* The smell of stale beer, cigarettes, sausage, urine, and sweat blended with the massed voices in the heat. It was like being inside a sinister tabernacle where unfamiliar and dangerous rituals were taking place. The voices reminded him of movies he had seen of the Nuremburg rallies. And then he thought of Luke, realizing that one of those guys could have been the one who killed him.

He climbed the stairs and looked down the row of tables along the left balcony. Charon was unmistakable. His black clothing contrasted with the green, brown and gray of everyone else. Old Sarge liked to make a statement. He stood as Blakely approached and held out his hand.

"*Wie gehts, Herr* Blakely," Charon said heartily. "Welcome to *Deutschland!* How was your trip?"

"*Gut, danke*," Blakely replied. "The flight over was smooth. I wasn't expecting Frankfurt to be so cold and dark, though." He spoke in his best Army Language School German, emphasizing the *ish* of the southern dialect.

Charon continued the conversation in German. "You'll get used to it. What do you think of this place?"

"To tell you the truth, it's pretty wild."

Blakely looked down at the crowd of old and middle-aged men. They were raising gray mugs of beer and shouting "*Probst!*"in the midst of singing. On the stage, a heavy-handed oompah band of seven guys in *lederhosen* whistled, danced, stamped their feet, sang, played their instruments, and shouted encouragement to the mass before them.

"Never seen anything like it." And he hadn't. The place was a mob scene. Small clusters of American GIs sat along one side, but the majority were German nationals.

"Plenty of old *Nazis* down there," said Charon in the steady, matter-of-fact voice Blakely had always admired. "They're just getting tuned up. An hour from now, they'll be singing all the victory songs when they were young and invincible."

Blakely leaned over the railing. "I guess I still have mixed feelings about *Krauts* and being here…"

"How so?"

"You know my half-brother got killed over Ploesti. I was just a kid. 1944. Ever since, I've had this thing about Germans. Guess that is why I went to language school and learned German. I wanted to understand what makes them tick…"

"Yeah. I had that problem, too, for a long time. It took years of being here before I could trust them. Now, with the cold war, I don't trust any of 'em again."

Charon had a silent intensity about him. His black hair, overgrown eyebrows and dark eyes always made him fierce looking. His lined face with its set, firm mouth and strong, chiseled white teeth, told people they had better take care around him. He was slender, yet physically powerful, even at forty-three. His demeanor often put people off until he spoke. He had a deceptively gentle voice, but Blakely had heard it turn explosive when Charon was provoked.

"How 'bout a beer and brat?"

He raised his chin abruptly, catching the eye of a heavy-set barmaid waiting the next table. She nodded back.

"Sure."

As they sat listening to the cadenced roar of voices and instruments, Blakely realized how Charon accentuated his silent power by wearing black. He stood out as utterly singular in a mass of nondescript bodies. He would have made a great priest!

"I'm looking forward to working with you again, Sarge."

"*Zwei beir und zwei bratwurst, bitte!*" Charon shouted into the ear of the waitress.

Turning to Blakely, his expression serious, "We won't be working together." He leaned closer. "I leave for stateside tomorrow."

"Why?" Blakely was genuinely shocked. "What's going on? The main reason I came over here was to work with you and Colonel Wafford."

"You won't be working with either one of us. We both got our walking papers because of our ages. Part of Eisenhower's reduction in force."

"I don't understand. I thought you had two more years here."

"Not anymore. I report to Fort Hamilton, New York, on Tuesday. Thank God I have my twenty in."

Sarge pulled a pack of Chesterfields from his pocket, flipped out a cigarette into his lips, and replaced the pack. He was looking away from Blakely. He absently pulled out a Zippo lighter and thumbed the wheel until it was lit. He held the flaming lighter as he spoke to the wall.

"Some poor bastards have only sixteen or eighteen years in service and are being forced out."

He turned back to Blakely as he drew on the cigarette, blowing a huge puff of smoke toward the wall. He snapped the lighter shut with finality.

"Jim's already been to Fort Hamilton and back again. He's a civilian. Wants to start an insurance agency here. Some way to treat a guy who knows a dozen languages, huh?"

"I don't understand."

Jim Wafford and the Sarge were genuine heroes of World War II. They served in the OSS behind the lines in France and

Germany, recruiting underground resistance groups, blowing up bridges, creating mayhem throughout the war.

Charon's coal black eyes were rimmed with water. He had never seen Sarge vulnerable, near to crying. This was a guy who once stabbed *Nazis* in their necks using ice picks, lived off scavenged food, would kill anyone in his way.

"I'm sorry for both of you," was all Blakely could think to say. "If I'd known, I wouldn't have come here…"

On stage, the musicians were doing a *Tyrolean* folk dance where they stamped their feet and slapped each other's faces and hands. Blakely recalled seeing the dance once at language school and thought how stupid it was. They got a standing ovation before launching into a favorite marching song. This brought an immediate roar of approval and voices singing as one.

"It wasn't something I wanted most people to know," said Charon. "Anyway, I thought Smitty or Cecil back at Mac would have told you fellas. On the other hand, I'm kinda glad they didn't."

Charon pulled a chewing gum wrapper from his pocket and began making little folds in it, watching his own hands with a look of growing despair.

"But how could Washington justify throwing you and the Colonel out?"

"Too much time in grade and being passed over for promotion." Charon tossed the wrapper on the table. "I once crossed a ninety-day-wonder second lieutenant after the war—got on the wrong side of him—and the son of a bitch wrote me up. Hurt me the rest of my career. That and my age were against me. Same with Jim."

The waitress delivered two mugs of beer with plates of bratwurst, mustard and rye bread.

"*Danke*," Blakely said. He raised the heavy blue-gray stein toward Charon.

"*Probst*," said Charon. They clinked the mugs together and drank.

The beer tasted thick and wonderfully sweet. The brat was toasted brown on the outside so that it crunched and popped juices into his mouth when he took a bite. Swishing the rye bread through the mustard and biting off a piece of crust, the mixture of sausage, bread and mustard tasted incredibly good.

"Still thinking about a career in the army?"

Blakely writhed in his chair, pushing the beer mug toward the middle of the table. "Sarge, if I ever did have any dream of being a career officer, I sure as hell wouldn't be one now... Not after what you've told me."

"You're smart to think like that," Charon said with renewed warmth. "That kind of thinking will keep you your own man. The army's changed from the war years. Now, every chicken shit peacetime lieutenant is looking to nail you and get more rank. You've got to watch your step over here."

"I can see that."

"Make any waves and some bastard will get your ass. You can't trust anybody to protect you here."

"I appreciate the advice."

The band struck up a new tune. The voices were louder than ever.

"Come here often enough and you'll learn them all," Charon said without looking up from his plate.

"All what?"

"The marching songs. Just a word of advice, though. Always come here with a buddy and get to know the bouncers. Between the two, you'll stay out of trouble. There are lots of characters hanging out here: smugglers, thieves, old *Nazis*, and undercover spies—theirs and ours. They're concentrated here in Frankfurt. Just watch your step."

"With all the GIs here, they can't do anything more than pick your pocket, can they?"

Charon threw his head back in an exaggerated laugh. "Hell, they'll find a way to pick your ass off the street. Next thing you know, you're in Bulgaria or East Germany."

"Really?"

"No crap, Ed. We lose a lot of our people here in Frankfurt." Charon leaned in with both elbows on the table, moving aside the empty plate. "Ordinary intelligence analysts like yourself. People just disappear."

Blakely thought about his friends from Army Language School who were assigned to covert intelligence. They must be out there some place.

"Look Ed, you are assigned to the most important intelligence base in Europe. You are forty-seven miles from the East German Border. It's easy to take people across. We're on a major river—the Main—that connects with the Rhine and Danube. Counter Intelligence folks say our people are nabbed off the street, put on a barge, and smuggled back into Rumania, Hungary or some-place so fast they don't know what happened. The most important operatives are taken to Russia for KGB interrogation.

Doesn't CID and CIC protect our people?"

Charon mashed his cigarette out in the ashtray. "All we know is a guy disappears. Rumors begin to circulate a few months later that he's in Prague or Moscow. Some end up killed or sentenced to Siberia. If they're lucky, they get swapped out for operatives we've caught on our side of the fence. By the time you arrived on German soil today, there was already a dossier being prepared by the Russians with your name, rank, serial number, prior assign-ments, schooling, and your new assignment."

"You're kidding!"

"No, I'm not kidding. We know the Russians get copies of orders cut in Washington practically before the ink dries."

It sounded like Sarge was purposely trying to put doubts in his mind. How could he do his job here, if he couldn't trust anyone?

"You mentioned my new assignment... What's it going to be?"

"Eventually, you'll probably be monitoring Russian air activity and missile testing—at least that's what Colonel Croft told me last week."

"Great. I can't wait to get started. Can I visit the office on Monday?"

"Not possible. You'll be cooling your heels at the *Gutleut Kaserne* for a few weeks."

"Why?"

"They're not going to let you near Army Security Agency Headquarters until your clearances are updated from your last assignment at Mac."

"How long will that take?"

"Let's see. With the holidays coming up, you probably won't clear until the first of February."

"What will they have me doing between now and then?" Blakely shifted his elbows on the table.

"There are so many transient people right now, you probably won't have anything to do. Maybe they'll give you courier duty to Berlin or someplace. If I were you, I'd do courier work rather than spend your time fooling around Frankfurt. Intelligence types with time on their hands tend to get into trouble here. And stay away from the whores on the *Romer Platz!*"

"Oh?"

"Yeah. They're clean and licensed, but you may be propositioning one of our Criminal Intelligence people or an East German spy. Either way, your ass is grass."

Blakely couldn't believe this conversation. It was surreal, being carried on above the growing din of *Deutschland, Deutschland Uber Alles.*

"You know, Jim might have some work for you if you have time on your hands."

"Really?" Blakely leaned in, thinking how great it would be to spend time after all with one of his heroes.

"Yeah. He's doing some research about World War II that might interest you. Something having to do with the *Gestapo* stealing people's gold after the von Stauffenberg bomb plot. Lives in a suburb of Frankfurt, a village called Eschersheim. Why don't you give him a ring?"

"I will."

Charon called a beer maid over, asked for a piece of paper and pencil and jotted down a number.

"He'd be glad to see you. Give him my regards." He handed Blakely the note.

"Thanks." Blakely felt cold and empty inside, yet he was perspiring. He wondered if there was any person within the agency—or in all of goddamned Europe, for that matter—that he might depend on.

"Sarge, since I'm new here and won't have you to lean on, who should I get to know so I can get off to a good start. I don't want to screw up."

"I wouldn't depend on any of the people who haven't been here more than a couple years. They're the new, political bureaucrats. I honestly can't tell you who'd be level with you. You might talk with Jim about it. Everybody is on the come, with the cutbacks and all. A bunch of whores. This cold war atmosphere has changed everything."

"Yeah?"

"Yeah. The Hungarian thing was sorta the last straw. The uprising has turned into a disaster. We had German nationals throwing stones at us just last month whenever we walked around Frankfurt in uniform."

"But why?"

"Our radio propaganda told the Hungarians to revolt. America would defend them. When they actually did revolt, our leaders were afraid to commit our troops. Afraid we'd have a nuclear war with Russia. The Russians had tanks lined up ten miles deep on all the main roads along the East German border. So, we basically lied to the Hungarians. We showed everybody—the Germans, the Brits, the French, the Russians, everybody—that we can't be trusted to do what we say we'll do."

"Damn."

"The entire organization is undergoing change; they're bringing in new equipment that will take away many of the intelligence analysts, translators, and interpreters. 1956 is not the same as it was in 1946."

"Guess not…"

And just between you and me, something's gone wrong with our covert operations. According to some of my contacts, we're losing bunches of people."

"To the Russians?"

"To everybody. All these iron curtain countries run their own spy networks. Then you've got KGB and all. Things are out of hand; not like the old days when you could trust your guys to cover your back.

"You mean our spies are being compromised?"

"Yeah. I suspect the Russians have moles high up in our State Department."

"Damn!"

"Then there's talk that Russia is about to launch a satellite into outer space, too."

"Is that right?"

"Yeah. Our people back at Arlington are putting a helluva lot of pressure on us to find out what's going on. And instead of cooperating with each other, every intelligence organization is competing with the other now. It's the latest intelligence game, new players, new rules. One of the rules is that nobody shares information with anybody else, unless you've got enough to put on a show for Arlington and score some points. That's the only way you'll get budget increases."

"Damn!" So, thought Blakely, he was going to be one of the pawns in a crazy game that he could not possibly understand.

"Just keep your nose clean. Do what they say. You can't screw up by doing that."

He knew Charon was trying to give him sound advice. Yet it all seemed so bizarre, out of keeping with all that he had been taught, all that he had learned about intelligence operations back at Mac. His hopes had been so high. Charon had dashed them one by one.

The loud singing stopped suddenly. Blakely and Charon both turned and looked down at the crowd. As if by some pre-arranged signal, everyone's attention shifted to a table near the back of the hall where eight middle-aged men stood up, tapped their gray steins together, and began to sing. There was total silence except for the voices singing in harmony.

> *Let us link arms together high above the clouds.*
> *We are prepared for whatever shall come,*
> *As we jump free of the plane in the sky.*
> *We live for the moment when we descend*
> *To earth and to meet our enemy.*
> *We are the brave paratroopers of the Seventh,*
> *Who are ready to fight the foes below.*
> *And, if we must, to die in the effort.*

"What's that about," whispered Blakely.

"They didn't teach you that song in Army Language School?"

"No. I'd have remembered it."

"It's one of the paratroopers' hymns. Veterans of the Seventh Division, the *Fallshirmjaeger*. They're held in special reverence."

"How come?"

"They were the ones who jumped in Holland and on Crete. They made the difference in winning the campaigns. Made them instant heroes. Later, Hitler used them to defend Stalingrad and against Patton on the Western Front. You always knew when you were facing them. A bunch of hard asses. They never gave up."

"Wow!"

"Whenever a few of them get together now, everybody listens. They'd sing this in the aircraft just before making the jump."

They both sat quietly, listening to the men singing as one. The group got a standing ovation when they finished. The band struck up another noisy tune and within seconds male voices were ringing the rafters.

"Can I buy you another beer for old time's sake?"

"Thanks, but I need to get going."

Charon threw a five *mark* note on the table.

"Still have packing to do. Tell you what... I found something this morning I used to carry around with me all the time..."

Charon reached into his coat pocket and pulled out a small, blue leather-bound book polished from age and use.

"I won't be needing this anymore. You can have it as a little gift from your old Sarge." He handed it to Blakely.

Blakely read the cover of the dictionary. *Langdorf's Universal Worterbuch: Englisch-Deutsch, Deutsch-Englisch.* Inside was an inscription, *Corporal Sylvester Charon, New Bedford, Mass. 1942.*

"Thanks, Sarge. I appreciate it."

The black fire in Charon's eyes flickered momentarily. He suddenly seemed self-conscious, separated from Blakely now by age, plans, and dashed hopes.

"I guess we'd better hit the road." Charon stood up. The singing and oompah instruments were louder than ever.

"I'll walk you to the trolley stop."

They walked down the steps, forcing themselves through the thick crowd standing at the entrance. They stepped into a clear, cold night and the perspiration on Blakely's neck made him shiver.

He couldn't think of any more to say. Charon was silent, too. The voices and music receded until only the grating of steel trolley wheels against rails echoed among the black buildings. They shook hands and nodded farewells.

"Take care and good luck," said Charon as he boarded the trolley.

"You, too."

Blakely watched his mentor disappear into the night. Now, he realized, he was totally alone in an alien place. He felt dirty even in his new clothes as he stood there sweating and shivering. He hadn't felt so bereft in a long time. Even without Charon's warnings, it wouldn't do any good to go to the American Bar and find a blond *fraulein*. Now, the whole thing of his being in Germany serving his country was perverse, wrong somehow, and he hadn't even gotten started.

Chapter 3

The Hit

Dying at the hands of a former SS non-commissioned officer would have been impossible to imagine. First, he–Georg Krusen–was a quiet man who, after the War was over, returned to Berlin where he was an engineer for the public works department. And second, he had no enemies that he knew of. In fact, he avoided confrontations, disliked talking about his war experiences, and was content to live out his days anonymously.

He enjoyed the engineering challenges of rebuilding Berlin. Replanting trees in the *Tiergarten* after the blockade. Reconstructing bridges. Modernizing the water and sewage systems.

He lived in a modest two room flat where he listened to recordings of Bach and studied Byrd's explorations of Antarctica. Most of all, he loved the time spent with Justina, the dinners at the *Menderhof Kafe* on *Linden Weg*, and their walks after attending a music recital.

Yet, here he was, bound and being tortured to tell a large, dark stranger about a relic he knew little about. He wanted to know how Georg had obtained it. His torturer insisted that he, Georg Krusen, was involved in smuggling a fortune in Habsburg jewels and gold out of Austria in July 1944. More, he believed that the wooden relic in Georg's possession contained a code that would lead him to where the treasure was stashed on the Greek island of Crete.

And as so often happens with SS interrogators—even the practiced ones—he had observed firsthand—they become impatient. They become heavy handed too quickly. Soon, the victim cannot talk or confess anything any more. This is what had happened to Georg Krusen. He found himself an observer of his own demise, unable to participate except in a totally helpless way.

During what seemed the final minutes of his life, Georg experienced great calm. He had known it before in similar circumstances when he had been wounded, frightened, dying. The feeling was one of total detachment. He could see his circumstances in his mind's eye, while withdrawing into a space deep within, a space out of harm's way. Reality appeared intermittently between floating mists of forgetfulness.

A white cloud passed. He was dragging his wounded and bleeding body behind the concrete abutment of a bridge. He pulled himself into a fetal position to wait for help or death. He could feel life seeping out of him no matter how hard he clutched at the wounds. He stuffed his wet and muddy parachutist's scarf into the hollow place at the back of his leg. His jumpsuit was torn and slimy feeling. When he tried to adjust his kneepad so that it covered the wound, the pain was too great and he felt faint.

His tormenter was shaking him. Threats echoed in the distance. Footsteps approached. Shadows. Something struck his jaw.

Even Justina was now distanced from him. He could hear her lovely voice calling. He tried vainly to assure her that he was okay…

Occasionally, he thought himself lying at the bottom of a well where from time to time groups of faces would appear as silhouettes in a shaft of light. They looked down at him. It was Schruns where he regained consciousness after the skiing accident. Strangers peered down at him, but he was too far away from them to be helped or harmed. They were merely animated faces and arms gesticulating meaninglessly. They disappeared in the mist.

He was being dragged to another place. Was it to the table of the Dutch surgeon who had saved his life in Holland? No. It was a darker image. A man jerked him upright and was now pressing a metal object to his left temple. There was another question. When he did not respond, the man struck him. Wetness in his ear was at once cool and sticky. He didn't know the answer. When the metal banged against the side of his head, the pain shrouded him in white again.

He had tried to duck the roundhouse right to the temple delivered by his boyhood friend Gunter. It was Gunter who had taught him how to box. He tried with great effort not to think about boxing, which caused him to recall the ineptness of his Jewish friend, Artur Goldstein.

Artur came floating across the basement room beneath his father's store in baggy knickers and white undershirt. His boxing gloves were poised in front of him, a look of brave determination on his round, sallow face. His fat lips were set tightly as he pushed out one glove and prepared to hit with the other. But his dark eyes betrayed his fear of getting hit back. Artur tried to throw a right cross, and Georg let Artur hit him. Artur flailed away, hitting him lightly about the head until Artur grew tired and gave up. Both knew Artur would never be a boxer because he did not want to be one. Artur did not like to fight, even in fun, and more importantly, boxing could damage his hands so that Artur would never be able to play the violin again. And Artur was too good a violinist not to be able to play it again.

Red and white flashes, sounds of gunfire, exploding shells brought Georg to a crouch behind a stonewall. A farmhouse near Potsdam, 1945. The final defense of Berlin. Russians were moving forward with first light, overrunning his position, and a heavy barrage of small arms fire sounding like overheated popcorn kept him pinned behind the wall. Next to him were a 14 year old boy and a 75 year old great grandfather. Both had been called up from the Home Guard in a desperate attempt to hold the Russians back. The boy and old man had arrived around midnight, just a couple hours before the artillery assault began. The two were visibly afraid. The old man was without teeth; the boy had never fired a weapon. Both had heard Russian troops were ruthless and took no prisoners.

Georg told them to pretend they were dead when the Russians arrived, knowing they could not defend themselves against an onslaught of heavy tanks and infantry. The Russians were streaming forward from the orchard and hemlocks beyond the pasture. He showed them how to breathe without showing they were breathing. The three slumped over together in a little pile as the Russians passed through the stone gateposts. But the old man and boy were so frightened they could not be still. He watched with half-closed eye as an infantryman, attracted by the movements of the boy and old man, lifted his rifle chest high and fired several rounds into the pile. He felt the jolts of warm bodies as metal slammed into flesh, bone and sinew; the old man and young boy twitching and snapping with each popping sound.

It was difficult to know whether he was watching from some other place or was still behind the stonewall when the white shroud evaporated and he saw bright pink and green flares, orange tracers, and the dull red glow of distant fires in the direction of Berlin. The crump, crump, crump of exploding bombs and artillery shells made his head hurt. The roar of heavy American bombers overhead was incessant. The boy next to him was dying all the while.

Georg fell into gentle sleep even as Russian supply columns passed through the gate nearby. A twinge of pain in his shoulder woke him. Two Russian officers were looking down at him as an infantryman was nudging him awake with the barrel of his rifle. He ordered Georg to his feet. Georg was aghast. He had fallen asleep and betrayed himself by his breathing. Now, he was being lifted, extricated from the tangle of dead bodies. He stood up. He feared the grimy infantryman standing over him would lose patience and shoot him on the spot. Only then was he aware that his field jacket was spattered with blood and pieces of the boy and the old man.

The dream slipped away along with lingering specks of his own life. His mouth did not hurt anymore. His teeth were broken. Pieces lay beneath his swollen tongue. An hour or a day or minutes earlier—he could not tell which—he had tasted his own blood and reckoned it a trivial thing. There was no longer pain in his arms from his wrists bound behind him. He had somehow mastered holding his body upright where he rested on bent knees with ankles tied together. His body was numb. He would have fallen by this time were it not for the person holding him upright by the hair.

He could no longer hear the harsh words and epithets, so it didn't matter that his inquisitor was threatening to shoot him. He had been shot before and nothing was so good as the feeling now of letting go—even of Justina whom he loved—and his thoughts turned to other people he had known.

Everyone, living and dead, was crowding into a low pasture of fresh, earth-scented grass above the village of Garmish. It was summer holiday. He was on his favorite walking path to the high pastures above. Porcelain-framed tintypes and photographs of dead loved ones as well as favored icons had been placed in small alcoves and wood and glass reliquaries along the way. The name of the deceased, birth date, place, and date of death, and brief prayers or comments set in handwritten or printed inscriptions identified each image.

Every summer he had come here since the war. He always stopped at the varnished picture of the youth who, according to the inscription, had been killed at Memel in 1944. The photo was official *Wehrmacht*, black and white. In uniform at age seventeen. Perhaps the parents had taken the photograph to a local shop to have it tinted. The boy was tan with pink cheeks and looked younger than his seventeen years. In Georg's mind, the image was the epitome of the futility of war.

From this vantage point, the village below with its church spires and famous ice rink looked like a quaint picture postcard. As the mist surrounded him, the boy's image faded and Georg felt the need to move on.

He turned away from the precipice and climbed a narrower trail up another several hundred feet, past the last of the reliquaries, before pausing to rest. He took off his jacket and gazed down the mountainside.

All his friends and acquaintances had stopped on the grassy ridge below. They pressed together like poor emigrants in the hold of a ship. He recognized the Dutch surgeon, Justina, his father, Artur Goldstein, friends from the engineering department, his oldest pals Heinrich, Joch, Freddie, his mother and grandmother and grandfather.

They were almost in black silhouette, as low clouds would at times obscure them. He waved. Everyone was waving back to him with arms raised. He heard the sound of a footfall in an empty room followed by an instant, all consuming burning flash of incandescence. His life filaments burst within him, like the sudden cracking of walked-on ice.

Chapter 4

Meeting the Colonel

Jim Wafford insisted they meet Sunday at noon. Blakely was to take the number seven *strassenbahn* to the end of the line, walk beyond the stop to the dead-end that was *Ginnheimer Strasse*, and turn right. The *gasthaus* with adjoining bakery was around the corner, across from the Catholic Hospital. Since he hadn't any idea how long the trolley ride and walk would be, Blakely found himself turning the corner into *Ginnheimer Strasse* half an hour early. It was treacherous walking on the ice and patches of snow.

As he approached the *gasthaus*, an American or Englishman— he couldn't tell which—was leaving the restaurant. He was probably in his late twenties, brown hair, pipe in mouth, and wearing an English-style brown tweed suit. The man looked both ways, crossed the iced cobbles, and entered the parking lot of the Catholic Hospital. He climbed into an old, brown Hillman convertible.

Blakely turned to look into a shop window and watched the reflection of the Hillman coming through the gate, skidding slightly as it turned in the opposite direction and disappeared around the corner. The Hillman bore U.S. military plates.

Blakely decided to walk back toward the trolley stop and look around the neighborhood for a while, just in case the colonel was meeting with other Americans. Perhaps the colonel was interviewing several guys for the job. He hadn't thought about competition. He took out a white handkerchief and wiped his brow. What's he like, he wondered? He sounded very southern on the phone. He recalled reading an article about him at Fort Riley. An OCS officer from Biloxi, Mississippi. Must now be in his late forties to early fifties. He felt sweaty beneath his trench coat, wool sports jacket and Oxford cloth shirt and regimental tie. Wasn't used to wearing such heavy clothes. Being from California, it simply wasn't his style. He felt trapped.

At noon, the bell tolled in the chapel tower of the Catholic Hospital. Blakely opened the door and entered the *gasthaus*. A few Germans sat at brightly polished oak tables. The colonel was the one identifiable American in the place, dressed in a tan gabardine suit and brown shirt buttoned at the neck. The telltale was his shoes: highly shined brown military desert boots. He sat in the back corner table, away from the others. He got up as Blakely approached.

"Ed Blakely?"

"Yes, sir!"

"Jim Wafford. Glad ta meetcha."

They shook hands.

"Have a seat." The colonel gestured to the chair next to his.

Blakely removed his trench coat and folded it over the other chair and sat down. Wafford was not what Blakely expected. He certainly wasn't the image of the super spy and former OSS officer. Rather, he was an old guy, fairly short, balding, over-weight, with heavy jowls and fat hands. A hangdog expression was accentuated by heavily hooded, pale blue eyes. His mouth had the appearance of pouting so that the whole aspect of the man was one of shyness. Was his appearance the result of dealing with the new bureaucratic, peacetime army for the past ten years? Was it from finally being kicked out of it? The guy looked tired, done in, Blakely thought.

"So you have some time to kill," the colonel said, glancing sidewise at Blakely.

"Yes, sir. Sergeant Charon said I probably won't be cleared for duty until the first of February. Seems there's a big transfer of personnel in each direction right now due to the Hungarian situation. A lot of people to process in and out."

"That's got nothing to do with you," snapped Wafford while drumming his fingers of his left hand on the table. "It's your clearance. FBI is swamped. Probably won't be done 'til last of January."

"Yes, sir."

The guy seems nervous, too, thought Blakely. Wouldn't expect that from James Wafford, OSS. And his voice was a high, nasal twang.

"You hungry? How 'bout something to eat?"

"Sure."

They ordered cheesecake and coffee from the waitress.

"So, Mr. Blakely, how would you like to do some work for me on the side while you are waiting clearance? I'd be glad to pay expenses plus your regular duty pay on an hourly basis."

"What sort of work?"

"I don't mean a job where you'd be wasting your effort. I'm talking about using your intelligence skills and making some money at the same time."

"Sounds good."

"I've got a little World War II intelligence project I'm doing with a history professor here at the University of Maryland Overseas Center. Tracking down some former German soldiers, their relatives, conducting interviews, that sort of thing. Would you be interested?"

"I'm not sure, sir. As Sergeant Charon probably told you, I was trained to be an intelligence analyst."

"Well, this is nothing more than interviewing people. It isn't cloak and dagger. I'd do it myself, 'cept I have plenty to do in the research area to keep me busy. I need a young man like yerself. Number one in his class at Fort Riley, a star athlete, a surfing champion, a good sailor, too, like ole Charon."

Blakely smiled appreciatively. "How'd you know all those things?"

The plump waitress delivered their coffee and cheesecake on a tray.

"*Danke,*" said Wafford, pulling his plate of cheesecake closer. "I've been following your progress ever since you attended Intelligence School. Bill Sommers at Fort Riley is a good friend of mine. So is Cecil at Mac. You come highly recommended. I was looking forward to you working for me at the Agency, but things didn't work out that way."

The colonel grinned slightly and shrugged his shoulders as he alluded to his forced retirement.

"You were going to be one of my new stars on the team. But maybe you and I can work together on my project."

"Can you explain it a little?"

"Glad to."

Blakely watched him scratching the surface of the cheesecake with his fork. Bits of cake collected on the tines, which he licked off before repeating the process. It was something a child might do.

"Do you remember from your history the unsuccessful plot to assassinate Hitler? I'm speaking of the one led by Count von Stauffenberg in 1944."

"Yes, sir. It was at the Wolf's Lair, in the map room. In July, I believe. I've read articles about it."

"Yeah, well, immediately after the attempt to kill Hitler failed, the German State Police and the *Gestapo* were given the green light to round up every person that was remotely suspected of being involved. The *Gestapo* offices became butcher shops."

The Colonel's face flushed and his voice rose higher as he spoke. "It's estimated that between six and eight thousand civilians and military personnel were killed as a result of the roundup. Hitler and Himmler used this occasion to wipe out their enemies. Some say that the actual death toll was much higher, maybe reaching eleven thousand. Nobody knows for sure."

Blakely set his coffee down. ."I know that several of the generals committed suicide to avoid being killed by the *Gestapo*, Rommel, for example. But I had no idea so many civilians were killed."

"Oh yes," Wafford continued. "It is difficult to estimate the actual murders because allied bombs were accounting for thousands more casualties. But what's most interesting to me, Ed, is that certain *Gestapo* units used this roundup of plotters to line their pockets. They simply began to prepare themselves for life after the war."

"Really?"

"They used the plot as an excuse to kill rich Germans and steal their money. It stands to reason. How else did so many former *Nazis* escape to South America after the War? The German *mark* was worthless. They needed gold or silver or precious jewels to buy their way out. We know whole bunches of 'em got new identities and became gentlemen farmers in Paraguay, Argentina, Bolivia and elsewhere. It took vast amounts of money to do that."

"I always assumed the *Nazis* used gold stolen from the Jews to pay their way out of Germany…"

"Yeah, that, too. But most of that gold was stolen much earlier by usually top-line officers. The thefts in 1944 were by mid-level *Gestapo* officers and non-coms."

"How'd you find out about this?"

Wafford stabbed a chunk of cheesecake with his fork and popped it into his mouth, talking with his mouth full. "We think we have a classic example. Professor Storey and I, with help from an archivist friend back in the states, have uncovered a *Gestapo* unit that appears to have robbed and killed a noble family just days after the Stauffenberg debacle."

"Yeah?"

"Royce Swain from Georgetown came across a sheaf of *Gestapo* papers that are quite incriminating. They include orders and reports concerning the von Etter family. As far as we can tell, the whole family was killed and their estate was looted by *Gestapo* under the command of Colonel Eugen Horst and two of his prime henchmen, Sepp Halder, a lieutenant, and an NCO named Heinz Beck. Only, this crime has a special twist…"

"And what is that?"

"The von Etter family was in the process of smuggling their family fortune in jewels, gold and silver out of Austria to the island of Crete right at the time of the plot. Unbeknownst to them, the *Gestapo*—Horst in particular—had been monitoring all their activities and planned to intercept the fortune when it arrived in Crete. But it seems Major von Etter, the young heir to the family estate, who was to receive the goods, outwitted the SS and hid the treasure somewhere on the island."

"How do you know?"

"The head of the *Gestapo* on Crete, General Gustav Kemft, was supposed to capture von Etter with the fortune and return them both back to Horst in Vienna. Something happened; we're not sure what. But the general disappeared the day the smuggled goods arrived. His aide-de-camp was found shot to death in the general's car a few miles from Iraklion. The general had disappeared."

"So, you think von Etter killed Kemft and his aide?"

Wafford toyed with his fork.

"We don't know. What we do know is that Major von Etter was arrested and returned to Vienna. Von Etter was tortured and put to death there by Horst. Neither Gustav Kemft nor the treasure was ever found that we know of."

"If Horst tortured the major, wouldn't he have found out where the fortune was hidden?"

"We know he obtained some information, that's for sure."

"How do you know?"

"In 1945 I headed a refugee processing center in a mountain pass above Salzburg. Harvey Gold, one of my interpreters, identified Horst and Beck as wanted *Nazi* war criminals. I had them arrested and searched. Around Horst's neck was a piece of relic on a leather thong. In his suitcase were the broken down parts of a *Schmeisser* automatic pistol, the type used by German paratroopers. Major von Etter was a paratrooper… None of it made sense back then. But that incident began my search into the meaning of it all. I could never put the puzzle together until recently, when Professor Storey and I began our investigations based on the documents. I can now say with almost one hundred percent certainty that Horst stole the relic and the *Schmeisser* from Major von Etter just before he killed him."

"Fascinating. But I still don't get the connection with the artifact?"

"Maybe there is none. But I think otherwise. Experts say the piece is genuine, 3,000 years old, made of cypress wood. Von Etter must have found the artifact or, perhaps, he purchased it as a memento. There are plenty of caves on Crete where Minoan artifacts are found—even today."

"How could wood that old survive?"

"Well, that is an interesting point. I did some research. Cypress produces its own preservative oil called cypressene, so it doesn't decay. Makes it ideal for pilings, docks, railroad ties. Legend has it Noah's Ark was built entirely of cypress. Did you know that?"

"No, Sir."

"Matter of fact, I read where the original church doors at St. Peter's were 1,100 years old when they replaced 'em. They were still in great shape. Made entirely of cypress."

"Fascinating. Can you tell me more about what the piece of wood is like?"

"Originally, it was part of a round disk, like a flat plate, about six inches in diameter, with fancy scrolls around the edges. It appears the disk was cut into pieces. The piece I took from Horst is approximately an inch and a half wide and almost six inches in length. On one side is a labyrinth design. On the back are fairly fresh perforations and marks."

"I don't follow you."

"Small perforations like you'd make with a scratch awl." Wafford smiled at his fork. "One fella we showed it to thought the holes were made by *Krauts* using the back of the thing as a dart board. There are also small cut marks like you'd find when somebody jabs a penknife into wood."

"I take it you think von Etter punched the holes and made the cut marks there?"

Wafford smirked. "Yes, but I have no proof. The holes were made to signify something, same with the longer cuts. I think the relic was split apart to make it more difficult for anybody to decipher the code, maybe where the stash is hidden... Why else would von Etter break a genuine 3,000 year old Minoan artifact into pieces?"

"Unless he didn't know it was old... But a good point. So... What makes you think there are several pieces?"

"The one I took off Horst is the second piece from the left side. There's one on the left and, if all were cut the same width, there's two more on the right, making four pieces in all."

Blakely nodded slowly, watching as Jim Wafford pushed pieces of pastry around with his fork.

"Makes sense."

Wafford glanced sidewise, smirking. "All I need is for you to help me find the missing pieces of the relic, that's all. I believe they are here in Germany. Just a matter of interviewing the right people. No covert activity."

"Just straight-forward interviews?"

"Yes."

"You'll furnish leads and backgrounds?"

"Exactly. You'll be tracing relatives and close friends of the von Etter family. They're well known because Otto von Etter was high up in the government of the Weimar Republic back in the twenties. Hitler, you know, tried to send all the democratic leaders to detention camps when he came to power in 1933. But ole Otto was so highly respected that Hitler didn't dare touch him. Otto, by the way, is Major von Etter's daddy. They were distant cousins of the Habsburg family, so they were very wealthy."

Wafford pushed his empty plate back and leaned toward Blakely.

"Whattya think, Ed? Are you interested?"

"Yes, sir. Very."

"I have some solid leads you can follow up. I think you'll enjoy the hunt. There's no danger involved. Not one iota! It'll also be an excellent opportunity for you to use your German."

The more Wafford talked, the more Blakely liked this man. He seemed so low key—even shy. His hooded blue eyes caught Blakely's momentarily, then shifted down and away again.

Blakely had also done his homework. Cecil Smith at Fort McPherson provided him with personal information about Wafford's personality and work habits. Between his OSS activities and listening to voice communications at the Agency, Jim Wafford knew eleven languages fluently and was learning four more. When it came to fulfilling mission requirements, he always exceeded expectations. He had the tenacious spirit of a bulldog. Wafford also had a reputation for being outspoken, even temperamental, but he was totally dedicated. He looked out for his troops. Drank beer with them, intervened on their behalf, encouraged them to stand out. He was a born leader who inspired his men.

On the flipside, Wafford protected his troops to a fault. He saw his fellow officers outside his own unit as competitors, not as colleagues. It was no coincidence that Jim Wafford's heroes were George Patton and Douglas MacArthur. Perhaps this explained why he never made it to full bird; he'd been passed over for talking when he should have been listening—just like Patton and MacArthur did with their superiors.

"What's our next step?"

"There's a German woman down yonder in Heidelberg I want you to interview. Professor Storey knows her—he's talked to her several times before—and he'll set it up for you. She was once the girlfriend of Major von Etter."

"If you don't mind my asking, sir… Why do you need me to interview her again, since Professor Storey already has the inside track?"

Wafford's face flushed. "I have new questions, Ed. And Dr. Storey's time is limited these days. Don't be second-guessing me. "

"Sorry, sir."

"I just learned that Estel von Etter, Heinrich's sister, wasn't slaughtered with the rest of the family like we thought. She lived another three months before Horst discovered her hiding down yonder in Trieste. The SS returned her to Vienna in October 1944 where she was shot. I thought perhaps *Frau* Schiller might be able to shed some light, since she and Estel were close friends."

"I see. How soon do you want me to go?"

"I'll have to let you know. And that brings up the matter of protocols. I don't want us making contact directly to one another. If I want to get in touch with you, you will get a telephone call from my friend Betty Crawford who owns the English Bookstore near the university. She'll tell you your book order can be picked up at a certain time and day. When you need to call Betty, just tell her to call me with the time and day when my book is in."

Wafford reached into the inside pocket of his jacket and pulled out a card and handed it to Blakely. It was a business card for the English Bookstore, showing the address, telephone number, and Betty's name.

"Why all the secrecy?"

"My former superior, Colonel Croft, didn't much cotton to my dabbling in recent German history, Ed. I'd just as soon keep what I do quiet, even though I'm retired now. That's why I want us to stay away from visiting one another or calling directly on military and public telephones. Croft keeps tabs on people. That's also why I'd like us to meet sometimes at the English Bookstore, here, or at the *Palmengarten*."

"The *Palmengarten*?"

"Nice place. It's a combination of zoo, park, botanical garden, and aviary. Its most notable feature is the large green house of palm trees. When you have something very confidential to share with me, then we ought to meet there because we can walk around the duck pond and not worry about listening devices. If you ever need to meet me there, it's easiest to wait for each other at the Kodak kiosk near the snack bar. You can't miss it. Check it out when you get the chance."

Wafford reached over and scattered the crumbs on his plate with his fork and then put the fork down next to the plate.

"How will I know whether to meet you here or at the book store or the *Palmengarten?*"

"Good point, Ed. That's where code words come into play "

Wafford's eyes sparkled. "*Beer* is for here. *Parsnips* the book-store. *Tropics* for the *Palmengarten.*"

"I don't follow you."

Wafford grinned.

"It's quite simple. You say, there's a book about *Parsnips* ready to be picked up at such and such a time. Or, there's a book about the *Tropics* to be picked up at such and such a time. Make sense now?"

Wafford's grin widened like he'd discovered what happened to the Holy Grail.

"Guess so, sir."

Blakely gazed at Wafford's face, which, for all intents and purposes, was closing down. His hooded eyes and sagging jowls were unreadable. Was Wafford a little paranoid or what? Wafford looked up.

"It may sound a little silly, but you never know who may be following you here in Frankfurt. I like to keep out of the way of our own counterintelligence and criminal intelligence people. They have a way of getting too nosy sometimes. You can usually tell from their clothes and demeanor that they're Americans."

"Sarge told me there are plenty of spies and thieves here, too."

"For sure," the colonel said solemnly. "West Germany is recovering, but there are lots of desperate people out here. Food shortages, rationing... Some people are willing to do most anything for anybody for any amount of money. So you need to keep your eyes peeled. If you do what I tell you, you won't have any trouble. Besides, from what I know about you, you can probably take care of yourself."

Wafford pretended to punch him in the arm, being careful to only graze his sleeve with his large fist.

"I hope so."

Blakely suddenly remembered the guy in civilian clothes who had left the *gasthaus* and gotten into the Hillman. He had little doubt in his mind that the guy—who looked a few years older than himself—had just concluded a similar meeting with Wafford. He wondered whether the colonel had several GIs working for him. He was tempted to ask, but decided that if Jim Wafford wanted him to know, he would tell him.

"Since this is a fairly sensitive project, Colonel, what are the protocols regarding telling other people about what I'm doing? I mean, I'll have to say something when my buddies at the *Kaserne* ask where I'm going or what I've been up to."

The colonel looked intense as he responded in even tones.

"Not one iota! I don't want you to discuss what I tell you with anyone—even Professor Storey, if you were to accidentally meet him. I've already told you more'n you need to know. And this is a *need-to-know* mission. Don't say anything to anyone. Make up whatever stories you want, so long as they are plausible and consistent. But don't use more stories than you have to. Understand?"

"Yes, sir."

"This is Q-clearance all the way. Are you okay with that?"

"Yes, sir."

Blakely sat back. There is more to this than he is telling me, Blakely thought. If he wanted to work with Jim Wafford, he'd have to be okay with Wafford's game playing. But what the hell. He decided to play along. Either the colonel was suffering from paranoia or else this so-called mission was a lot more complex than the colonel was letting on.

"By the way, what should I wear when I go visit the lady?"

A subtle smirk grew on Wafford's face as he gazed at Blakely.

"Civies. Same as what you've got on will do," motioning toward his new jacket and trench coat. "There's no way you won't be recognized as an American GI unless you buy German clothes that are a size too small and you take about six weeks to grow some extra hair."

"Will you provide a list of questions?"

"I'll prepare a list of topics you will explore with her. It will be your responsibility to develop lines of questions based on her responses. You know all that... Use all the techniques you learned at Riley. And I want you to use the five point reliability scale, too."

"Okay. What about identification? Do I show this lady my military ID?"

The colonel sat back, shaking his head at Blakely while almost laughing out loud.

"Naw! You won't need to go through any identification process. I'll have Professor Storey describe to her what you look like. He'll tell me what she'll be wearing and where you will meet for the interview. Probably some public place such as a library or restaurant. Just let me take care of all the details. I'll give you a thorough briefing after final arrangements are made. Okay?"

Yes, sir. I just want to do everything the right way."

"You'll do fine, son. You'll do just fine!"

"I can't help asking you, sir. I've read and heard so many stories about what you did during the War. What was it like to work behind enemy lines for weeks at a time?"

Wafford pulled himself taller in his chair while grinning at his plate. He looked up slowly.

"I hafta confess, Ed, it was the most thrilling time of my life. I was fortunate enough to have plenty of good people protecting me. The best people in the world. Otherwise, I'd a been dead the first day out."

"You mean other American operatives?"

"Uh, uh. I depended entirely on Dutch, German, French, Polish Underground. Fine men and women. I still keep in touch with the few that are left"

"Did you really kill Germans using ice picks and piano wire?"

Wafford looked down momentarily, then looked back at Blakely.

"Reporters have a habit of exaggerating truth, Ed. I only used an ice pick twice. Never used wire. I don't believe in torture."

Wafford looked across the room toward the large window. "Guess we'd best go."

They both got up from the table and pulled on their overcoats. Wafford paid the bill while Blakely stepped out into the cold air. The ice hadn't melted. The leaden sky was already beginning to darken and Blakely could smell snow in the air. The colonel joined him.

"I'll have Betty call you sometime tomorrow morning,"

"Do you mind if I ask another personal question, sir?"

Wafford's eyes flickered as he grinned and said, "No, not at all."

"Why'd you come back?"

"Come back?"

"I mean, sir, why'd you come back to Germany rather than retire stateside?"

The colonel's face flushed. He seemed flustered. He looked down at the slick gray ice on the sidewalk, pushed some of the loose granules of rock salt into a little speckled pile with his shiny desert boot, seeming to collect the pieces of his answer carefully before responding in an almost wistful way.

"Hell, Ed, Germany is more home to me now than any place in the whole world. I grew up in Biloxi and loved it there, but when I used to visit from time to time, well, everybody there forgot ole Jimmy Wafford. I'd been gone too long. Once I got into the military, I gave up my home place, you might say. I guess I never gave it a second thought about staying here in Germany. This is where I fought for my country. Where I gained a certain amount of notoriety. Frankfurt is where I've been assigned since 1946, 'cept for attending Army War College and short stints at Holabird and Riley. My home is here. Louise, my wife, is happy here. All my closest friends are here. I've got my little project here. It gives me a reason to keep my skills sharp, keeps me useful."

The two men started walking slowly down the sidewalk as Wafford talked. The colonel placed his hand on Blakely's shoulder.

"You see, Ed, ole bastards like me who've spent all their time in the military don't have anywhere much to go once the army is done with 'em. We're just old, obsolete, useless. I'd go nuts back stateside. There wouldn't be anything for me to do."

"What about consulting?"

"Hell, the whole military is in transition. From planes to missiles. From covert operatives to fancy computers and tracking devices. My knowledge isn't worth a penny to the government. At least here, I can keep up with things and conduct my own investigations."

"Sergeant Charon said you plan to open an insurance agency."

"Yeah, well… It makes a good cover. Don't plan to do much of that unless I can hire it done. Maybe eventually I'll hire part-timers like yourself who want to make extra money."

The colonel stopped and touched Blakely on the arm.

"You want to know something? I have my own war room down in the ole wine cellar of my house. Why, I can keep up with anything going on in the world from down there. It matches any war room I've ever seen. One of these days, Ed, you'll have to come over to the house and see it."

"I'd like that. I hope you don't mind my questions."

"Naw. You'll understand these things better when you get my age, Ed. Now, I guess I better hightail it to the Commissary. Louise gave me a list of things to pick up before I go home. I'd give you a lift, but I think it's better for both of us that we not be seen together 'cept in places I know are secure."

What was so secure about a *gasthaus*, Blakely wondered. "I understand. I'm looking forward to working with you."

They shook hands, said goodbye, and walked in different directions. Blakely was touched by the colonel's sadness. It had somehow bonded them. Maybe working for him would make Jim Wafford feel important again. He hoped so.

When Blakely arrived back at the *Gutleut Kaserne,* he still felt a thrill of excitement about doing assignments in secret for the colonel. At the same time, he had a lingering doubt about how Colonel Croft—the commander of the Agency—would look upon his working for Wafford under these circumstances. But there was no way to find out. Contact with the Agency would not be possible until his clearance came through and he was permitted past the military police with their electronic devices. Still, Nash down in the Orderly Room said everybody waiting for clearance could do as they pleased unless they volunteered or were called upon for courier duty. The great thing, he thought, was that Wafford could expose him eventually to covert intelligence work. Perhaps the experience would lead to a different job here in Germany. It was worth a try.

He sat down on his bunk and turned off Sergeant Lester's radio. Heidelberg would be fun to explore. And this would be his chance to use German with a national in an extended conversation.

Chapter 5

News from Berlin

Despite eating cheesecake with Blakely, Jim Wafford was famished when he arrived home mid-afternoon. He sat at the kitchen table playing with the knife, fork and spoon Anna had placed before him. His fingers moved the pieces into different positions and designs. It was a nervous habit. And from years of practice, his fingers could change the pattern with a single flick of thumb or forefinger. He had been impressed by young Ed Blakely. The boy had character and wasn't afraid to ask questions. He had the spunk to go someplace in life.

From time to time he would glance out the frosted window to see whether Hans had arrived with the papers. He also watched Anna stack thick slaps of turkey and slices of canned cranberry jelly on pieces of toasted whole wheat bread. This was his favorite sandwich. Things were going well. He enjoyed being in the warm kitchen with faithful Anna and inhaling the aroma of brewing coffee with chicory. Chicory and eggshells; you couldn't make good coffee without them. The news on Armed Forces Radio at Hanau broke his thoughts.

> *President Eisenhower's order to air and sealift 21,500 Hungarian refugees to the United States by January 1, 1957 is being implemented, according to General Brewster at SHAFE Headquarters. US Air Force transports based at Rhein-Main and Wiesbaden are expected to participate in the operation during the next several days. Meanwhile, heavy fighting continues between the Hungarian rebels and Soviet armored units...*

He half-heartedly listened to the radio newscaster's latest report on the fighting between Soviet troops and Hungarian rebels at Miskolc, near the Czech border. The radio news was merely a confirmation of what the colonel already knew from his own order of battle: the Hungarians were being slaughtered. It's a disgraceful thing, he thought to himself, when the most powerful nation in the world can't reach out and aid freedom fighters when it was our own propaganda on Radio Free Europe that inspired them to revolt in the first place. Now, after the bloodbath, we're saving face by taking some of the refugees stateside. Just too many Harry Crofts running the country these days, he thought ruefully. A helluva mess we created over there.

"Could you add a little more cranberry jelly, Anna?" he asked with a sheepish grin, just as she was starting to place the remaining jelly into a storage container.

"*Ja*," said Anna, glancing across at him momentarily. "*Und vould* the Colonel today like coffee or milk *mit* his lunch?"

"Coffee, please, Anna."

He reached over to the *Blaupunkt* and turned up the volume. The news was over. Bing Crosby was singing *White Christmas.*

Wafford slid further down in the wooden chair so he had a better view out the window. Small, fluffed-out black and white winter birds flitted among the frozen limbs of the two apple trees.

"We need to put some food out for the birds, Anna. Maybe some cracker crumbs or something."

"Ja, Colonel. I'll sprinkle some on the snow."

Anna cut the thick sandwich into two halves and placed them on a plate and poured steaming coffee into his favorite red mug.

"If you'll put it on a tray, Anna, I'll have it down in the war room."

The muffled crunch of tires on the iced driveway announced Hans had arrived. The colonel watched as Hans came around the back of the Mercedes, all bundled in black overcoat, scarf and wool hat, to the passenger side. He opened the car door and began stacking newspapers into the crook of his left arm as though they were cordwood for the fireplace. The colonel got up and opened the door as Hans moved carefully up the iced steps to the kitchen.

"Got all the early editions, I see," said the colonel, speaking German. "Have any trouble with the roads?"

"*Nein,* colonel. The roads clear are; only small ice on the little streets."

"Good. Let's take everything down to the war room."

He crossed the kitchen toward the hallway and noticed Anna was already bringing the tray with his lunch. "Thanks, Anna."

The procession, led by the colonel, entered the door to the old wine cellar. They descended the long flight of wooden steps to the black steel door at the bottom. The colonel dialed the combination and lifted the lever upward. He flicked a switch and the war room was instantly bathed in bright fluorescent light.

The cellar had been built entirely of stone with two-foot thick granite walls. The colonel had taken great delight in refurbishing the cellar into a war room that he shared with very few people. Anna and Louise hardly ever went down there, except to bring him coffee or a snack. He had rigged a telephone between his war room and the kitchen. A separate, outside line connected the war room with the German public telephone system.

The room contained all that was of value to a career intelligence officer. The right wall was filled with maps covered with acetate. He could apply grease pencils or erasable ink markers to draw lines, order of battle symbols, or follow an operation across topographic sectors. Pushpins of many colors were placed here and there denoting certain types of installations. The largest of the maps were of East and West Germany and Hungary, site of current military activity. Smaller maps of Berlin, Frankfurt, Vienna, Prague, the Island of Crete, and the Middle East were arranged neatly under shiny acetate.

Along the left wall were shelves filled with green library boxes, each labeled and arranged by subject and chronologically. They contained order of battle information about most of the major fighting units of World War II, Korea, and the world's current armies. Above the bookcases was a world map.

The colonel kept pace with current military activities through his vast network of contacts as well as using common newspapers and wire reports. He deduced the outcomes of skirmishes in Hungary, for example, based entirely on wire service reports.

The wall to the left contained memorabilia from his happier days. There was a commendation certificate signed by then Brig. General George Patton. Photos of him when he graduated from OCS at Fort Benning. Another as a captain at the border crossing near Salzburg in 1945 with his favorite interpreter, a German Jew and concentration camp survivor named Harvey Gold. Plaques identified him as Officer of the Month in 1943, 1944, and 1946. A commendation in 1950. A framed letter congratulating him on his performance carrying out intelligence missions signed by General Dwight D. Eisenhower.

The central piece of the display, however, was a prized weapon of the German *Fallschrimjaeger*, the famous *Schmeisser* automatic pistol. It was mounted under glass in a walnut frame. A full clip of ammunition and another clip and accessories—including the attachable shoulder stock and sling—surrounded the pistol. The weapon was in mint condition and would have fetched the highest price, if he had wished to sell it.

An old, roll-top desk and a four-drawer file cabinet next to the entrance contained his special cache of documents about the Stauffenberg fiasco. In separately marked files were fold-ers of materials about General Kurt Student's Seventh Airborne Division of the *Wehrmacht*, the command structures of the German Army in Prague and in Vienna during 1944, and copies of documents concerning *Operation Mercury* and *Task Force Crete*. Other files contained order of battle information on the *Gestapo*, including biographical sketches, orders and other items about the well known, the infamous, and the lesser-known *players* as he called them.

In the center of the room was a large mahogany table upon which were spread recently acquired documents and photo-graphs. Most of the items were German newspaper accounts of the recent murder of Georg Krusen. The colonel had managed to collect nearly every edition of the newspapers carrying the story, even those which reported the incident in brief, single paragraphs buried inside among advertisements and unimport-ant news.

The colonel subscribed to so many newspapers from Germany, England, and the United States that it took him nearly three hours each morning to scan the headlines and read pertinent stories. And there were days when, following a gut feeling to do so, he read the classified sections, looking for any suspicious announcements or ads that could provide a clue to some covert activity. He seldom found any of import, but it was a game he had practiced for many years to keep his instincts sharp.

"Put the papers here on this end of the table, Hans," he said, pointing to the left side of the great table. Anna placed the tray in front of the brown leather swivel chair.

"Anna, you might go up and tell Louise that Hans is back. I think she wants to do some Christmas shopping this afternoon. Maybe all of you could go together and spend the afternoon in Frankfurt."

He noticed Hans and Anna glance at one another.

"*Ja*, I'll tell her, Colonel. Is there anything more I can get you before we go?"

"No. Close and lock the upstairs door before you leave, okay?"

"*Jawoll.* There is strudel and fresh milk in the refrigerator in case you get hungry."

"Thanks."

As the two servants disappeared up the stairs, the colonel opened and stacked the newspapers according to name, date and edition. Hans had picked up all of yesterday's editions he could find from the largest newspaper shop in Frankfurt on *Frederick Ebert Strasse.* He then went to the *Hauptbahnhof*—the main train station in Frankfurt—to obtain the latest morning editions.

Sitting down in the swivel chair, he pulled the first stack in front of him and began scanning the first section of the *Berliner Zeitung* while lifting half of the turkey sandwich to his mouth and biting off a sizable chunk. He reached for the coffee and washed the food down, enjoying the mixture of chicory, coffee, and sandwich. On the second page, his eyes fastened upon a headline: *"Murder Suspect Held at Charlottenburg Precinct."* The story said Heinz Beckmann was the main suspect in the torturing and killing of Georg Krusen, a citizen of the allied sector of Berlin.

"Beckmann… Beck…" he mused aloud. "Surely, it is not a coincidence."

The article described Krusen as being an employee of the public works department for the city. He was an engineer with the city from 1946 until his death two days ago. No surviving family members. A World War II veteran. Paratrooper. Wounded in Holland. Yes, thought Wafford, I know all this. Let's find something new.

Thumbing through the early morning edition, the colonel found an update. According to Berlin Police Inspector Krebs, Heinz Beckmann may be Heinz Beck, a former SS non-commissioned officer, identified through Interpol and Israeli Intelligence as a resident of Paraguay and a war criminal.

"Yes! Bingo!" cried Wafford. His excitement grew as he realized what Beck's presence meant. "If Beck's back in Germany, Horst must also be here," he said aloud. So far as he could see, Beck never acted without orders directly from Horst. Wouldn't it be great, thought Wafford, if he could capture the bastard and bring Horst before a war crimes tribunal? He's got to be nearby. Probably hiding in East Germany, slipping into Berlin with Beck just for the Krusen event? Hm, thought Wafford. If they were after Krusen, Horst would also be gunning for the man who took the relic and *Schmeisser* away from him in that mountain pass at the end of the war. A wave of uncertainty caused Wafford to run his hands through his thinning hair. Yes, he acknowledged, Horst would be coming after him, too, probably sooner than later. Perhaps Major von Etter had told Horst more than he had suspected about the relic and the whereabouts of the jewels and gold. Ah, well, Wafford thought, I can match Horst's game any day of the week.

He read on. Beckmann was apprehended after he attempted to authenticate part of a broken antique relic. Dieter Lenhardt, an employee at the Museum of Egyptology, recognized the relic as belonging to an acquaintance. Lenhardt alerted police about the possibility of foul play. Krusen was found beaten and shot to death at his flat in the Charlottenburg section of Berlin. Lenhardt would give no details except to say he was certain the relic belonged to the victim.

The museum curator, Dr. Kurt Schaus, was quoted as saying Heinz Beckmann came to the museum to find out whether the relic had any historical value. Beckmann was also asking questions about what the carvings and marks on the object signified. The curator confirmed that the object appeared to be the same as that belonging to Krusen, and that it was originally part of a larger wooden relic probably of Minoan origin.

The colonel painstakingly sorted through the various newspaper accounts, tearing off whole pages where articles appeared and marking the stories with a black grease pencil. It was in this morning's edition of *Das Bild* that he found what he was looking for: a photograph of the relic in the hand of Inspector Krebs.

Wafford glanced toward the cabinet beneath the framed *Schmeisser*, got up, went to the cabinet, and opened the glass door. He lifted out a small bundle wrapped in green velvet, and tied with a brown cord. He couldn't suppress his elation as he placed the tiny bundle on the table, sat down, and unwrapped it slowly.

Removing the velvet, he drew out the piece of wooden relic with its leather thong and rubbed the polished surface with thumb and forefinger. He placed the relic next to the photograph showing the small object held by the inspector.

"Jim, dear, we're leaving now. Do you want me to get anything else for the boys?"

Louise was calling him from the top of the stairs and the colonel hardly heard her voice.

"Jim?"

"Uh, no, Louise. I can't think of anything. Maybe you can find some small things we can carry on the plane. You pick out whatever you want. I'm sure the boys'll be happy with anything we bring them."

"All right. We'll be back around seven o'clock."

"Fine, dear. Why don't you treat Anna and Hans to a snack at that new place on *Goethe Platz*?"

"That's sweet of you, Jim. I will. Are you sure we can't get something for you?"

"No, dear. Will you lock the door on your way out?"

All right. Bye."

He listened for the firm closing of the door and the click of the deadbolt before returning to his work. Taking a large magnifying glass from the table drawer, he focused upon the object Krebs was holding up for the photographer.

"Jackpot!" he cried as he compared the relic in his hand with that shown in the photograph. Krusen's was apparently the third piece of four. It joined his from the right side, which meant there was one more on the left edge and one more on the right edge to make the round disk complete.

"Thank you, Inspector Krebs! You don't know it yet, but you have in your hand a little piece of antiquity that will lead me to a fortune in gold and jewels. And you, SS Sergeant Heinz Beck, came all the way from Paraguay just to find it for me. You stupid *Kraut*! You and Horst made a serious wrong choice. I've got to call Harry and share the good news."

He swung his chair around to the desk and dialed Harry at his home.

"Harry?"

"Yeah, Jim. How are things going?"

"Fine, Harry. Great, actually."

"And Louise?"

"Louise is fine, too. She's out shopping presents to take when we visit our boys."

"Well, I hope you have a terrific holiday back in New York."

"Thanks. Listen, Harry, I just wanted to let you know I appreciated the lead you gave me the other night on this murder in Berlin. It confirms everything. I'm close to breaking the whole business wide open."

"You're welcome. Just don't get carried away with it, Jim. Those old *Krauts* don't play around. I was sharing the news as a matter of interest, not to get you involved there."

"What's that?"

"What I'm saying is, stay out of this murder business. Don't get your ass in a sling at this point in your life."

"Well, no. Naturally, I'll follow all the protocols, Harry. You know that. Hell, I wouldn't do anything foolish at my age, any more than you would."

"I know. But metaphorically, we both understand how easy it is to go too far beyond our sources of supply, so to speak. You've got to keep your ass covered."

"Right!"

Wafford could feel the heat rising in his cheeks.

"Well, Harry, metaphorically speaking, I guess that's all my news…"

"Just remember that you're retired now. You can't pull strings any more like you used to."

"Yeah. I realize that, Harry. I won't be pulling any goddamned strings any more."

"Good. Give my best to Louise."

"Okay."

"Is the Christmas party still on?"

"Yeah. I believe Louise has sent out all the invitations, so we'll see you before we leave."

"Terrific. Take care of yourself."

"You do the same."

The colonel placed the receiver in the cradle, swung back to the table and instantly felt a wave of disgust. The conversation had taken a false turn at the git-go, not leading where it should have.

"Son of a bitch!" the colonel whispered. "I try to share some exciting news and ole Harry has to give me the same old metaphorical bullshit. 'Now, Jim, let's not go out of bounds on this, Jim' 'Don't do anything you'll regret, Jim! 'Protect your ass, Jim.'

He thought, Harry just can't give up the idea that I don't work for him anymore. Besides, he doesn't have the balls to do what I am doing. Never did!

The colonel toyed with the black grease pencil with his stubby fingers. He flicked it across the polished surface of the table where it pinged against the brass nameplate from his days in G-2. Oh well, he thought, I never could rely on Harry.

He ate the remainder of his sandwich. It was clear that Horst had gotten von Etter to talk. Why else would he kill von Etter's friend twelve years later and confiscate the piece of relic? No question about it, the punctures and cut marks on the back tell where the stash is hidden. He lifted the mug of coffee in the air. 'Here's to you, Krebs. And to you, too, Beck and Horst, you *Nazi* bastards. And as for you, Harry, you can go straight to Hell.' He swallowed the coffee down to the last dregs and turned back to his desk. He must let Blakely know there was a change of plans. If Cunningham wouldn't do the job, he'd ask Blakely to do it. He needed him to be in Berlin more than down in Heidelberg. He would set up a meeting ASAP.

He listened silently. He thought he heard something upstairs. Pulling out the left drawer of his desk, he removed his loaded U.S. Army issue Colt .45 automatic and moved deftly up the wooden staircase. He unlocked the deadbolt. There, another scratching sound coming from the front rooms. He crept forward, into the vestibule. Nothing. Then something! Scratching on the porch. He quickly moved into the living room, holding the .45 above his head. He drew the curtain back while lowering the gun at the window. A wind had come up. A branch was scratching the downspout on the porch. He gathered himself, catching his breath. A single set of human footprints in the snow mounted the steps, crossed the porch to the window, then went in the opposite direction, returning down the steps and out to the road. All was clear. No cars. No foot traffic.

Had Hans walked there this morning? The footprints were man-sized. He would have to ask Hans about it. He dropped the automatic down to his hip and slumped into his favorite chair. Was he getting this young man Blakely in over his head? Naw, he thought. They could handle it.

Chapter 6

The Palmengarten

Blakely huddled next to the Kodak Kiosk, stamping his feet to keep them warm. An icy knife of wind swept across from the pond beyond which he could hear the howling of many zoo animals. A man in a tan overcoat and brown slouch hat emerged from the far entrance. It was Wafford.

"*Guten Morgan, Herr* Blakely," said Wafford, pulling a leather-gloved hand from his pocket.

"*Morgan*, Colonel," Blakely replied as they shook hands.

"Cold as Hades this morning!"

"For sure," although Blakely thought something was very wrong with the simile.

"Oh, by the way, I'd just as soon you didn't call me colonel when we're out like this," Wafford whispered while looking around the empty park.

"If you say so, sir." Blakely wiped a smirk from his face with his gloved hand. "How should I address you?"

"And don't call me sir anymore… That's too military. Either Jim or Mr. Wafford will do, depending on the circumstances."

"Yes…" Blakely nearly said 'sir' out of habit. What circumstances, he wondered. He watched as Wafford continued to scan the patches of snow and crescent of ice on the pond. There wasn't a soul to be seen.

"Have a change in plans."

"Oh?"

Wafford rubbed his hands together.

"No need to go down to Heidelberg right now. More important you go to Berlin."

"Yeah?

Wafford leaned in, hunching his shoulders against the cold.

"One of Heinrich von Etter's war buddies—a Georg Krusen–was murdered there a couple of days ago. He was killed by a former *Gestapo* NCO by the name of Heinz Beck. Remember me telling you 'bout him?"

"Who?"

"Beck."

"Was he one of the *Gestapo* guys you caught with the gun at that checkpoint in the mountains?"

"One and the same. He came all the way back from Paraguay to make the hit. Just got a clean ID on him yesterday afternoon."

"But why after all these years?"

"Von Etter apparently sent a piece of the relic to Krusen. Horst and Beck got Heinrich von Etter to tell what he'd done with the pieces. Horst found out Krusen was living in Berlin and came after it with Beck. He and Beck murdered Krusen *Gestapo*-style. That's my take on what happened."

Holy shit, Blakely thought. This is big-time. He shivered and pressed his arms against his sides. What in hell was Wafford getting him into?

"How do you know?"

"Beck was arrested yesterday. It's in all the papers. He did a stupid thing. He took the relic to a Berlin museum for identification purposes. The archeologist who examined it was a friend of Georg Krusen and realized Beck must have stolen it. He notified authorities and they arrested him. It was a piece of cake to link Beck to the murder."

"So, where does Horst come in?"

"Beck was his NCO. He wouldn't know when to piss, if Horst weren't there to tell him. I can assure you Horst was there directing Beck every step of the way."

"Then… Why are you getting involved in this?"

"Well, hell, Ed… The murder validates it…The relic holds the key to where a fortune in gold and jewels is hidden. Why else would Horst and Beck risk their lives coming back to Germany and kill a man for it? They probably ran out of money and were desperate."

"But won't they be coming after you, too? You've got part of the relic."

"Ed, you're jumping to too many conclusions... You're forgetting that intelligence work requires taking one step at a time. Either you are willing to work with me and trust me or you're not. Which is it, Ed?"

Blakely shrugged.

Well, sir... Sorry. I mean, well Jim, as I said before... I'm not into covert work. That's not what I'm trained for. And I don't necessarily want to mix it up with a bunch of *Gestapo* guys no matter how old they are."

"It's just fact-finding. That's all. No danger. Believe me, Ed. I wouldn't put you in the line of fire. That'd be crazy!"

"Yes, s... What is it you want me to do?"

"I'm having orders cut as we speak. Want you to take the *Milk Run*—the Frankfurt-Berlin train–tonight as a courier. I want you to spend a couple days in Berlin doing some interviews for me. I also need photographs of the relic: front and back."

Wafford touched Blakely on his coat sleeve. "No danger, Ed. You needn't worry one iota 'bout that Beck fella. He can't hurt you 'cause he's in jail. And his former commander, Eugen Horst—if he was in Berlin helping Beck—he's probably back in East Germany and afraid to come out of hiding."

"How would I get photos? You mean I should take a camera with me?"

The colonel grinned sardonically while looking away. "Naw! I don't want any amateur pictures, Ed. Dr. Shaus at the museum and Inspector Krebs of the Berlin Police must have professional photos. Just want copies is all..."

"And these guys will talk to me?"

"Absolutely. You'll be on official military business. As I say, you are doing fact-finding for a government agency. Only...you don't hafta tell 'em which agency. Your orders will say explicitly what your mission is... Just show 'em copies of your orders is all."

Blakely looked questioningly at the colonel. He wondered whether Wafford had his own printing press in his war room to print out fake orders. Certainly, his so-called mission could not be officially sanctioned by the Army Security Agency or anyone else.

"What if they want to keep copies of my orders. Is that okay?"

"Oh, sure," said Wafford. Blakely's eye was drawn to an elderly man being pulled by a large German shepherd toward a cluster of ducks on the far side of the pond.

"Perfectly proper. I'd be surprised if they didn't ask for copies."

"So I wear my *Class B* uniform as a courier and change into civilian clothes to do the mission?"

"For sure. Take at least two changes of civies with you. You can change clothes at Berlin Command Headquarters. I have a couple of hotels in mind where you can stay. I'll put it all on paper for you."

"Should we meet back here later for your instructions and orders?"

"No. I'll leave a package for you at the English Bookstore. Ask for Betty Crawford. She'll give it to you anytime after 1400 hours."

"Any other words of advice, Jim?"

"Naw. I trust you'll do what's necessary. Just follow my checklist. It covers every contingency, including aborting the mission—just in case something unexpected comes up… Are you okay with it?"

"Yes…" Blakely almost said 'sir' again. It would be a difficult habit to correct.

"Oh, one more thing… and this is very important. Under no circumstances are you to mention my name to anyone you contact."

"May I ask why?"

"Let's just say I have my reasons. Okay?"

"Yes."

"Good luck, then. Leave a message for me with Betty when you return. We can arrange to meet back here. Remember the code for *Palmengarten*?"

"Uh, *tropics*."

"Very good. I'll need a written report and the photos. The report should be a point summary based on my checklist. Not a lot of verbiage. Understand?"

"Yes."

"Oh, one more thing. When you leave Berlin Command Headquarters to be on your own, they usually send a tail to see where you go."

"Oh. Really?"

"Yeah. Usually one fella. You can't miss 'em. Counter or criminal intelligence. They know it's a game. Hop on a *strassenbahn*, then jump off quickly and get on another. Repeat as necessary. You'll lose him within a few blocks. That's standard procedure."

"Wouldn't losing him raise suspicions?"

"Naw. They don't want to report that you were clever enough to give 'em the slip."

"Well, if you say so."

"I say so," he said with a grin. "*Vedersehen!*"

"*Vedersehen.*"

Sounded like a recipe for disaster. Blakely nodded in disbelief. He had entered a new, surreal world: the world of Wafford, where one cannot tell the difference between fact and fiction. And his mission was fact-finding... or so Wafford would have him believe. He turned away. He walked toward the exit gate nestled between high, snow-covered hedges. He glanced over his shoulder. Wafford was moving slowly across the iced walk in the opposite direction, toward the man and the dog, holding his hat by its brim and leaning into the cold wind.

Chapter 7

The English Bookstore

Blakely entered the English Bookstore. A little bell tinkled over the door. There didn't seem to be any customers. A woman sat behind the counter. She was tall, wispy, fortyish, with hair pulled into a bun, spinster-style. She smiled and held out a slender hand. "I'm Betty Crawford... and unless I'm mistaken, you must be Mr. Blakely."

"Yes, ma'am. Glad to meet you."

Her smile was filled with British reserve, what Blakely felt was 'carefully friendly' as she seemed to size him up. Her hand felt thin, cool, smooth, before releasing it. She reached under the counter and produced a manila envelope. She handed it to him.

"May I call you Edward?"

"Please do."

Blakely looked around. He was the only customer. A muted *Hark the Herald Angels* played from a backroom behind the counter.

"And I want you to call me Betty."

"Yes, ma'am. Mind if I browse?"

"Oh, most certainly. I would be disappointed if you didn't."

Most of the books were inexpensive, paperback editions published by Penguin, Modern Library and Everyone's Library.

"Do you happen to have Hemingway's *A Farewell to Arms?*"

"Yes. I'm sure we do. Let's just look over here."

She came around the counter and walked to a stall.

"We should look here."

She bent down to a bottom shelf.

"Here we are."

She pulled one of two copies of *A Farewell to Arms* from the shelf with all the care of lifting a baby in her hands. It was a Bantam paperback edition. The price on the cover was thirty-five cents.

"Would you like something else from Mr. Hemingway as a gift for someone?"

"How do you know this is not a gift for someone?"

He was amused by her slight audacity.

"I can always tell the difference." She smiled broadly while slipping the book into a bag.

"How do you tell the difference?"

"It's quite easy, you know. My new customers—strangers like yourself—are very deliberate when they are buying a book for themselves, because they have already decided what they want most of the time before they come here."

"Really?"

"Yes. You came here and said you would like to browse, then immediately asked whether I had this novel. This had to be personal choice."

"But suppose I had come here to buy a gift of Hemingway for a friend?"

"Then you wouldn't have said you were browsing, would you?"

Blakely scratched his head.

"No, I guess not."

"Most people do spend much time browsing when purchasing a gift book for a friend or relative—unless they truly don't like books."

"Oh?"

"Book lovers must take time to find the appropriate match between a book and the person they wish to receive it, so I suppose it to be a deliberate sorting out process. Or at least that is what we have observed."

There was that 'we' again. Blakely glanced toward the rear office. There was nobody there.

"And what about those who do not like books? What's the difference?"

She laughed self-consciously, pulling her hand up in front of her mouth. She leaned toward him conspiratorially.

"People who don't like books buy my most expensive ones—the large hardbacks you see here and in the window. I believe they do so out of guilt."

She pointed toward the large display of coffee table books on the counter before writing out a receipt.

"That will be one *mark*, fifty *phenigs*, please."

Blakely drew several coins from his pocket and fished out the proper amount.

"Thank you. Here's a little gift for you at holiday time."

She handed him a red leather bookmark with gold printing upon which *English Bookstore* was embossed along with a crest and the address and telephone number.

"That's very nice, Betty. Do you give these out to all your customers?"

"No," she replied again in conspiratorial tones. "These are only for people who care about books—such as yourself."

"Thank you."

"Would you like a cup of tea, Edward?"

Blakely felt the envelope containing his orders. It was the thickness of a *Collier's* magazine, and he couldn't wait to open it.

"I think I should be going. Could I have a rain check on the tea?

"Most certainly."

Betty clasped her hands like a schoolgirl before extending her hand out again. "I am sure we will be seeing much of one another."

Blakely smiled and shook her hand gently. "Yes, I am sure."

Upon getting on the *strassenbahn*, Blakely tried to remember the entire sequence with Betty Crawford. She seemed a prudent, careful, but warm person. One who wouldn't risk losing a business it probably took years to develop. How did she come to trust Wafford? And how was it that Wafford came to trust her? Was she CIA or sponsored by one of the agencies? Certainly, her shop was a perfect fence for black market, intelligence swapping, smuggling, you name it. He reminded himself again what Charon and Wafford had said: Don't trust anybody. Don't share any information.

After glancing around the car to be sure nobody was watching, Blakely opened the envelope and examined the contents. Clearly, Wafford had left nothing to chance. There were Army orders, Russian orders to be used on the *Milk Run*; checklists of questions he was to memorize for the interviews; copies of news stories about the murder of Krusen; addresses, phone numbers and contact names; maps showing streets, contact locations, districts of Berlin; diagrams of trolley and underground routes and stations showing off-limits cars and lines entering the Russian sector. It must have taken weeks for Wafford to gather all the information here. Still, the entire scheme of Wafford doing all this seemed to him quite bizarre.

Blakely got off the *strassenbahn* at the *Hauptbahnhof* and headed toward the *Gutleut Kaserne*. On impulse, he decided to get the latest editions of the Berlin papers inside the station. They would make great reading on the train. Besides, there might be some late-breaking information about Beck or Horst or the relic Wafford was so excited about.

Chapter 8

The Milk Run to Berlin

Blakely checked in at Headquarters, US Army Security Agency Europe, at 1600 hours. He was directed to a room just off the main corridor. A tow-headed blond sergeant was cinching a cartridge belt around the waist of his Ike jacket. He looked up and grinned.

"You my date tonight?"

"Guess so."

"Tom Kentop. You must be Ed Blakely."

They shook hands.

"Is this your first *Milk Run*," asked Kentop.

"Yup."

"Waiting on your clearance to catch up with you?"

"They say it takes at least six weeks. You been doing this long? "

"I've been up and back about twelve times. It's fun at first, but it's getting old. I've seen just about everything you can see in Berlin outside the Russian sector. Did you bring any snacks or playing cards?"

"No. I didn't think about that."

"Honeymoon Bridge is fun, but I didn't bring my cards either. Well, I've got enough snacks and sodas for both of us. I also have a couple of *Newsweeks* and a *Life* in case you want something to read."

"Sounds like you're prepared for everything."

"Well, I don't know about you, but I find it's hard to sleep on a train. And when you travel all night, you need some snacks and stuff."

Kentop filled a clip with .30 caliber shells and snapped the clip into the carbine.

"How come we're using carbines instead of Army .45s?"

"Guess not everybody's qualified for pistols. The officers who fly in and out of Berlin with top-secret pouches carry them. Us peons who carry confidential stuff are limited to carbines."

Blakely began loading ammo into two clips.

"How's the scenery? Can you see East Germany at night?"

"Lord no," said Kentop. "The Ruskies don't want you to see nothing. We have to keep the curtains drawn while crossing the Eastern Zone. I guess they don't want us reporting any military activity. And now, they've taken to stopping trains. Been three in a row stopped."

"What happens then?"

"Nothin'. Just harassment is all. They just hold the train up for a couple hours, then let us proceed."

"Why do they do it?"

"Military maneuvers mostly, I guess. They don't want us to see what they're doing."

A master sergeant entered, dragging four large leather and canvas pouches with padlocked tops behind him and a folder tucked under his arm.

"You boys sign for these, please…I also need a copy of your orders and ID."

"Okey-doke," said Kentop.

Kentop and Blakely signed the forms, slung the carbines on their shoulders, and hauled the pouches and personal bags out the doors to where a black 1949 Mercedes sedan waited in the iced half circle drive. A German national got out of the car and opened the rear doors.

"Ed, this is Oscar, our driver."

They shook hands. Oscar took their bags and put them in the trunk while Blakely and Kentop climbed in the back with the pouches next to them.

"Oscar has been picking up couriers for three years, Ed. He's a weather expert and can tell you when the train will be late leaving and when it'll arrive in Berlin. Isn't that right, Oscar?"

"*Ja*! Except those damn Russians are now fooling with our trains so you can't count on anything these days. Just last Monday, the train arrived three hours late into Frankfurt, keeping me standing there waiting for it without word as to when it would come in. So, you can't count on anything from those damn Russians."

With Russian and American military orders in hand, Kentop and Blakely left Oscar's car in front of the *Hauptbahnhof* and hauled their bags and pouches through the ticketing area and waiting room directly to the departure area. The train was open and ready for them to step aboard. A cluster of GIs and civilians and a few children stood behind another gate, obviously ready to board the same train. A second lieutenant armed with a holstered .45 pistol waited for the couriers at the steps of the first car behind the engine. They saluted.

"I'm Lieutenant Robert Jackson. I will be the officer in charge of this train tonight." He examined their orders, glanced at the pouches and weapons. "I want you to know that you are to keep the safeties set on those carbines and lay them on the floor of your compartment, barrels pointing away from the compartment door. Is that clear?"

"Yes, sir."

"Furthermore, you are not to touch your weapons unless I command you to do so. Understood?"

"Yes, sir."

"When you enter your compartment, be sure you lock the door after you and stay there until we arrive at Kastel. At that point, a courier will come aboard to pick up one pouch—the one with the green label—and deliver another one to you. Are you clear about the procedures?"

"Yes, sir."

"In the event we are stopped inside East Germany, do exactly as I command. If I ask you to open the door, do not draw any weapons. Just follow my orders."

"Yes, sir."

The lieutenant took copies of the Russian orders and attached them to his clipboard. "Now climb aboard so I can process the other passengers. You're in 1C tonight."

Blakely pushed the door open. The compartment was spacious, comfortable. It had a toilet, lavatory, mirror, and two fold-down beds. The upholstery of the seats appeared to be new. The maple wood interior was finished to satin-smoothness. What a difference between this train and those he used to ride between Los Angeles and San Diego. There was no comparing them.

Kentop settled back in the seat and opened his mobility bag. He pulled out two magazines, offered one to Blakely, and then took out two boxes of snack pretzels and one of cookies.

"Here. Help yourself." Kentop handed him a box of pretzels. "It's going to be a long trip, so you might as well enjoy it."

Blakely pulled two newspapers from his bag and offered them to Kentop. "Got last night's editions of the *Zeitung* and *Bild,* if you care to read one."

"No thanks. My German's not so red hot."

The train pulled out of Frankfurt half an hour later. The four cars and diesel engine moved along swiftly to the northeast. At Kastel, it stopped and voices were heard. A few minutes later, there was a knock on their compartment door. Kentop opened it and greeted the courier as Lieutenant Jackson and Blakely looked on. They exchanged pouches, signed transfer forms, said goodbye, and the door was again closed and locked.

"Now we'll see whether the Ruskies stop us at the border again," Kentop said as he sat down and closed the window curtains after taking a brief look outside.

"From now on, we can't so much as raise a corner of these curtains; that's how much the Ruskies and East Germans want to hide what they're up to."

The train began moving again, traveling at a slower pace until it arrived at the East German border. It came to a stop. Blakely could visualize Jackson climbing down from the first car to greet his Russian and East German counterparts. He could hear them talking, but couldn't determine what they were saying. An interpreter was speaking Russian, German, and English in between. Discussion went on for as much as fifteen minutes.

"What's going on," asked Blakely.

"I don't know. From the sound of it, they don't seem to be communicating on the same wavelength. This is different from the way they acted last week. They took a long time, but our train commander said they held us up because of some military convoy up ahead. This time, it sounds like a basic difference of opinion over something. I think we should be on our toes and ready to use our weapons."

Instead of being frightened, the idea of pulling carbines on Russians in the compartment of a train car seemed to Blakely utterly absurd. He nearly laughed aloud, imagining the comic yet possibly very serious situation. Blakely sat back, munching on a pretzel and listening. Lt. Jackson began cursing under his breath as he walked down the aisle and stopped outside their door.

"I told the son of a bitch that he was not allowed on board this train, that this train belonged to the United States Government, and that he would have to seek permission from our officials before I would let him on it," Jackson said heatedly.

"Sounds like you did exactly the right thing," was the reply. "Is he going back to get permission?"

"That's what I understand, sir. I have also radioed headquarters to get advice, but haven't gotten a response."

The two voices faded again as the two men evidently stepped out of the car and onto the platform. There was silence except for the sounds of nearby trains stopping and starting during the next hour. Blakely realized most of the engines were steam rather than diesel. He finished his Orange Crush and slipped the empty bottle into his B-4.

"I don't know about you, Tom, but I'm about ready to pull down the bed and try to get to sleep before we begin rolling again. Which bunk do you want?"

"Bottom."

Blakely checked his watch. 2300 hours.

"How do these work?"

Kentop showed him how to pull down and lock the upper berth while he flipped the lower birth out from the seat.

"Hope you don't mind the veteran courier getting the bottom bunk, Ed. That's the one extra benefit old hands get over new ones," he chuckled as he climbed in.

Blakely glanced through the newspapers, finding it hard to concentrate. He lay back and put the papers aside. Just about the time he was dozing off, he heard voices again. Suddenly, Lt. Jackson's voice blasted the air.

"Attention! Attention, Everyone on board this car. Prepare to open your compartments and be ready to show your ID and copies of your orders in Russian to the local commander here. I am asking everyone to cooperate. Those of you who are on special duty, please cooperate to the fullest. Disregard any prior instructions you have received. In five minutes, I will be coming through the train with Major Vladimir Shenko, who will ask you for an identification card and a copy of your orders. Please get these documents ready now. You are to give him one copy of your orders when he asks you for it."

"Well, damn!" exclaimed Kentop as he jumped out of the berth. "This is a new twist. What are we supposed to do?"

They cleared the bunks.

"Guess we have to stay calm and let the lieutenant tell us what to do." Blakely rinsed his face in the lavatory.

Tom was clearly agitated and paced back and forth in the narrow space. "I'm assuming that when Lieutenant Jackson emphasized people on special orders, that meant us. Right? So, if that's what he says, and he is the train's commander and we are under his command, then that's what we've gotta do, right?"

"Right." Blakely rubbed a hand towel over his face.

"But what if this Shenko guy asks us for the pouches? Then what are we to do?"

"Damned if I know."

"But maybe Jackson can answer that one, too, since he'll be right there. I agree with you… I'm not going to do anything unless Jackson isn't there. If he isn't with the bastard, then it is up to us to tell him what we'll do and not do. That right, Ed?"

"Right."

Blakely twisted the towel in his hands, appreciating the fact that they could be in deep shit in the next few minutes. He heard approaching voices, a knocking at the door of the compartment next door, a muted discussion. The door closed again. A few seconds later, there was a loud knock on their door.

"Well, brace up ole buddy, here we go," whispered Kentop as he grasped the door handle and looked down at the two carbines on the floor. "Are you ready?"

"Sure."

Blakely was not sure at all. There would be no chance to retrieve the weapons. It was stupid not to have pistols that could be pulled in split seconds. Kentop swung the door open. Lieutenant Jackson stood in the doorway. Behind him was a Russian officer who appeared to be in his early thirties. They saluted. The Russian was short, trim, athletic, with head erect, broad shoulders, a tailored gray uniform. His shiny black boots came to the knee like cavalry. His dark eyebrows were in stark contrast to smooth white skin. Holy hell, thought Blakely, I am staring into the eyes of the new enemy. The Russian stepped forward.

"Orders, please." Shenko said it quickly but with a certain politeness, holding out his hand to receive them. As he spoke, he nodded slightly in military fashion, showing square white teeth and unflinching blue-gray eyes.

"Gentlemen," said Jackson, "please cooperate with Major Shenko here. He will also want to see your military identification card. And if you will, please relax a bit and not concern yourselves about your weapons."

Blakely and Kentop handed their identification cards to the Russian. He glanced at Kentop and returned his ID, nodding affirmatively, saying, *"Danke."*

He spent a few seconds more in examining Blakely's ID, pausing once to look from photo to face, then back to the card again. Returning the card, he looked into Blakely's eyes as though he expected to read something in them. He glanced around the compartment, seeming to note the pouches in the far corner and the two carbines on the floor, but he never changed expression. He turned away, saying again, *"Danke"* as he moved on. Jackson, now behind the Russian officer, glanced at Kentop and Blakely with a sigh and an eye roll that suggested all this was silly but very serious nonsense everyone would have to put up with.

Blakely locked the door and leaned against it. Sweat was dripping down his ribs. Kentop slumped onto the seat.

"Now, just what the hell do you think that was about?"

"Scary," said Blakely. "But it wasn't as bad as I thought it might be."

The impression the young officer made upon Blakely was not easy to dismiss. He had looked carefully at me, he thought, studying me so he would remember me for a future time. Was he really a local commander or was he from Russian Intelligence? He was probably both. Blakely pulled pencil and paper out of his bag and set about describing the officer. He would report this episode to Wafford and see what he thought. Perhaps Shenko—if that is really his name—is responsible for the new policy of stopping all the trains.

They pulled the bunks down again and climbed into them. The train did not get underway for another hour. It was good to stretch out on the bunk, but Blakely was wide-awake. He retrieved Wafford's instructions and studied them for the next two hours. He memorized the directions to the museum, studied the maps of Berlin and trolley routes. His plan was to buy a small suitcase at the Post Exchange and check into a small hotel near the museum before conducting any interviews. He counted the money Wafford had given him: 800 *marks*. He stuffed the notes into his wallet and slipped all the papers back into the envelope. Then, he tried to sleep, but Blakely could not erase the image of Major Shenko's face when their eyes had locked.

He awoke to the sound of Lieutenant Jackson announcing they would be arriving in Berlin in fifteen minutes. He glanced at his watch. They were running an hour and a half late. He looked forward to getting rid of the pouches, checking into quarters, having a nice shower and shave, some breakfast, and starting his investigation into the backgrounds of Georg Krusen and Heinz Beck.

He realized he had never met a *Nazi* that he knew of. He wondered how he would handle his emotions. It was one thing to stare into the eyes of an enemy like Shenko, who was essentially a political enemy. It was another to come face to face with a cold-blooded killer like Heinz Beck. The scent of tobacco smoke broke his reverie. He opened his eyes. Kentop was already dressed and smoking a cigarette. Blakely swung down from the bunk and pulled on his shirt.

"Morn'n."

"Morning."

"How 'bout we take in a flick this afternoon. *The Man in the Gray Flannel Suit* with Gregory Peck is playing downtown."

Blakely ran his hand through his hair.

"That'd be great, but I made plans to visit a museum today."

"Really."

"Yeah. I'm interested in ancient history."

"No shit. You a teacher or something?"

"No. But I always admired Schliemann."

"Don't know 'im. Who's he?"

"An amateur archeologist from right here in Berlin. He's the guy who dug up Troy and Mycenae. Found gold masks, shields, all sorts of stuff."

Kentop moved the pouches to the door just as the train stopped.

"Guess I'll be seeing you tonight, then."

"Actually, I'm staying over a couple days. I've always wanted to explore Berlin."

"Oh?" Kentop seemed disappointed. He picked up his bag and two pouches and moved out the door. A whiff of icy air struck them as they moved down the aisle toward the exit door. "Our driver will be waiting at the top of the stairs."

"Is it true that CIC or CID guys follow you when you leave headquarters on the *strassenbahn*?"

"For sure. Sometimes we try to ditch 'em. Other times we just let 'em follow along. Most of the time, I think they get bored. They disappear by lunchtime."

"So it's not a big deal?"

"Nah."

Blakely shook his head. It made no sense. Why would the U.S. Army spend time and money on a monitoring program that didn't work? Unless... Unless they were decoys and there were other operatives following them who were much more clever. This was no time to be cute... He wouldn't play any games with them. If they wanted to follow him, so be it. He wasn't breaking any damned military laws or rules before he even got to his intelligence assignment. Jim Wafford's face came involuntarily to mind. At least not yet...

Chapter 9

The Museum of Egyptology

Berlin was vibrant and to Blakely's surprise, rebuilt. There were still open, snow-filled lots where tall buildings had once stood, but there were very few ruins left in the downtown area except the notable ones like the burned out *Reichstag* and the *Kaiser Wilhelm* Church. A lively flow of traffic filled the streets. Many shoppers were out on *Kurfurstendamm Strasse,* mostly plump women with their net bags. Stores were decorated for Christmas, showing wooden toys, metal trains, snow scenes, and fashionable clothing. West Berlin seemed prosperous even with rationing.

The three cars of the *strassenbahn* were crowded mostly with young and older women. And despite it being 14 degrees above zero, men and women wrapped in woolen coats and mufflers and hats sat in outdoor *kafes* sipping coffee and eating pastries.

After checking into the *Grunewald* Hotel, a block away from the Museum of Egyptology, Blakely reviewed the questions Wafford had prepared. He was supposed to meet Dr. Dieter Lenhardt at 1100 hours. At 1055, he departed the hotel. There was no sign of anyone trailing him.

The museum was impressive. Two huge, golden Egyptian cat figures guarded the entrance. And just inside was a sarcophagus handsomely decorated with carved and brightly colored designs. Standing next to it was a uniformed policeman. He nodded and asked the lady behind the ticket counter for Dr. Lenhardt.

"He's expecting you."

She escorted him up the stairs to an office where a scholarly man was slumped behind a small desk, reading a typed paper. He arose and greeted Blakely.

"Please sit down, *Herr* Blakely. And excuse my desk. I'm in the midst of a research project."

Blakely sat down and opened his zippered notebook and pulled a pencil out of its holder.

"And just how do you know Dr. Storey?"

Blakely was nonplussed. He quickly surmised that Storey had set up the interview for Wafford.

"I don't, actually. He's part of a research team that I work for…"

Lenhardt was probably in his late forties, tall, thin, almost gaunt in his dark suit. His most arresting features were his aquiline nose upon which were perched metal-rimmed glasses that seemed too small in size to be practical.

"Ah, yes. Tracking down old soldiers. Yes, Gerald has visited me a few times in the past. But now, I must say I cannot discuss with you anything concerning *Herr* Beckmann."

"Why, if you don't mind my asking."

"It is a criminal murder case. Mr. Krebs of the Berlin Police Department took a deposition just yesterday. I am not to discuss any part of what took place until the investigation and trial are over. Sorry. I know you came all the way from Frankfurt. Perhaps you can obtain more information directly from the inspector. I can give you his phone number and address, if you like."

Blakely already had this information, but said, "Yes. Please do."

Lenhardt pulled out a card from his desk drawer. He copied the information on a piece of paper and handed it to Blakely.

"What about Mr. Krusen? Can you tell me anything about him, how you came to know him?"

"Only that he brought part of an ancient relic here, seeking information."

"How long ago?"

"A little over four years ago, I believe. It was soon after I came to work here fulltime."

"And what were you able to tell him?"

"My colleagues and I deduced that it was of Minoan origin, approximately 3,000 years old, and was part of a decorative object of some sort. Of course, we were observing only one section of the complete artifact. It had obviously been split into pieces rather recently."

"By Minoan, are you saying it came from the island of Crete?"

"Most likely."

"How did Mr. Krusen obtain it?"

"I understand it was sent to Mr. Krusen by a German officer stationed on Crete in 1944."

"Oh?"

"Yes. Mr. Krusen told me a close friend, a Major Heinrich von Etter, sent him the piece with instructions to keep it in a safe place."

"Did the major explain why he sent it?"

"*Nein.*"

"What else can you tell me about Mr. Krusen?"

"Only what you can read in the newspapers. Georg was a very nice man. Indeed, a kind man. A civil engineer by occupation. A paratrooper during the war. He played a large role in rebuilding Berlin's water and sewage systems after the war. He was a most quiet fellow. Interested in geography, history, music. All of us here got to know him well over the years. He would often visit to see what we were researching. He became like a father figure to one of my colleagues. We are all shocked and saddened by his death, particularly because it was so brutal and undeserved. That is all I have to say…"

Lenhardt's lip quivered slightly as he pushed his glasses back firmly.

"Thank you, Dr. Lenhardt. I appreciate you taking time to talk with me, especially under these circumstances."

"Sorry I cannot share more… Please give my best to Dr. Storey, if you should meet him."

"I shall. Would you happen to have photos of the artifact?"

"Hm. I don't suppose there is any harm in sharing ours."

Lenhardt stood up and went to a set of files just outside his door. He returned with two black and white photos and handed them to Blakely. The photos showed both sides of the artifact, reproduced to one-to-one scale.

"They are yours to keep. Sorry they aren't in color, but we've run out."

"Thank you so much. I'd be happy to make photostat copies and return these to you."

"That's not necessary. We have a dozen or so more."

Blakely studied the photos. The piece of wood seemed in excellent condition considering its age. A leather string had been pushed through a hole at the top and knotted to form a loop.

"You mentioned a colleague had become very close to Mr. Krusen."

"Yes. That would be Dr. Justina Schmidt. She was quite fond of Georg."

"Would it be possible for me to interview her?"

"Hm. I'm not sure she is up to it. She's taken Georg's death quite hard. Wait here. I'll see whether she would be willing to meet with you."

Lenhardt left the room. Blakely listened as Lenhardt opened a door and spoke with someone. He returned.

"She is unable to see you now."

"Oh."

"However, she would be available at one o'clock this afternoon, if you would like to come back."

Blakely felt relief. "Fine. I'll do that. Thanks again!"

Blakely descended the staircase and explored the many glass cases filled with scarabs, small statuary, potsherds, and carved stones. The place was empty except for the cop and the lady behind the entrance counter. It's time for lunch, he thought. Pulling on his trench coat, he opened the glass door and nearly bumped into a man in a brown overcoat who burst through the door in a rush.

"Uh, so sorry," said the man under his breath.

Blakely was stunned. It was the same guy—the guy who came out of the *gasthaus* in Frankfurt the day he met Wafford. The guy who drove the Hillman! What in hell is he doing here? Is he tailing me? No, I would have spotted him at some point. No. More likely, Wafford hired him to conduct the same interviews so he could compare results, see if Easy Ed Blakely was the right guy for the job. Yeah. Made sense. Expensive but expedient. Blakely crossed the boulevard and entered a café. He suddenly felt hungry.

Chapter 10

Dr. Justina Schmidt

"I must tell you at the outset, *Herr* Blakely, that I agreed to meet with you only out of my friendship with Dr. Storey."

"Yes, ma'am. I understand. I appreciate that."

She was quite beautiful even with swollen face and red eyes. Her dark hair had a wonderful shine. Great breasts. Dark brown eyes. Pert nose. No rings on her pretty fingers. Probably in her late twenties or early thirties.

"And I am under the same constraints as Dr. Lenhardt. I cannot discuss with you anything related to the current investigation."

Blakely decided to tack until he found decent wind. She was too emotionally undone to discuss Krusen even without police constraints.

"I understand. Can we talk about the relic?"

"That depends… What do you want to know?"

Blakely took the two photographs out of his notebook and placed them on the desk before her.

"Where did you get those?"

"Dr. Lenhardt gave them to me. He believes the relic is Minoan."

"I believe that also."

"Can you tell me in a brief sequence how you arrived at this conclusion?"

"*Ja.*" She seemed to brighten at the prospect of sharing her expertise. "When the artifact was brought to us by Mr. Krusen, Dr. Schaus thought it was similar in style and design to Greek pottery shards. I am a specialist in Greek antiquities, but I could not really identify it as mainland Greek. Comparisons with Minoan pottery, on the other hand, showed similarities in the designs at the top and bottom. Right here and here, for example."

She pointed an index finger at the designs on the photo. Her nails were cut neatly, painted using clear nail polish.

"On the obverse, the labyrinth, while not symmetrical, also suggested that it is Minoan. But I suppose the best evidence is the possibility that it contains some *Linear B* inscriptions on the reverse."

She picked up the second photo and pointed to two sets of very small marks at the bottom of the piece. They looked like innocent scratches forming two rows.

"Sorry, I'm not familiar with *Linear B*. What is it, exactly?"

"We can't be certain. It's all new to us and unconfirmed. An Englisher by the name of Michael Ventris recently published a paper describing *Linear B*. His theory is that it is a counting system used by the Minoans 3,000 years ago. Ventris based his theory on marked clay tablets found in the grain storage areas at the Knossos palace by Sr. Arthur Evans. He determined that the symbols stood for quantities of grain stored there. However, it is only a theory at this point. What we do know is that these marks were purposely made a very long time ago, probably at the time the relic was incised."

"So what do they mean?"

She shrugged. "Unfortunately, Ventris never lived to decipher these particular symbols. He was killed in an auto accident just a few months ago."

"That's too bad. So it is possible this is not really *Linear B* writing?"

"*Ja*, that is correct."

"And what about the perforations and other marks?"

"They are fresh. I suspect they were made at the same or nearly the same time the relic was purposely split into pieces."

"Purposely?"

"*Ja*. The cut edges are too uniform to be accidental. Someone cut them, using a sharp knife, or perhaps a bayonet or hatchet.

"How long ago, would you say?"

"Ten to fifteen years ago. Not more than that."

Dr. Schmidt picked up a pencil and tapped the eraser end on the green ink blotter, then set it down. In addition to looking sad, she seemed quite self-conscious.

"And how do you explain the perforations?"

"I have no explanation. They appear to be random." She smirked. "Dieter and Dr. Schaus think soldiers used the relic for a game of darts."

"But what about the longer cut marks?" Blakely pointed to five cuts of various lengths.

"They appear to be made using a small knife, such as a soldier might carry in his pocket."

"You don't think they have any significance?"

She shrugged and shook her head. "We simply don't know."

Blakely was tempted to tell her about Wafford's belief that the marks signified where a stash of gold and jewels was hidden, but he held his tongue.

"Based on the size and shape of this piece, how many pieces would make a complete artifact?"

"Given they were split into nearly equal parts, there would be four in all."

"I see. And you say you have never seen another artifact similar to this one?"

"No. Hardly any wooden pieces this old have survived anywhere, especially on Crete. There were fires caused by invading warriors, lightning, and earthquakes. Dorians sacked and burned most of the great palace cities. Therefore, we have no other example of Minoan art like this one."

"Is there anything else you find unusual about the relic?"

"*Ja*, there is. Virtually all of the designs of labyrinths on vases and coins from Crete show a stylized design in which all the lines of the mazes are uniform. This partial maze is not uniform. See how the passage is wide here and narrow there?"

"Yes. How do you explain it?"

"Perhaps this was due to the lack of skill of the artist who crafted it. Or, perhaps it was caused by the imperfections of the wood. Naturally, it is much easier to get a perfectly symmetrical maze design when you are dealing with a pottery or coin mold than it is when attempting to carve individual wood."

"So, you don't believe that this maze might actually be a true representation of a cave system or man-made labyrinth located somewhere on Crete?"

"I would say not."

"Why?"

Dr. Schmidt raised her right arm and ran her hand through her hair. The movement shifted her breasts slightly. She glanced at him and dropped her arm suddenly.

"We have no precedent for such a depiction."

She shrugged; her breasts jiggled. "Certainly, it is within the realm of possibility. But I doubt it."

"I know this is stressful for you, but could you share with me the name of Mr. Krusen's friend who gave him this relic?"

"*Ja*. His name is Heinrich von Etter. Heinrich was stationed on Crete and sent him the artifact from there."

"Did the package contain anything else?"

"In the same package was one of those imitation stone seals which are common curios sold at tourist shops on Crete. This particular seal was of an octopus design. I determined it was made in 1940 or 1941—nothing valuable or even interesting. It is a crude example of something that was quite beautiful in its original form. We have several Minoan seals downstairs, if you care to see them."

"Thanks. In your view, there is no significance in sending the two items together?"

"How do you mean?"

"Like, for example, the octopus would be a clue that ties in with a code of some kind on the piece of wood?"

"It is possible, but not probable. There were no marks on the seal whatsoever. We have speculated that Heinrich wanted to put off antiquity authorities by making both objects look like cheap curios. Hence, the loop of leather shoestring making the artifact appear as an amulet such as a tourist might wear around his neck. Georg told me the box and wrappings were from a tourist shop in Iraklion, suggesting Heinrich had the store mail the package for him to avoid detection."

"Detection?"

"By the antiquity authorities. They are always on the lookout for smuggling antiquities, even during the war. The *Wehrmacht* more or less cooperated with Greek authorities."

"I see. So Heinrich von Etter must have known that the relic was old and very valuable. Otherwise, he wouldn't have gone to such trouble to make it seem like a cheap curio before smuggling it out of Crete?"

"*Ja.* That is probable."

"Dr. Lenhardt said von Etter gave instructions to Mr. Krusen. That he should keep the relic in a safe place. Can you tell me exactly what the message said?"

"*Ja.* Georg told me it was a brief sentence written in pencil on the inside of the cardboard box. Nothing else. Something like, *Keep this safe for me.*"

"That's all?"

"*Ja.* Georg eventually paid it no attention. He displayed the fragment in his flat."

"Displayed it?"

"He hung the fragment on a nail in the hallway to his bedroom."

"That right?"

"*Ja.* That is true. Georg did not place any value on it."

"Did von Etter send Mr. Krusen any other packages or letters around this time or later?"

"No. Georg surmised Heinrich died sometime after the package arrived because he never heard from him again. Many soldiers on Crete were sent to the Russian Front around that time."

"I see..."

Blakely looked at his watch. He wanted to stay longer and listen to her lovely Berlin accent. She was gazing at him intently, seeming on the verge of saying something. He waited. She didn't. He tried to think of any other relevant questions. None came to mind. What else could he do here, he wondered.

"Would Dr. Schaus be available for interview?"

"He is not here for three days," she replied. "He's on holiday in England."

"Dr. Schmidt, I do appreciate your giving me this interview. And I'm sorry for your loss."

"*Ja.* Thank you."

"Under other circumstances, I would invite you to dine with me if you were free. I will be staying in Berlin for a couple of days."

"That is sweet of you. But no, I couldn't do it just now."

"If I happen to have more questions, would you mind me calling you?"

"No. Feel free, *Herr* Blakely. I wish you luck in your quest. Where are you staying? I can recommend a good hotel."

"Just down the street. Hotel *Grunewald.*"

"Ach! That is what I would have recommended."

"Thank you."

She extended her hand. Blakely squeezed it softly as he looked into her eyes. Beyond the sadness and grieving was a mischievous energy, he thought. A delightful, playful energy that could take you to paradise. He reluctantly pulled his hand away.

"*Vedersehn.*"

"*Vedersehn.*"

Blakely descended the stairs. The ground floor gallery was quiet. He found a pay phone in the lobby and called Inspector Krebs for an appointment. Krebs' desk sergeant said he would be available at 1530 hours for interview. The woman at the entrance counter was knitting. The cop was now standing outside near the front door, leaning against one of the two golden cat statues. Two young men in alcoves along the far wall were busily reading and writing.

Blakely wandered among the glass cases filled with Egyptian scarabs, small statuary, carved stones, and funeral masks. He discovered a glass-topped table beneath which were a couple dozen Greek and Egyptian stone seals. There were two octopus-shaped seals. He had to agree with Dr. Schmidt: they were indeed simple and quite beautiful. He glanced at a golden sarcophagus. Fascinating stuff, he thought, as he pulled on his trench coat. He nodded at the lady knitting as he pushed the glass door open.

Chapter 11

A Cat and Mouse Game

"Come back this way," commanded Inspector Krebs as he quickly shook Blakely's hand and absently muttered a greeting. He followed Krebs into a small office crowded with file cabinets.

"Sit there, please." He beckoned with an arm toward the one chair as he moved behind a metal desk piled high with folders to sit in a secretarial chair.

Blakely figured Krebs was probably a former German army officer, since he was tall, fortyish, strongly built, and possessed the self-assurance of somebody who was always in charge. His crew cut suggested a no-nonsense approach to life. Krebs leaned forward, lighted a Chesterfield while offering one to Blakely.

"No thanks."

"Now, tell me again who you are and what you want."

Krebs blew a perfect smoke ring toward the doorway and scrutinized Blakely.

"I'm Ed Blakely, sir. I'm assigned to Intelligence in Frankfurt."

"Let me see your ID, please."

"Yes, sir."

Blakely took his military ID card from his wallet and handed it to Krebs. He studied it carefully.

"Would you mind if I copied this?"

"Not at all, sir."

Krebs swung around to the photostat copier behind him and made a copy of each side of the card before handing it back. Blakely felt unnerved. He took a deep breath to steady himself.

"I assume you have orders?"

Blakely unzipped his notebook and handed Krebs a copy of the orders Wafford had given him. Krebs nodded affirmatively.

"May I keep these?"

"Yes, sir."

Krebs flipped the paper onto his desk and inhaled deeply on the Chesterfield.

"Your orders are signed by a Colonel Thomas Cahill. Normally, orders such as these are signed by Colonel Luther North. Has Cahill replaced North?"

He blew another smoke ring.

"I don't know, sir. I'm new to the command."

"Who do you work for, Sergeant Blakely?"

Blakely was caught. He shifted his weight forward in the chair and took a chance.

"As I said, I'm assigned to Intelligence."

"Give me a person, Sergeant. Who is your boss?"

"I'm really not at liberty to say, sir. It is classified information."

Krebs turned slightly in his chair and mashed the half-smoked cigarette in the ashtray. Blakely detected a smirk.

"Then, how the hell am I supposed to help you, if you can't provide me basic information? I like to know who I'm dealing with. And unless you tell me, I won't tell you anything."

Blakely felt a rush of warmth in his cheeks. He had to figure some way to come about.

"As my orders state, I am gathering information on possible criminal activities during World War II."

"And as you mentioned to my desk sergeant on the telephone, you believe Heinz Beck is one of these criminals?"

"My commander thinks so."

"I see. And why does he think so, Sergeant?"

"Heinz Beck, if this is the same man, was an SS NCO in Vienna during the time von Stauffenberg attempted to kill Hitler. Beck worked under a colonel named Eugen Horst. During the roundup of plotters, my commander believes Horst and Beck killed several innocent people."

"How would he know this?"

"War archives, mainly. There's also circumstantial evidence suggesting Horst's unit killed a well-known politician and his family during this time."

"And who would that be?"

"Count Otto von Etter, who was a relative to the Habsburgs."

"Interesting." Krebs lighted another Chesterfield and jotted something down on a legal pad using a bright green pencil.

"Interesting…" he repeated.

"My commander thinks there is some previous connection between Beck and Krusen."

"Ah, we finally get to the nub of it all, don't we?" Krebs smiled ruefully.

"What do you mean?"

"The piece of wood. The Minoan trinket Heinrich von Etter mailed from Crete to Georg Krusen."

"Yes, sir."

"Tell me what you know about this piece of history, Sergeant Blakely?"

Blakely shrugged. "Very little. That is another reason I am here, sir. I had hoped you would allow me to see it."

Krebs tilted his head and smiled. "But you already know what it looks like."

"I don't understand."

"You were given photos of it this morning or do you forget?"

Blakely grinned. He was impressed. The guy is a master of control.

"How did you know?"

"I make it my business to know everything that happens here in Berlin."

Blakely was awed. Krebs broke into a laugh.

"Just kidding, Sergeant. Coincidence, really. I had a call from Dr. Lenhardt just before you arrived here. He told me you had visited him this morning. He wanted to be certain it was okay that he gave you the photos."

"And was it?"

"Oh, sure. No problem. Those photos were taken when Krusen first brought the fragment to the museum a few years ago. No problem there."

Blakely was unsure how to proceed. "I'd still like to see the relic, if that is possible."

Krebs sighed and stood up. "Why not? Come with me."

He followed Krebs out of the office and down the hall to a closed door. Krebs fished through a ring of keys, selected one, and unlocked the door. He turned on lights. They were surrounded by steel file cabinets. Krebs opened a drawer and pulled out a cellophane bag containing a flat piece of gray, decorated wood.

"I will allow you to look, but I won't allow you to touch it," said Krebs, holding the bag flat in his large hand.

Blakely leaned in closely. There were tiny bits of red coloring here and there in the lacy design at the top and bottom, suggesting it had once been painted bright red. The part of the labyrinth showing in the middle was dark gray as though it were originally black in color.

"Quite impressive. Would you mind turning it over?"

"Sure."

Blakely examined the small perforations and compared them with the markings at the bottom of the piece. Yes, they do look like they were made with darts, he said to himself, but the two little groups of marks at the bottom—the ones thought to be *Linear B*–looked much older.

"Thank you, Mr. Krebs. I appreciate your doing this."

"Not at all. Sorry I can't give you more information."

"Yeah. Me, too…" Blakely paused at the door. "Was this the only thing Beck took from the apartment as far as you know?"

Krebs shrugged as he put the cellophane bag in the drawer and locked the file.

"Don't really know. I can tell you that someone ransacked the apartment at the time Krusen was murdered. Everything was topsy-turvy. Gutted upholstery, mattresses. Closets and drawers emptied onto the floor. A huge mess."

They walked down the hall to the reception desk.

"Wish I could share more about our investigation, but we have rules. You may not believe it, but I do cooperate with you military people. I have a very close relationship with Berlin Command."

"I understand, sir."

"Surprising how many military chaps I know down in Frankfurt…You wouldn't happen to know an old Intelligence officer by the name of James Wafford, would you?"

There was that smirk again.

Blakely grinned.

"The name's familiar."

They shook hands.

"I thought it might be… Good luck, *Herr* Blakely."

Blakely turned toward the double entrance doors.

"By the way," said Krebs, "If you were hoping to interrogate Heinz Beck, forget it. For security reasons, we transferred him temporarily to Spandau Prison. Nobody is allowed to see him right now."

"Thanks for letting me know."

Chapter 12

Confrontation

So far, he figured he was batting zero. Lenhardt and Schmidt couldn't talk. Krebs wouldn't talk. And Dr. Schaus and Heinz Beck were unavailable to talk. Blakely peered out the cab window. Only 1650 hours and it was nearly dark. A flurry of large snowflakes suddenly danced crazily as the cab pulled into the entrance of the Hotel *Grunewald*.

Blakely paid the driver and got out. It was getting colder, too. Must be around ten degrees. He entered the hotel lobby and glanced in the lounge. A man in a U.S. Air Force officer's uniform was reading a newspaper. The hotel clerk handed Blakely his room key. As he approached the lounge, the officer turned the page and Blakely immediately recognized him. It's the same guy–the Hillman guy he bumped into at the museum. He's a first lieutenant. Maybe I can get to the bottom of this. I'll introduce myself and see what happens.

"How are you, sir? I'm Sergeant Ed Blakely."

The guy put down the *Berliner Zeitung* as Blakely offered his hand. The officer did not get out of his chair. Rather, he seemed annoyed at Blakely's intrusion.

"Do I know you?"

"I believe we bumped into one another this morning at the Egyptology Museum."

The lieutenant's face softened. He stood and shook hands.

"So sorry. Tell me again who you are."

"Sergeant Ed Blakely, sir, U.S. Army. I'm based in Frankfurt."

"May I see identification?"

"Yes, sir."

Blakely pulled out his wallet and handed him his Army ID card.

"Hm." He handed back the ID. "You can't be too careful in Berlin. Tell me, Sergeant, what brings you here?"

"Sightseeing. Always wanted to see Berlin. And you, sir?"

"I'm an archeologist on the outside. So I spend lots of time visiting various museums."

"And what do you do in the Air Force?"

"I'm a courier for SHAFE. I fly out of Rhein-Main every four days or so."

"Nice job."

"Yes, it 'tis." The lieutenant glanced at his watch. "I have a night flight to catch at *Tempelhof* in a few hours."

"Sir, I don't believe you told me your name."

"Ah, sorry. Name's Cunningham. Christopher Cunningham."

"If you don't mind my saying so, you sound more English than American."

The lieutenant beckoned toward an armchair next to where he had been sitting. "Sit down, Sergeant. Yes, I do have a bit of Oxford about me, don't I?"

Affectedly so, thought Blakely. They sat down.

"I spent three glorious years at All Souls on a Rhodes scholarship before attending OCS."

Cunningham pulled a pipe and a tin of Prince Albert from his jacket pocket. He packed the tobacco and lit the pipe using one of those tubular metal English pipe lighters. Definitely an anglophile, thought Blakely.

"So, did you enjoy the exhibits at the museum today, Sergeant?"

"Yes, sir, very much." Justina's breasts jiggling in the red sweater came to mind. "I especially liked the collection of Greek seals."

Cunningham heartily puffed and puffed until there was fragrant blue smoke enveloping Blakely. The lieutenant removed his pipe from his mouth.

"You don't say!"

"Yes, sir. My favorites are Minoan."

"Really?" The lieutenant seemed flabbergasted. "And why would you favor those?"

Blakely tried to put on a studious air. "I guess it's their simplicity. The smoothness of the stone. The lack of ornamentation. Like, for example, the octopus design. I think that is the best example of…"

"Sergeant, you are most astonishing. I wouldn't have dreamt in a million years someone like you would have a passion for stone seals when there are so many more beautiful collections of scarabs and carved gems. Are you quite serious?"

"Quite."

Cunningham puffed his pipe while gazing suspiciously at Blakely.

"By the way, sir… Do you drive a brown Hillman ragtop?"

Cunningham again removed his pipe and smiled wryly. "I think you are more than you say you are, Sergeant Blakely. Really, now, what is your game? Who are you? Are you following me?"

"No, sir. I guessed you were either following me or checking up on my assignment."

"And just why would I be doing that?"

"You tell me, sir. I saw you last Sunday leaving a *gasthaus* on *Ginnheimer Strasse* in Frankfurt. You drove off in a brown Hillman convertible. There was only one man in that *gasthaus* you would have been meeting."

The lieutenant's face flushed. "I say, Blakely. You are getting a bit too cheeky. Come to the point. Which agency are you? CID? CIC? CIA? NSA? Or what?"

The guy acts like he knows nothing about me or what I'm doing here. "With all due respect, sir. I have reason to believe you are working on the side for a certain retired Intelligence officer."

"Look here, Blakely… I might have conducted some interviews and provided scholarly advice, but I've done nothing wrong. My purpose in meeting James Wafford was to tell him I wanted to cut off our relationship."

"Oh? Why, sir?"

"Really, Sergeant, why don't you ask Wafford himself?"

"I will, sir. So you no longer work for him?"

"That is correct. And I've never violated laws or military codes during our association."

"How long did you work for him?"

Cunningham looked trapped. His left hand holding the pipe was beginning to shake slightly.

"Six, perhaps seven months."

"What did you do for him?"

"I've already told you. My work was above board."

Cunningham tapped the pipe on the ashtray nervously, emptying the half-spent coals and ashes into it. He seemed in a quandary as to whether he should say anything more.

"You're CID, aren't you?"

"Why would you think that?"

Cunningham shrugged and looked away. The blush had disappeared from his cheeks, leaving his face pale and haggard.

"What has he done now to cause you to investigate me?"

Blakely looked sternly at the lieutenant. "You tell me, sir… Has the colonel stepped over the line?"

Cunningham fidgeted, pulled out a pipe cleaner and began reaming the pipe stem. "I felt he was about to. I'm afraid his judgment has become faulty."

"You felt he was sucking you both into dangerous activities?"

"One could say that… Yes."

"How did you leave it, when you met with the colonel?"

"I don't follow…"

"Did he agree to cut off your relationship?"

"He insisted I think it over for a few days. I told him I'd be back to him in one week. But my answer will be no, despite the fact I could use the extra money."

Blakely glanced at the lieutenant's ring finger. "I take it you are single. A first lieutenant's pay isn't enough?"

"Hardly. I intend to marry a German national when I am discharged next year. We plan to live here on the economy. Right now, I have no job prospects. So, I'm building a nest egg to tide us over."

Blakely studied the lieutenant's sullen face. The guy seemed doomed. "What if I asked you to hold off telling Wafford for a while?"

Cunningham looked hopeful. "Why?"

"I can't tell you right now."

Truth was, Blakely didn't know why. He only had the vaguest idea that he wanted to keep the lieutenant in limbo for the time being. "Do you know him well?"

"I thought so until recently."

"Do you like him?"

"James has been most kind to me. Yes. I'm quite fond of him. I've just thought he's pushing the limits beyond where I can go."

"You know he is a big war hero?"

"I've gathered that. Everyone in Germany seems to know him."

Blakely leaned forward and looked around. There was nobody in the lobby except the clerk.

"Do you think the old guy has all his marbles?"

"Who?" Cunningham looked around.

"The colonel."

Cunningham's brown eyes widened and a half smile crossed his face.

"You think he's daft?"

"I'm asking you."

Cunningham shook his head and pulled out his tobacco again.

"He does act a bit queer, doesn't he? Obsessed. Yes. Obsessed with that damned Minoan fragment. Yes. I believe you are absolutely correct, Blakely. He is losing his marbles. Why else would he want to get caught up in this—I am sure you know all about it—this murder business and the *Gestapo* thugs?"

"Tell you what, sir. I won't turn in any report about our conversation until we can talk more back in Frankfurt. How does that sound?"

"I suppose I should thank you, but I have no earthly idea as to who you are or what you're up to."

"Next time we meet, it'll all be clear to you, sir. I promise."

"Mind you, I've done nothing wrong. You understand that, don't you?"

"That's not my call, sir. Thanks for your time."

Cunningham looked at his watch. "I must call a cab."

"Give me your work number in Frankfurt and we'll set up another meeting."

The lieutenant handed Blakely his card.

"Thank you, sir."

"Should I bring my lawyer next time?" He seemed serious.

Blakely grinned as they stood up.

"Believe me, sir, that won't be necessary."

Cunningham reached out his hand. "I must say, Sergeant Blakely–or whoever you are–this has been a most bizarre encounter."

"Same here."

They shook hands.

"Have a safe trip."

"Thank you."

Cunningham picked up a B-4 bag at the desk and waited in front of the door for the cab. Blakely entered the elevator and punched number three. After the doors closed, he peered into the mirror and winked at his own smiling image. It was a helluva kick to play CID interrogator and watch an officer's hands shake.

Chapter 13

A Dinner Surprise

Blakely finished editing a first draft of his report. What would Wafford think, he wondered. He read over the summary of interviews. There was not much new information, merely corroborations of facts. Still, he had obtained photos of the artifact. The most important information could not be reported: his chance encounter with Cunningham. His mind was still reeling from their confrontation.

Why was Cunningham so frightened? Ah, the SHAFE courier job. Of course! Cunningham was no doubt restricted from accepting money for work outside his SHAFE duties. After all, he was hauling TOP SECRET information around. CIC and CID were always up tight about our people being blackmailed. That must be it. Cunningham was stepping over the line because he was in love with a German *fraulein* and needed money for a wedding and job search. But why would Blakely encourage Cunningham to continue working for Wafford? Strange, but he had had an immediate gut feeling about it, that they–he and Cunningham—could work together to keep Jim Wafford inside the bounds, maybe even save his ass.

Yeah. It was almost like Holden Caulfield, he thought, wanting to be a catcher, keep people from going off the edge. And he didn't know why he wanted to do that, except that Jim Wafford was a hero who did a lot of brave things for his country over many years. Now, a much older Jim Wafford needed somebody to protect him from himself and others. Yeah. He had felt Wafford's vulnerability from their very first meeting. Funny he should feel that way about a guy he'd met only twice. On the other hand, he had admired Jim Wafford from the time he was a kid, reading about his war exploits in *Life* magazine. He heard firsthand stories about Wafford's heroics at Intelligence School and later, at Fort Mac. Wafford was a legend. He was an icon like Audie Murphy and Mitch Paige. You don't let guys like that fall off the edge, if you can help it.

Blakely showered. He wished he could call Colonel Smith at Mac and talk about his situation. But he knew the call would be monitored. He dressed quickly and went down to the mezzanine where, he had been told, there was a dining room with excellent food.

It turned out to be old world with a Nazi twist: a mix of odd furniture and décor in the reception area, mostly faux rococo and faux art deco. Taped violins were playing. An elderly waiter wearing a tuxedo greeted him and showed him to a corner table. Very few diners. It was too early. He looked around. An interesting room. Fat, squat, inlaid chests with marble tops, above which were art deco sconces with indirect white and pink lights adorning the outside walls. Linen covered tables, deco flatware, old-looking silver salt cellars, thickly cushioned Victorian chairs, heavy blue velvet curtains–the sort of ersatz prewar style so cherished by the *Nazis*.

He ordered a glass of Vouvray from the wine list and half a dozen cold boiled shrimp with cocktail sauce. The menu was pricey, considering that four *marks* equaled a dollar. After what he had been through today, he figured he deserved to splurge a bit. He looked up just as another waiter was escorting a customer to a nearby table. He recognized her. It was Dr. Schmidt from the museum. Blakely stood up and beckoned to his table.

"Dr. Schmidt! Would you care to join me?"

She turned. Her mouth opened in surprise. She smiled and nodded to the waiter.

"*Herr* Blakely! Yes. That would be nice."

Blakely pulled a chair back. She sat down. Her black hair shone and there was just a hint of light perfume with a clean, lavender scent. She seemed happy that he was here. She touched her hair momentarily and smiled again. She was still in office clothes and had obviously come directly from the museum.

"I just couldn't bear the thought of cooking dinner tonight," she said, shifting the silverware and stretching the linen napkin across her lap.

"I've ordered a glass of white wine and some boiled shrimp. Would you like the same for starters?"

She nodded affirmatively at the waiter.

"I take it you come here often."

"*Ja*. I do. It is so convenient. However, there is an even better restaurant a little farther down in *Linden Weg*."

"Oh?"

She brushed her black hair back from her face. "Ja. It is the *Menderhof Kafe*. Very nice. I recommend it to you."

"I'll have to try it. Is it better for lunch or dinner?"

"Either one. My friend Georg and I would dine there after a concert sometimes."

"You spent a lot of time with him, then?"

"Oh, not so much. Once a week we would do something together. He became like the father to me that I never had. And he treated me like the daughter he never had…"

"So he never married?"

"*Nein*. A confirmed bachelor after his war experiences."

"Oh?"

"*Ja*. He wanted a very quiet life." She paused.

"You say you didn't have a father. Were your mother and father divorced?"

"Ah, no. My father was taken away soon after Hitler came to power. A political prisoner. That was in 1933, when I was a very young. I remember nothing about him. My mother and I presume he died in a detention camp."

"Sorry. Was he a professor?"

"He was an elected member of the Weimar government. Ironically, he worked closely with Otto von Etter, the father of Heinrich. Unfortunately, my father did not have the popularity of Otto, so Hitler could arrest him without any consequence."

"What was his crime?"

"He was outspoken against the *Nazis* even before Hitler came to power. He tried to get the *Nazi* Party banned in 1926. I've read newspaper accounts of his bravery. He called Hitler a liar and a thug, which he was, of course."

"A courageous man."

"*Ja.* My mother told me many stories about him facing down the *brown shirts.*"

"So, you never learned what happened to him?"

"*Nein.*"

"I think not knowing is the worst, isn't it?"

"That is true."

"I suppose you lost many of your relatives during the war."

"*Ja.* All that was left was my mother and I. What about you? Do you have much family?"

"Funny you should ask. I never knew my father either. I was born out of wedlock. My mom was sixteen. My father was in the merchant marines, according to my mom. He was on leave in San Diego, spent a week dating my mom, and I came along nine months later. I don't think she ever knew his real name or where he came from. So I can appreciate your situation. I have no idea who he is, whether he is still alive, or what. I call him *Father No Name.*"

"Ach! That is a worse tragedy than mine. At least I know my father was a *gut* man."

"Yeah. I was raised by my grandparents. Eventually, they adopted me so I would have a legal name. As a result, my mom became my sister."

"No! You must be joking!"

They both laughed.

"I'm not joking. From that time on, my mother always sent me birthday cards with verses to 'my loving brother' or 'from your loving sister.'"

"Unbelievable! You remained close to her, then?"

"I was really never close to my mother. She was too busy working. She did send my grandparents money for my food and clothing though."

"She did not live with you?"

"Just after the war started, she got a job at an aircraft factory up in Long Beach. She seldom came home after that."

"And where is Long Beach?"

"California."

"Ah so! You must know surfing?"

"Yeah. I'm a sailor, too."

Justina's brown eyes opened wider. "Fascinating! How did you learn sailing?"

"Mostly on my own. We lived on a small cove on the Pacific Ocean. One day when I was a kid, I found a wrecked sailboat. I fixed it up and learned how to sail the hard way."

"The hard way?"

"Yeah. By being tossed into the water every time I did something wrong. You learn very quickly that way. The Pacific Ocean is quite cold even during summertime."

They laughed.

"Were you close to your grandparents?"

"The closest person in my family was my half-brother Luke. He was ten years older. I truly worshipped him. Then the war came. He was shot down over the Ploesti oilfields in Rumania."

"He was killed?"

"Yes."

Justina placed her hand on Blakely's arm and patted it.

"I am so sorry. Like me, you, too, have great sadnesses."

"Yeah," said Blakely, tilting his head. "It's taken a few years to get over, but you have to go on with your life. Right?"

"That is so."

Tell me, how'd you become a—I don't know what you call yourself—a curator?"

She laughed. "Dr. Schaus is the curator. He's in charge of the museum. I am called an archeologist."

"Ah, you are a digger of history. Like Schliemann!"

"*Ja*. We dig and hopefully find important things."

"So, how did you become an archeologist?"

"My mother was a history teacher. She used to read me stories about Schliemann, Carter, Evans, and many others. It amazed me how one could piece together tiny fragments and be able to explain how people lived a thousand years before. There was never any doubt in my mind what I wanted to do with my life. From early age, I wanted to be an archeologist. And you?"

Blakely shrugged. "I never wanted to be anything except a sailor."

"Why didn't you join the navy rather than the army?"

"Good question. I felt like there was more adventure in the army. There's a big difference between sailing a racing yacht and living on a battleship with hundreds of other guys. I don't like to feel cramped."

"I see. You speak excellent *Deutsch*. Did you learn from your grandparents?"

"Army Language School."

"Very *gut*."

The waiter brought their wine and boiled shrimp on ice and placed them on the table. "Have you decided what you'll be having this evening?"

Justina and Blakely looked at one another and laughed. They hadn't glanced at the menu.

"Give us a few minutes, Jacob," said Justina. "Do you have any recommendations this evening?"

"I can recommend the venison. It is done in an excellent wine sauce."

"That sounds tasty," said Justina, looking at Blakely. "I'll have that."

Blakely put the menu down. "I'll have the same. What wine would go with the sauce?"

"It was made with a *Chateau Langa*, 1952. Would you like a bottle?"

"Yes, please."

Justina had both elbows on the table and was resting her chin on her hand. She seemed entranced, her lips and eyes forming a delightful smile.

"You are so urbane for a GI, *Herr* Blakely. I don't believe I've ever met an American quite like you."

"Really? I've never in my life been described as urbane."

"Well, you are. How did you become so?"

"I can't really say. Maybe it was working during my teen years at the San Diego Yacht Club. I raced boats there. I also taught beginning sailing to kids, did boat repair and maintenance. Made good money. Hobnobbed with some very rich people. I showed the kids the ropes and their parents showed me their culture. Guess I developed a taste for good wine and food early in life."

"What is hobnobbed?"

Blakely grinned. "It means I spent a lot of time with rich, educated people—even though I was just a teenager. I guess I learned how they do things."

"I am impressed."

"Thank you."

Blakely shifted in his chair. She kept looking at him with sparkling eyes, unlike earlier in the day when she appeared to be so sad. He felt a slight tingling sensation.

"I am impressed with you, too, Dr. Schmidt."

She tilted her head pertly. "In what way?"

"You seem to have a passion for your work."

"*Ja.* It is my life. I love what I do. And please call me Justina."

"Call me Ed."

She wrinkled her nose. "If you don't mind, I shall call you Edward. Yes. You are more an Edward and less of an Ed."

Blakely smiled. "Actually, most people who really know me call me Easy Ed or Captain Easy."

"But why?"

"Nicknames I picked up surfing and sailing. I sometimes make difficult maneuvers look easier than they really are."

Justina smiled broadly. "Yes, I imagine you can maneuver quite well… Nevertheless, you are an Edward to me."

The tingling sensation was growing. He felt a blush rising in his cheeks. This woman is lovely and quite sexy.

"Fine with me, Justina."

"*Gut!*"

Jacob appeared. He presented the wine bottle to Blakely, who examined the label and nodded approval. The old man opened the wine and presented the cork. Blakely took the cork and sniffed, then nodded again. Jacob poured a small amount of red wine into Blakely's glass. Blakely swirled it around, but instead of tasting it himself, he handed the glass to Justina. She beamed, sniffed the glass, and tasted.

"It's very *gut,* Jacob."

Jacob poured more wine for both of them.

"To our futures," said Blakely, looking into Justina's lovely brown eyes. "May you discover the secrets of the past and become a world famous archeologist."

"*Ja*," said Justina breathlessly. "And may you some day win America's Cup!"

They both laughed as Jacob brought the entrée and salad. They ate their salads in silence.

"I'm curious, Edward. Why are you not an officer?"

She peered at him over her glass as she sipped the dark wine.

"I enlisted mainly to avoid the draft and to get the GI Bill. Never thought about being an officer 'til I got to my last assignment at Third Army Headquarters."

"Ah, so now you want to become officer?"

"Some of my superior officers want me to, but I don't think so."

"Why not?"

Blakely swirled his wine and examined its legs forming on the sides of the glass. "There's a lot of uncertainty in the military these days. In peacetime, you can't count on being promoted because of budgets. Besides, I don't believe I'd fit in the new Army..."

"Hm. What about Air Force? Isn't Air Force better than Army?" Justina seemed quite serious about his prospects.

"Not much different. I think all the services are going through the same budget problems. And twenty years is a long time."

"I see."

They ate in silence. What happened? Why her sudden interest in military careers?

Jacob poured more wine. The venison in the wine sauce was delicious, especially mixed with the beans, onions, parsnips, carrots, and small dumplings. He took a thick crust of bread and slathered it with butter.

"If you don't mind my asking, why are you so interested in my military career?"

"Oh, just curiosity. I see so many American officers here in Berlin. They appear very successful and rich by our standards. I believe you would make a good officer, Edward. You'd be very successful."

"Thank you."

He wiped the napkin across his mouth. "Problem is," he continued, "if you get passed over for promotion just one time, you are doomed to stay in a lower rank for the rest of your career. And when you retire, you get less retirement pay."

"What is passed over?"

"Receiving a bad report that goes on your record. Any bad report can keep you from being promoted. It's pitiful to see a guy who's been passed over walking around as a major at age 45. You see more of them now, especially with the Eisenhower reduction in force."

"But I thought with the Hungarian revolution and cold war, this would be the perfect time to be military officer."

"Not so, Justina. Truth is, it's a very bad time to be a young officer. The military is in transition, changing from how things were done in World War II to a new and more technological organization. And frankly, I'd just as soon not be a part of it after my enlistment is up. I'd rather be racing sailboats and drinking wine in California."

"*Ja.* If what you say is true, I cannot blame you."

The bloom had left her face. Justina seemed to take Blakely's views to heart, as though she somehow had a stake in all this.

"How about a nice dessert and coffee to finish off the meal?"

"I think that I had better now go home. I must check on my mother always by nine o'clock."

"Can I walk you home or get a cab for you?"

"Jacob will call a cab for me. You stay and have coffee. Oh, and have one of their torts. They are simply wonderful."

"I might try one."

"Yes. Please do... Well, this has been a very nice and unexpected pleasure, Edward."

Blakely pulled her chair back as she stood up. She held out her hand. He took it in his and squeezed it gently.

"It was my pleasure. I hope we can meet soon again, maybe on my next trip to Berlin."

"Me, too."

She turned and walked across the dining room to where Jacob was standing near the entrance.

Blakely looked at the dregs of wine at the bottom of his glass, then back to the entrance. She was gone. He tried to reconstruct their conversation in his mind. It had been like a tide coming in, warm, swift, enveloping, then suddenly receding, replaced by small, unexpected riptides that were at once nothing and something, surprising and diminishing. The tingling was gone. He couldn't remember exactly her facial features. For some strange reason, they were blurred in his mind.

Chapter 14

First Report

During the return trip to Frankfurt, Blakely made several decisions. First, he would make photostat copies of everything he intended to give to Wafford. Second, he would copy every document, set of directions, and orders Wafford gave him. Third, he would store all the documents plus his notes in some safe place away from the *Gutleut Kaserne*. Fourth, he would make arrangements to meet Wafford in the afternoon at the English Bookstore.

* * *

Blakely entered the *Gutleut Kaserne* Orderly Room and stood in First Sergeant Easterling's doorway. "Come in, Blakely. What's up?"

"I met a guy up in Berlin by the name of Christopher Cunningham, a first lieutenant in the Air Force. Says he's a courier for SHAFE. Is there any way I can check him out? I just want to be sure he is who he says he is."

Easterling scratched the side of his face. "I can call CID. You gotta problem with him?"

"Oh no, Sarge. Nothing like that. No. Please don't call CID. I think he's on the up and up. My old friend Sergeant Charon—I think you guys know each other–said I should check on people before becoming friends with 'em. That's all. Any chance you or Corporal Nash could call over to SHAFE and confirm that he works there?"

"Sure." Easterling nodded his head toward the door. "Ask Nash to call Master Sergeant Betts at SHAFE administration. He's got a directory."

"Thanks, Sarge."

"So how'd you know Charon?"

"Fort McPherson. I worked with him until he transferred over here. A great guy."

"They don't make 'em any better. I already miss him."

"Yeah, me too."

* * *

Nash confirmed that Cunningham had worked for SHAFE as a courier for nearly three years. He mostly worked out of Rhein-Main Air Base. He had time in grade for a promotion. Blakely momentarily considered calling him for an appointment, but decided to wait until after his meeting with Wafford. Now, he found himself standing on the corner of *Fredrich-Ebert Strasse* attempting to find the perfect place from which to operate. He gazed at the multi-story stone building across the boulevard. The *Schumann* Building. What could be better? He crossed the street and entered the wide stone portal. Businesses were listed in alphabetical order within a metal and glass case next to an elevator. *Geschaft Dienst.* It was located on the second floor. He took the elevator. One of those new office centers catering mostly, Blakely thought, to businesses that were just starting up. He crossed the lobby and entered the door. There was a bank of five public telephone booths, a telegraph, two photostat copiers, postal supplies. A stationer was next door. A young clerk stood by to assist. A small but steady stream of well dressed men and women came in and out as Blakely set about his tasks. Nobody seemed interested in what he was doing.

He copied his report and photographs of the relic and placed the copies back in the large envelope Wafford had given him. He purchased a smaller envelope in which he placed his single page report along with the photographs and an itemized account of expenses. He contacted Betty Crawford who called him back confirming a meeting with Wafford in the next hour.

Blakely crossed the wide boulevard with its many trolley tracks, avoiding half-frozen puddles, and entered the train station. There were plenty of lockers available along the wide hall leading to the ticket counter. He placed the large envelope in an upper locker, inserted a coin, and locked the door. He put the key in his pocket and decided to buy a Cadbury bar of chocolate with almonds and watch the throngs of people getting on and off the trains until it was time to meet Jim Wafford.

* * *

Blakely found Betty Crawford in good spirits.

"How are you and Mr. Hemingway getting along?"

"Well, I am where the *Tenente* just got the closest shave of his life from the Italian barber and Catherine has arrived in his room at the hospital."

"Is that where you stopped reading?" She wore a look of mock incredulity on her face.

Blakely grinned broadly, knowing she expected him to have finished reading *A Farewell to Arms* by now.

"Yes," he explained. "I read like Hemingway writes, stopping at an exciting point so that when I start up again, I look forward to the experience."

"That is good, Edward. I'll have to remember that. Very good, indeed. I'll suggest that to some of my university students who are attempting to read English stories. It would help them in their reading, don't you agree?"

"I suppose so. Truth is, I've been too busy to do much reading."

"A pity. You must work on your priorities."

The little bell over the door tinkled. Wafford strode in, removing his slouch hat and smoothing down his thin hair. He nodded to Betty and Ed.

"Afternoon, Betty, Ed. How's everything?"

"Fine, thank you. How are you, James?"

"Great. Just wish these holidays didn't creep up on me so unexpectedly. I haven't bought a present for my wife yet—or anything for my boys back in the States."

"You are an awful husband and father," Betty chided. "Shame on you for neglecting them so close to Christmas."

"Louise always takes care of those things. Guess I'll end up sending the boys their usual check."

Wafford turned to Blakely. "They're both in college. They appreciate my cash more'n anything else."

"But what about your neglected wife," Betty pursued.

Wafford threw her a scowl and sauntered over to the counter where the large, coffee table hardbacks were displayed. He picked one up and leafed through the colored pages.

"Betty, do you think Louise would like this one on famous English gardens?"

Blakely and Betty exchanged glances and nearly burst out laughing.

"What did I miss? What are you two grinning about?"

"Oh, nothing James. Edward and I were just having a discussion recently about who purchases what types of books. I predicted you would buy one of these high quality books here. I am sure Louise would love to have a book for the living room on English gardens."

Betty can be devilishly playful, thought Blakely, as he turned away, unable to suppress his widening grin any longer.

"Okay. How much is it?"

"That would be, let's see, one hundred *marks*."

"Hm. Expensive. I guess I'll take it anyway. She'll like all the nice pictures."

Betty placed the book in a bright green paper bag. She did not offer a bookmark. She was true to her word. As she handed the package to Wafford, she glanced at Blakely. There was that conspiratorial look again which told him he would be in serious trouble if he ever mentioned to Wafford that he really didn't like books and, therefore, did not deserve a handsome leather bookmark from the English Bookstore.

"See you later, Betty." Wafford turned toward the door. "We need to take a walk. Ed and I have some business to attend."

"Cheerio."

Blakely closed the door and followed Wafford up the boulevard toward the university. The wide sidewalk was covered in gray ice except for a single path down the center, which was bare and showing wet, black asphalt. They entered a student canteen at the edge of the campus where dozens of backpacked young people in jeans and canvas coats milled about sipping coffee, smoking, and munching pastries and homemade sandwiches.

"There's a table over in the corner, " said Wafford pointing.

They sat down. Wafford leaned expectantly across the table. "Well, watcha got for me?"

Blakely unzipped his notebook and pulled from it a manila envelope. He started to open the hasp when Wafford laid his hand on Blakely's arm. "No, no, Ed. Not here." Wafford whispered as he looked around suspiciously. "I can look at all that later. Just give me a brief summary of what you found out."

"I guess for starters, Berlin police have pretty much shut down our sources for now."

"How da ya mean?"

"The inspector you read about in the papers?"

"Yes. Krebs?"

"Right. He's moved Heinz Beckmann to *Spandau* Prison temporarily and won't allow anyone to see him. He also has everybody else connected with Georg Krusen under court order not to discuss the case until the investigation is over."

"Damn! How long will that be?"

"I don't really know. Probably weeks."

Wafford's face was turning crimson. "So, you went up there all fer nothin'."

"No, sir, I mean Jim… I got the photographs you wanted. I also corroborated quite a bit about Krusen's fragment from Drs. Lenhardt and Schmidt."

"Ah. At least you got something out of it. So what did you learn that we didn't know before?"

"The piece is definitely *Minoan*, probably found by von Etter or someone else on Crete. It was recently split into probably four pieces."

"How recently?"

"Lenhardt and Schmidt agree it was split using a hatchet or bayonet probably during the German occupation. There are some marks near the bottom edge of the piece, which suggest numbers or a count of some sort. Dr. Schmidt says the unusual maze design…"

"Wait. What kinda numbers?"

"They're more like counting marks. Just a few along the bottom edge. Dr. Schmidt thinks they might be *Linear B* writing, which the *Minoans* may have used to count inventories. *Linear B* writing would also confirm the piece is 3,000 years old."

"Very interesting. What'd Dr. Schmidt say the writing means?"

"She has no idea. Especially since there are so few marks and the guy who discovered Linear B died without confirming what the symbols mean."

"Okay, go on."

"Uh. Dr. Schmidt says the unusual maze design was more accidental than intentional, probably due to the poor skills of the artist. The…"

"How can she be so sure?"

"She's never seen another instance where a labyrinth design was so crudely made."

Wafford shook his head and sighed. "No imagination whatsoever. Not one iota! So what else did she say?"

"The piece was originally painted red except for the labyrinth design, which was painted black."

"That, we know."

"The punched holes and cut marks on the back were made around the same time the complete relic was split into pieces. Lenhardt and Schmidt agree that it would be impossible to determine what the punctures mean, if anything, even if all four pieces were put together."

Wafford shook his head sadly. "None of these people have any imagination. Is that it?"

"I learned that Georg Krusen has no living relatives. He did receive the relic in a package sent from Crete by Heinrich von Etter along with a cheap seal stone curio with an octopus design in 1944. The seal was from a tourist shop. The only message in the package was a handwritten note on the inside of the box saying, *Keep this safe for me.*"

"What'd they say about the seal stone?"

"Dr. Schmidt thinks it was sent along with the piece of wood to put off antiquity authorities. Otherwise, it is meaningless. Heinrich even had a curio shop to wrap the package for him so it would appear that he was just sending mementos to friends. He probably put the leather thong on the relic for the same reason, to make it look like a common curio."

Wafford's jowls were an admixture of red and purple. "What else?"

"Krusen was a loner. Well respected. He enjoyed classical music. Thought of Dr. Schmidt as a daughter. They became close friends over time after he brought the relic to the museum. That was approximately four years ago. Had no enemies that Dr. Schmidt was aware of."

"Ever married? Divorced?"

"Never married. Krebs did tell me Beckmann or somebody totally trashed Krusen's belongings, apparently looking for other things besides the relic. Krebs said even the couch and stuffed chairs were pulled apart. His mattress was turned inside out. Everything was pulled out of shelves, drawers, closets and thrown into piles on the floor."

"How do you know Beck and Horst were searching for, as you say, other things?"

"Because, according to Dr. Schmidt, the relic hung on a nail in Krusen's apartment—in clear sight. There was no need to look elsewhere, unless they were searching for other things."

Wafford looked away from Blakely and seemed to be watching students playing chess at the next table, thinking about what to say. There was no question, Wafford was furious. Blakely zipped up his notebook and placed the manila envelope on top of it and waited. Wafford finally turned back and scowled at the tabletop, avoiding any eye contact.

"Guess you should go down to Heidelberg and see the Schiller woman. After that, we'll see what can be done in Berlin."

"When should I go?"

"Tomorrow. I'll have a package waiting for you later this afternoon at Betty's."

"Jim, I'm sorry I wasn't able to get more information. I know you are disappointed."

"Yeah, well, you did your best, Ed. I don't fault you." Wafford reached across and took the manila envelope while keeping his eyes lowered. "Did you give me an expense report?"

"Yes, sir. Oh, sorry. I didn't mean to use 'sir'."

"You should have enough money left over to pay your expenses down to Heidelberg and back, right?"

"Plenty. I have over five hundred marks left"

"Good. Oh, by the way. I wouldn't share anything with Miz Schiller 'bout your trip to Berlin—including Krusen's death. Okay?"

"I understand."

"Don't worry, son. You can't help it if you run into roadblocks. We just need to think of a different angle of attack up in Berlin. Take care. Give me a couple minutes before you leave."

Wafford pushed his slouch hat down on his head and pushed through the crowd of students and out into the cold. *'Schackmatt!'* (Checkmate!) shouted the kid with the stringy hair as his opponent slumped in disbelief while angrily scattering the chess pieces.

Chapter 15

A Coming Together

Blakely watched as Cunningham parked the brown Hillman across from the *Neuer Wall Kafe*. The guy nearly slipped down as he crossed the *strasse*. There was something totally clumsy about Cunningham, he thought. He was so caught up trying to be an Englishman that he couldn't walk straight. He came through the door and removed his tweed hat and overcoat and approached with a grim expression. His brown hair was ruffled and out of place.

Blakely got up and extended his hand. "Good to see you again, Lieutenant."

Cunningham avoided his hand. Both sat down. "Now, you tell me what this is about," Cunningham hissed. "Who are you and what do you want?"

"I don't want anything, really, except your confidence," Blakely said in a soft voice as he sat back in his chair. "I recently came over from the states. I am a Sergeant and an Intelligence Analyst. I am awaiting assignment to the Army Security Agency Headquarters."

"I'm confused, Sergeant. How in blazes did you get involved with me?"

"I can explain."

"Do you know that I could report you for being insubordinate to an officer? Your behavior in Berlin was abominable."

"Sorry, sir, if I offended you."

"No matter, you were most rude in carrying out your charade, pretending to be CIA."

Blakely grinned and held out his hands. "No, sir. I never said that. You were the one who assumed I was CIA. Anyway, I am glad you are here so we can clear the air."

"I'm still in the dark. How did you know I was meeting with Colonel Wafford unless you were following me?"

"Quite simple. I was on my way to meet the Colonel myself. Just happened to see you leave the *gasthaus*. Running into you again in Berlin was, it turns out, accidental. I thought at the time you were following me."

Cunningham was leaning forward, both hands on the table, seemingly trying to decipher the truth from Blakely's face. "How do I know anything you tell me is the truth?"

"You don't. Can I call you Chris?"

Cunningham stiffened. "Why not," he hissed, "since you obviously do not understand basic protocols between officers and enlisted. Go right ahead. I don't give a groat. Be my guest. Call me what you like."

"Sorry. I'm used to officers and enlisted working together on a first name basis. In intelligence work, your skills are all that matter."

"That's no excuse for your treatment of me."

Blakely grinned. "I do apologize for giving you such a hard time, but I had to be sure you weren't following me."

"Why would I have been doing that?"

"Could be several reasons. I have to tell you in greatest confidence. I also work for Jim Wafford. Truly, I'm not with CIA or CID or CIC. You needn't worry about that."

Cunningham's chin dropped and he crossed himself. "Ah. Mother of God!"

Cunningham's thanks changed to indignation. "But why in hell's name did you lead me on? I must admit I was quite frightened you were going to turn me in—still am, in fact."

"I had to figure whether I could level with you or not. And I wanted you to feel like you couldn't go back and confront Jim Wafford or confess what you had been doing for him to your superiors at SHAFE."

"Well, you bloody well succeeded on all counts. Just what is your game?"

"No game. I've been trying to figure out how you can continue working for Wafford without violating your own principles."

"But why in bloody hell do you care?"

"I guess I'm selfish, Chris. I need your help. By the way, you can call me Ed or Edward or whatever. Maybe, together, we can keep Jim Wafford out of trouble."

"And why should you care what happens to him?"

"I like him. I also admire what he's done for our country. He's one of the real warriors from World War II, a true hero. He's highly respected by people I respect. But, I don't think he realizes how vulnerable he is. He's past prime. Sorta out of touch with the reality of the situation."

"You said as much in Berlin."

"Yeah. Just between us, I have a strong sense that Jim Wafford is going to over-reach and find himself up to his ass in trouble."

"You mean from these *Nazi* thugs?"

"Yes, sir. They're playing for keeps. And I think Jim is too proud to call in his chits so he'll have protection. He seems bent on keeping his little operation top secret—even secret from all those agency people who could help him. Jim doesn't have a clue as to how many people are out there gunning for him."

"So, Edward, if you are so bloody worried about him, why don't you pay a visit to CIC and CID and tell them what you know?"

"He would lose face. He could even be arrested for all I know. I don't want to see him shamed after all he's done. Look, Jim and his wife are supposed to leave for the states soon. Visiting their boys in New York over Christmas. If we can work at keeping him in bounds 'til he leaves for stateside, maybe by the time he gets back all the *Nazis* will be in jail."

"If you ask me, you are being foolishly optimistic. These fellows did not come all the way back here from South America to murder Krusen and take their leave again. I suspect they are right now planning how to get the second bloody piece of relic away from Wafford."

"I'm sure you are right. But that is my point. Maybe we can keep them at bay just by sticking with the Colonel. If they try something overt, then we report it. Maybe they can be arrested by civil authorities before they commit any harm."

"I don't follow you."

"Well, if Horst shows up, we can report him to authorities. He's an escaped war criminal and murderer."

"Sounds too dangerous to me. I would advise you not to get involved. Anyone who tortures an innocent man like Krusen is a psychopath." Chris sat back, crossing his leg and reaching for his pipe and pouch. "I suppose you've deduced that James wanted me to investigate the death of Georg Krusen in Berlin. Even wanted me to interview my fianceé about it. I told him then, that I could no longer work for him."

"Your fianceé?"

"Yes. You interviewed her. Justina Schmidt. The Museum of Egyptology."

Blakely was stunned. He sat back in disbelief. He recalled the conversation he had had with her over dinner. He connected the dots. Well, damn. She was asking about Chris's possible future in the military, not Blakely's. He forced a grin. "Gosh, I guess congratulations are in order."

Cunningham sputtered, "Well, not quite yet. I say she's my fianceé. I do plan to propose to her at Christmas. We've talked about it. Made plans." He lit his pipe nervously, using the aluminum push-pull lighter.

"Dr. Justina Schmidt. She's one pretty lady. You certainly have excellent taste in women."

"Yes, well," Cunningham looked away, "we've been dating for a year and a half. Only made sense, you know. Both of us archeologists. Me looking to stay on the continent rather than returning to the states. She being an established archeologist with a good reputation. Dr. Schaus being willing to assist me in finding a position. It was all very convenient. We seemed well matched for marriage. It all fell into place."

A strange way to describe the love of your life, Blakely mused. A marriage of convenience? "So tell me, Chris. Since you obviously visited Dr. Schmidt often at the museum, did you also know Georg Krusen?"

"No. I ran into him two or three times, but we weren't friends. Nor did I know he had a part of the relic until the murder happened. No one at the museum ever discussed the relic business with me. It was an extraordinary coincidence, but one which woke me up to the gravity of what I was doing for the Colonel."

"I take it that is when you met with Jim at the *gasthaus* on *Ginnheimer Strasse*. to say you couldn't do any more work for him."

"He had just heard about the murder and asked me to meet him there. He wanted me to confirm an early report that there was a Minoan artifact involved by going to Berlin and—of all things—interviewing Justina and Dieter Lenhardt."

"You refused?"

"Yes. I did not want to embarrass Dieter or Justina by implicating myself—and by association, them—in a half-baked scheme hatched by James Wafford."

"But now it isn't half-baked. Murdering a guy for a piece of Minoan wood proves Jim is on the right track."

"Quite right. On the right track to getting us all murdered."

"So Jim still does not know about your relationship with Dr. Schmidt?"

"No. And I pray he never does."

"What types of work did you do for him, if you don't mind my asking. I believe you said you worked some six months with him."

"Oh, following various leads primarily concerning the von Etter family. I interviewed a young Jewish boy who had actually witnessed some of the executions. I corroborated some of Professor Storey's information that neither Heinrich von Etter nor Jochim Grenz had anything to do with the von Stauffenberg plot. That sort of thing. I did locate Fredrich Braun, another close friend of Heinrich's. He was living just outside Frankfurt."

"Oh?"

"He was quite ill at the time, so I really could not interview him per se. I reported where he was living to the Colonel. He visited him in Hanau, I believe, just before Braun died."

"How long ago was that?"

"Four months? Yes, around four months ago."

"Jim ever share what he found out?"

"No. Data and information are one-way with James, as I am sure you know. He doesn't share."

"Which brings us to the present. Would you consider continuing to work for Jim—provided I'll be there to back you up? And keep in mind that you can always refuse to do anything you feel would be too dangerous. Really, Chris, I agree with you. I don't want to try mixing it up with these *Nazi* guys any more than you do. We would play it one day at a time and see how it goes. Hopefully, it is only a few days until the Colonel's plane takes off. Then, we're done with it."

Cunningham pulled on his pipe and blew smoke at the large window. "As I said before, Justina and I could use the money. But I don't know. If there's any chance I'd be caught up in some scandal or blackmail, I won't do it."

Blakely looked closely at Cunningham's tweed suit. It was expensive. "I'm a bit confused, Chris. You're wearing a handsome suit. You have an undergraduate degree. A doctorate from Oxford. Surely, there's got to be some money in your background. What Wafford is paying you is small change by comparison."

Cunningham grinned sardonically while looking down at his fingers. "If you must know, Sergeant, my father is threatening to disown me if I marry Justina. I hope you will never tell another soul."

"Yeah? Honest?"

"Honest."

"I won't tell anyone. I promise."

"My father comes from a long line of Chestnut Hill attorneys in Philadelphia. They go back to the American Revolution. He always thought I'd follow tradition and go to Yale, join the practice, and marry a proper graduate of Radcliff or Vassar, have precisely two children, and live happily ever after."

"I can understand his feelings about traditions. But what's wrong with becoming an archeologist?"

"Not only did I wish to break tradition, I chose to marry the enemy."

"The enemy?"

"Of course. A *Kraut*. A *Nazi*. It broke my father's heart. He won't tolerate it."

"But Justina is no *Nazi*."

"In the eyes of my family she is. That is another reason I plan to stay abroad. I do not wish to return home unless my family accepts Justina."

"Well, damn." Blakely wondered how a father could think of disowning his kid, no matter what he'd done. A truth dawned and he ruefully thought about how his own father had abandoned him without ever knowing he had a son. "Well, damn," Blakely muttered again.

Chapter 16

Declining An Invitation

Blakely retrieved Wafford's instructions from Betty and returned to the barrack. He was packing an overnight bag in case he needed to stay over when he was called to the Orderly Room for a telephone call.

"Sergeant Edward Blakely here, sir."

"Sergeant Blakely, this is Captain Tom McCloud up at headquarters."

"Yes, sir."

"One of our couriers came down with the flu at the last minute. We'd like for you to pull courier duty tonight to Berlin. You'll be going up with Sergeant Kentop again. Sorry I couldn't give you more lead time."

"Sir, if that is an order, I'll be glad to do it. If it is not an order, I've made plans to go to Heidelberg this morning, sir."

"Oh? Well, Sergeant, it's not an order. Most young men coming over from stateside jump at the chance to visit Berlin. But if you have other plans, I guess we can get somebody else."

"I'd be happy to go sir, if you can't get someone. But I've got train tickets for 1000 hours, sir."

"That's okay. We'll get somebody else."

Thank you, sir. Please call me again anytime. I'd like to do whatever you need me to do."

"Talk to you later, Sarge."

"Yes, sir."

Blakely replaced the receiver and slowly climbed the stairs to his room. He slumped on the edge of the bunk and glanced at Sergeant Lester, who was stretched out on his own bunk reading a book. Lester closed the book. "What's up?"

"Oh, I was asked to do courier duty to Berlin and turned it down. Had another engagement. I feel really bad about not doing duty for headquarters."

"Never got to Berlin, myself. Must be a heavy date or something special to give up that chance."

"Yeah, well, I promised a friend that I'd do him a favor. Just wish they'd given more notice."

"Hell, man, they're used to having it their way. You belong to Uncle Sam, buddy. When Uncle says go, you'd damn well better get your ass in gear and go."

"Yeah. You're right, Frank. I'm heading out." Blakely picked up his overnight and trench coat and walked out of the room and down the steps. He didn't need Lester to make him feel worse than he already felt. He pushed open the heavy door and strode out across the hard, iced cobblestones toward the *Hauptbahnhof.* The excitement of the trip to Heidelberg was spoiled. His helping Wafford was already getting him off to a bad start at headquarters. They kept records of such things. Even after boarding the train and watching it pull out of the station and past *Gutleut Kaserne,* he felt empty. It was no good. He couldn't concentrate either on the scenery or on all the instructions Wafford had given him. It was no good at all.

Chapter 17

Frau Katrin von Rosenheim Schiller

They were to meet at *Das Alten Fenster Restaurant*, a place hidden away among the narrow medieval alleys of Heidelberg. *Frau* Katrin von Rosenheim Schiller was described as thirty-eight, tall, blonde with blue eyes. She would be wearing a navy colored dress and hat. She would be sitting at a table in front of the famous mullioned window, which had withstood centuries of war. He had the impression he would be looking for one antique sitting beneath another, the window and the woman sharing age and decay in common.

Blakely entered the restaurant and removed his trench coat. The interior was semi-dark. A low-hung ceiling with varnished old beams glistened in the half-light. A waiter bowed slightly and accompanied him through a gallery of lit oil paintings to a well-lighted room beyond. Well-dressed Germans were quietly eating and being served by tuxedoed waiters. There was no mistaking *Frau* Schiller, sitting beneath the great window. Light poured down upon her hair, turning it nearly white in contrast to her dark hat and dress. She certainly knew how to present herself in the best light. Her eyes were shaded by the hat brim, but Blakely was aware of her aristocratic bearing, high cheekbones, creamy complexion, thin nose, and splash of bright red lipstick. She was fashionable and still quite attractive.

Although she had been looking slightly away, the moment Blakely approached, her head turned and the red splash of color grew into a carefully modified line of polite smile. Her back straightened as she watched his approach. Put on your best charm, Easy Ed, for you are about to meet your first honest-to-god aristocrat.

Blakely held out his hand. "*Frau* Schiller?"

"How do you do, *Herr* Blakely?" She extended her hand. A sonorous voice, not shrill, but of singing quality—like Peggy Lee's.

"How do you do, *Frau* Schiller," Blakely responded in his best German and took her hand firmly in the German way. "I am delighted to meet you," using the *"ish"* of South German dialect.

"Ah! You speak *Deutsch,* then, *Herr* Blakely. Do please sit down," she said in English, motioning him to choose either the side chair next to her or the one opposite. He audaciously chose the side chair, noting that her face was pert, even elegant. There was challenge and serious playfulness in her demeanor. Professor Storey was wrong. Her eyes were blue-green, not merely blue.

"So tell me a little about yourself, *Herr* Blakely. I have an aversion to talking with strangers."

"Well, ma'am, I've just come over from the states. I'm a sergeant in the Army. Before I joined, I was a professional sailor working out of San Diego, California. Sailing's been my passion ever since I was a kid. I'm a graduate of the Army Language School. That's about it in a nutshell."

Her eyes shone brightly. "Your life in a nutshell."

"Yes, ma'am." Blakely grinned confidently.

"Not married?"

"No, ma'am."

"Lots of pretty girlfriends though?"

Blakely shifted toward her. "Not really. There's always room for one more…"

She laughed. Pretty white teeth. "What is your connection with Gerald? How did you meet?"

"We didn't. I am doing some interviews for one of his colleagues."

"Ah. I take it you work for Colonel James Wafford then?"

So, Wafford is not as anonymous as he thinks he is. "Do you know him?"

"*Nein.* Gerald has spoken of him many times. I recall meeting a man some years ago at a reception that may have been him. I can't be sure. I simply don't remember. You say you are a professional sailor. What does that mean?"

"In civilian life I raced boats for money. I also taught sailing and did charter day sailing. Took a lot of people over to Catalina Island and back."

"Interesting."

"Yes, ma'am."

"If you and I are to have lunch together, I want you to refrain from calling me ma'am. You make me feel ancient."

"Sorry, *Frau* Schiller. You certainly are not ancient." Blakely looked around the room. "Fact is you're the prettiest lady in the room."

"I was not intending to draw a compliment from you, but thank you all the same."

"I promise not to call you ma'am, if you promise me I can pay for your lunch."

She laughed, pulling her hands together at her chin. "You may do that, sir."

Blakely looked around, not sure what to say next. "This is a nice place."

"*Ja.* Quite old. You probably noticed the ceiling when you first came in. The beams are from an eleventh century chapel that once stood here. This window," she turned and pointed, "was constructed in the fifteenth century. It was once part of the castle. The mullions are quite fine for the period. When they renovated, they removed it to here."

"Wow."

Two waiters arrived. One poured water into goblets. The other presented menus.

"What do you like, *Herr* Blakely? They serve excellent Bavarian rabbit in white wine with apples."

"Sounds like a winner. Would you care for wine?"

"A light one. Are you familiar with wines?"

"To some degree. Why don't we find out what wine they used to prepare the rabbit?"

She gazed at him carefully. "An excellent idea."

Blakely nodded to the waiter who retraced his steps from the other side of room.

"Yes, sir?"

Blakely spoke in German. "Yes. Can you tell us the name and vintage of the wine used to prepare the rabbit today?"

"It is a *Sylvaner*, 1952. A *Franconian*."

"Does that suit you, *Frau* Schiller?"

"*Ja*. I won't be drinking but a small amount. Probably less than a glass."

Blakely looked up at the waiter. "We'll have a bottle of the *Sylvaner* and two orders of the rabbit, please."

"Very good, sir." The waiter retreated toward the kitchen.

Frau Schiller leaned closer. "You seem very confident for such a young man. And quite worldly, too."

Blakely placed his elbow next to her arm and smiled. "Well, thank you, *Frau* Schiller. I am still in the early learning stages."

They laughed. She drew back and turned serious. "I understand from Gerald that Colonel Wafford has new questions?"

"Yes. They concern your good friend Elsa von Etter."

"Oh? And what about her?"

"It seems everyone believed she was killed along with the rest of the von Etter family in July, 1944. There is new evidence that she fled to *Trieste* and wasn't captured by the *Gestapo* until October."

Katrin blinked her eyes and gazed past Blakely as though in a trance.

"In honest truth, Mr. Blakely, I did not know that. We all assumed she was killed at the same time as the rest of the family. And insofar as she was fleeing, that isn't true. She was invited to go there by her cousin for a vacation. Even so, what difference would it make if she were put to death in July or in October?"

"I don't know. Do you recall when she left to visit Trieste?"

"It was several days before the atrocities took place. I helped her pack."

"Did she pack like she wouldn't be returning to Vienna? Like, maybe she was leaving Vienna to escape the *Gestapo*?"

"All of us were fearful of arrest by the *Gestapo*. But no, I can assure you, she packed only one large case as I recall. Things one would take on vacation: her cameras, film, sportswear, a few dresses for evening, walking shoes. Nothing out of the ordinary. I remember she was quite excited and happy because she was to meet her boyfriend in Graz, on her way down there."

The waiter brought the *Sylvaner* and two small green-stemmed glasses and opened the wine. Without fanfare, he poured the glasses to the brim and set the bottle on the table.

"Would you mind if I took some notes, *Frau* Schiller. Otherwise, I'm likely not to remember things properly."

"No. Not at all."

Blakely opened his notebook and began jotting some cryptic notes. He stopped and looked up. "You didn't see her putting anything unusual in her case, such as a piece of wooden relic?"

"No. Gerald asked me that question several times. I am bored with this relic nonsense. No. Nothing of the sort."

"I see. Was that the last time you saw her?"

"*Ja*. She sent me a postcard soon after she arrived in Trieste. I responded with a letter, but never heard back. I always assumed she was arrested and murdered along with the rest of the family."

"That doesn't seem to be the case. Do you recall what she said on the postcard?"

"*Ja*. She said she was enjoying swimming and that she had met Joch in Graz. That they had a gay time together. That is all."

"Joch?"

"Joachim Grenz. He was a close friend of Estel and Heinrich."

"I see. There was no other communication?"

"*Nein*."

"Was her cousin's name Swartzlander?"

"*Ja. Frau* Hilda Swartzlander. She was a young widow living alone. Lost her husband in a boating accident. Had a lovely brownstone home overlooking the Trieste Yacht basin. Elsa took me down there one summer before the war. Trieste is quite charming. Have you been there?"

"No. So *Frau* Swartzlander was slightly older than you and Estel?"

"Perhaps five or seven years. If she were alive today, she would probably be in her mid-forties."

"Do you still have *Frau* Swartzlander's address?"

"I would have to look for it."

"That would be very helpful. So, you heard nothing more from either Elsa or *Frau* Swartzlander?"

"*Nein*. As I said, I assumed both were killed by the *Gestapo*."

"There is no evidence *Frau* Swartzlander was arrested with *Fraulein* Elsa von Etter."

"No?"

"Estel von Etter was, according to *Gestapo* documents, arrested alone and brought back to Vienna October 16, 1944. She was shot the following day."

Frau Schiller shook her head and gripped the edge of the table with both hands. "I see."

"And what about Joachim Grenz? Have you kept in touch with him?"

"I saw Joachim last during summer, 1943, when he was being transferred from Crete to the oil fields in Rumania. He was on furlough. We used to correspond rather regularly."

"So Mr. Grenz was with Heinrich von Etter on Crete?"

"*Ja*. They parachuted together during the invasion and were stationed there as engineers."

"Construction engineers?"

"*Ja*. They built an airfield, various facilities."

"Were you good friends with Mr. Grenz?"

Frau Schiller raised her head and smiled wanly. "*Ja*. We were star-crossed lovers before the war."

"Star-crossed?"

"*Ja*. We were very much in love, but could never be married. He was the son of shopkeepers. I was of noble birth. My family would never approve such a union." She smoothed the folded napkin, stroking the linen with her fingers. She wore a wedding ring on her left hand and a pink gemstone on the ring finger of her right hand. "He was the true love of my life…"

"That is quite sad, *Frau* Schiller. If you don't mind my asking, what was it like to meet Mr. Grenz again in 1943?"

Her eyes lit up momentarily as she drew her hands together as though she were about to pray. "We spent the afternoon together. It was a lovely day. Bright sunshine. We mostly walked in the Belvedere Gardens and talked about our lives and those of mutual friends. What would happen to us after the war. He said he had fallen in love with Estel and was intending to propose to her over her family's objections. I remember his joking with me and making me smile. Joch always had a wonderful sense of humor."

"Sounds like it was a special day."

"*Ja*. It was…"

"Then, a year later, Joch was on furlough again and meeting Estel in Graz?"

"July, 1944. *Ja*."

"Was he on leave from the oil fields?"

"I learned later from mutual friends that he was on his way to the Eastern Front when he met Estel in Graz."

"Did he continue writing letters to you?"

"*Nein*. I never had a forwarding address."

"And what about Georg Krusen? Did you know him well?"

"*Ja*. Fairly well. He was engineer like Heinrich, Joch and Freddie Braun. The four were inseparable. They became parachutists together. We spent many wonderful times together attending parties, hiking, boating, mountain climbing—all that was before the war, of course. Georg was seriously wounded during the invasion of Holland."

"You mentioned Freddie Braun. Have you kept in touch with him?"

"*Nein*. Freddie was the brightest of the four, but a total introvert. Very sweet, however. We never corresponded. He was a graduate of the University of Frankfurt."

"You've had such an exciting life. Did you actually know Count von Stauffenberg?"

"*Ja*. I attended several parties before the war where he was also a guest. We were not close friends, although I remember waltzing with him at a friend's home in Saltzburg. Quite a handsome man. Very outspoken."

"Have you considered writing a *memoir, Frau* Schiller?"

The two waiters reappeared at table with two plates of rabbit, apples, potatoes and cabbage along with bread and butter.

Blakely raised his glass and *Frau* Schiller did the same. "Here's to more adventures in your life. *Probst*."

"And yours too, *Herr* Blakely. *Probst.*"

They sipped the wine and began eating.

She sighed. "No, I never considered writing a *memoir*. I am truly tired of talking about the war."

"May I ask why? The rabbit, by the way, is excellent."

"I'm pleased you like it. Not everyone does. I've gone over and over the same things with reporters, investigators, Gerald, and persons like you. I feel myself exploited. Every time Gerald or someone else I've talked with publishes a new article about the von Etter family, the Rosenheims or von Stauffenbergs, it causes some reporter or another to track me down to see also what I know about it. Before Gerald and the newspaper reporters, the police and military officials interviewed me countless times over the years—especially before the Nuremberg trials.

"I really have nothing more to say than what is already on hours of tape recordings and in hundreds of pages of depositions. The truth is, *Herr* Blakely, Gerald knows more about me than I know about myself."

Blakely leaned in, watching Katrin's face become serious, resolute. She was shaking her head from side to side, lines drawn tightly at the corners of her mouth.

"Besides," she added, "Gerald hasn't kept up his end of the bargain."

"Oh?"

The waiter arrived and poured the wine glasses full to the brim.

"*Ja*, that is true. We had an agreement. No money was involved, of course. I would put him in contact with important people he wished to interview. In return, he would find out what happened to members of my family. Unfortunately, I helped him immeasurably while he never found out what happened to my family and closest friends."

"I'm sorry to hear that, *Frau* Schiller. I really am."

"Thank you. I especially wanted to confirm how my husband died. He was a pilot transporting supplies to the armies at Stalingrad. It is said his plane exploded upon being hit by anti-aircraft guns. But we never know for sure what to believe, do we?"

"True. We really don't. I lost my half-brother that way over Rumania in 1943. They say his B-24 was shot down with no survivors. I guess you have to trust the official reports and move on with your life."

"After living under Hitler, I trust nothing in official reports. Nor, for that matter, those who write history."

"Really?"

"I have observed how my own words have been used and misused in articles and books. I often find serious errors, misunderstandings of what I've said—to say nothing about my statements taken out of context and used inappropriately. Even Gerald makes horrible errors in reporting what I, or someone I know, have said. Not on purpose, mind you, but errors all the same. And the difficulty is, once they are printed you cannot ever get them corrected. The errors take on a life of their own."

"That's too bad. I understand from my training how it happens. It can hardly be avoided, though. Don't you think?"

"I agree. Only God is perfect. We, as imperfect human beings, tend to cause great harm to one another, even as we think we are doing good."

"But most of us try to do our best. Don't you think? I've always thought you can improve things in the world if you really try hard. You can make a difference, make the world a better place."

"Your philosophy, *Herr* Blakely, is one of being young, hopeful, just getting started in life. My own is very different. I have come to believe that things on earth do not improve with time but are merely different, like the ebb and flow of waves upon the beach. Each wave brings new life and death along with elements of the past, some of which are most ancient. Each wave is at once different and the same."

"I like that. I've never thought about waves in that way. And I suppose you're right. Maybe things don't change as much as we think they do. Perhaps it is our own ego thing—to believe what we do is important. It gives us a reason for living."

"*Ja.* Precisely. That's been my experience."

"You mentioned going boating a while ago. Do you like sailing?"

"Long before the war, when Heinrich and I first met, we went sailing many afternoons on the Swansee in Berlin. You know, they were only little boats with one sail. He would purposely catch the wind a certain way so that the boat would tip, and I would be laughing so much that I would sometimes topple into the water. Yes, I liked to sail, but I never cared to do it without Heinrich."

"Ah. You were in love with him too, then?"

"*Ja*. Unfortunately, Heinrich's family was already allied with ours for many years. My family intended for me to marry a man from another aristocratic family, which would broaden the alliance and wealth, so to speak. I know that must sound strange to an American, but that is how aristocratic, Catholic families in Germany and Austria were before the war."

"We have the same thing in Boston and Philadelphia. People in old families don't like the idea of marrying beneath themselves or with outsiders. As for me, it wouldn't make any difference, so long as I loved the woman."

"A typical American romantic! Totally democratic. You American men fall in love with nearly every woman you meet. Not true?"

She seemed amused, but was watching him intently.

"Yeah. I guess we're easily attracted. Especially when the lady is quite pretty and charming."

She laughed and leaned toward him while sipping her wine. "Tell me, *Herr* Blakely, how do you like the apples?"

"Kinda sweet and sour. Different, but very good. They go well with the rabbit. Speaking of which, I used to cook rabbit over an open campfire on a spit."

"Hm. I suppose you shared it with some pretty young woman." Her eyes danced as she said it.

"Not necessarily a young woman, *Frau* Schiller. Just so they were pretty and liked a bit of adventure."

"You are clever, *Herr* Blakely. I am beginning to like you. Tell me more about rabbits on spits."

Blakely grinned, feeling like she had him on a spit and was throwing another log on the fire. "To tell you the truth, most of the time, it was just a group of fellows I sailed with. We'd take off on a Friday afternoon and go camp out on the Anza Berrega Desert for the weekend. That's in Southern California. We'd catch some rabbits using snares or with a .22 rifle and cook them over a fire. If any girls went along, they had their own campsite. We'd sometimes join them around the fire and sing, have a few beers together. Share food. That's mostly it."

"Those times are not unlike happy times we spent before the war. Everyone was young and took pleasure in the mountains and on the lakes. All of us loved adventure."

"That's the nice thing about adventure. It can take so many different forms."

"I can tell you speak from experience, *Herr* Blakely."

He laughed. "What do you do here in Heidelberg?"

"I have since 1942 worked with a Catholic relief agency helping survivors, orphans, pensioners. We provide food, locate jobs, train people for occupations." She reached into her purse and pulled out a card and handed it to him. "This is my agency address and telephone number in case you would like to contact me."

"Thank you. Do you have any children from your marriage?"

"I lost my only son in a bombing raid. We were living in Dresden. The bombers came so suddenly we had no time to get to the shelters. My little boy and his nurse were killed instantly. He was just two."

Blakely leaned closer, shaking his head negatively. "So tragic."

"*Ja.* There hasn't been more time in my life for another marriage or kids. Besides, there are so many children without parents to care for that I haven't had time to think about what I've missed."

"No time for romance?"

The waiter arrived and poured the remaining wine into their glasses and disappeared with the empty bottle.

She laughed and looked up toward the ceiling—like an embarrassed teen-aged girl—pulling air into her lungs so that her breasts expanded beneath her blue dress. "You are getting entirely too personal, *Herr* Blakely." She said it with a broad, coquettish smile. "Not very much time for that either."

She touched her wine glass and looked at him pensively. "I only occasionally see a man I wish to know better. Otherwise, I stay content with my role in life now. It is what God has intended for me, I believe."

"No dancing?" Blakely leaned closer, almost touching her arm with his own. "I think God loves dancing."

She laughed wistfully, moving her shoulders and touching the top button of her dress where the hollow of her skin made a shadow. "No dancing. Perhaps one day I will take time to learn those American dances you do, with all the turns and twists."

"You mean the jitterbug?"

"*Ja.*" She giggled. "The jitterbug."

"I'll be glad to teach you, *Frau* Schiller. Just tell me when and where."

She drew back slightly and pretended to be shocked. "For shame on you! You are much too eager, *Herr* Blakely, even for an American."

"Sounds like you know a lot about us Americans. I think you'd find it fun," Blakely whispered conspiratorially.

They both finished off the wine and set the empty glasses next to one another.

"I am sure I would." She touched her blonde hair lightly with her hand while seeming to search for the right reply. Blakely waited. She finally pursed her lips and looked into his eyes. "Well, *Herr* Blakely, I have enjoyed our lunch."

"Thank you, *Frau* Schiller. So have I. Would you care for a dessert?"

"I think not. But you go ahead."

"No." He patted his stomach. "I eat too many sweets as it is."

She smiled.

"I appreciate your seeing me. Can I escort you home or get a taxi for you?"

"That won't be necessary. A dear friend of mine is coming up from Stuttgart this afternoon. She will be stopping by here any moment. I think I'll have a cup of coffee while I wait for her."

She held out her hand. Blakely arose from the table and shook her hand firmly before letting go. As he pulled on his trench coat, he felt a little foolish, flirting with a woman he didn't know who was nearly as old as his own mother. He thought he had accomplished very little for the colonel, but felt totally good about himself and his meeting with Katrin von Rosenheim Schiller. She was one enticing woman, no matter that she had a few age lines here and there. Her pretty mouth and flashing blue-green eyes were all he could think about as he paid the bill and headed out.

Chapter 18

Breaking Protocols

Betty had called and left a message. The book on *Parsnips* would be available at three o'clock today. At 1450 hours, Blakely entered the English Bookstore, carrying his report and expense statement from the Heidelberg trip in a manila envelope tucked under his arm.

"Afternoon, Edward. Have you finished the Hemingway?"

Blakely rolled his eyes and grinned. "Not quite. I am into chapter 31. He's in deep trouble. The *Tenente* is swimming in a freezing river, up to his neck, and clinging to a heavy timber. I'm not sure he is going to make it."

"Ah, the perils of fiction." She smiled. "I was hoping you had finished it so we could discuss it."

"I have less than a hundred pages to go. Is the ending a good one?"

"That depends on what you mean. If you mean how it turns out, it turns out rather awfully. I cannot imagine a less happy ending. I am certain it will surprise you. On the other hand, in terms of its success as art, I would consider it a masterpiece. But I want you to finish it and tell me what you think."

"I will."

She reached beneath the counter and handed him an envelope. "Did you know that Hemingway wrote forty-four different endings to *A Farewell to Arms* before selecting one?"

"No. That's incredible. I wouldn't think it'd be possible to come up with that many alternatives. Thank you." He took the envelope and slipped it into his pocket.

"I attribute it to ambiguity."

"I don't understand."

"Ambiguous experience. There is so much ambiguity and irony in American life as reflected in your fiction, don't you agree?"

Blakely shrugged. "Never gave it much thought."

"Oh, James said for you to open and read the contents immediately." She pointed at his pocket.

"Thanks." Blakely opened the seal and pulled a note from the envelope. It said Hans, Wafford's driver, would be parked in a black Mercedes behind the English Bookstore at 1505 hours. Hans would be wearing a dark hat, muffler, and overcoat. He was to get in the back seat. Hans would take him to Eschersheim. Blakely strode toward the door, wondering what this was about. Must be some emergency for him to be invited to the house.

"Good to see you, Betty. Hope you have a very merry Christmas."

"And merry Christmas to you, Edward."

* * *

To say Jim Wafford was effusive and light-hearted would have been an understatement. He was like a kid showing off the new toys he had gotten for Christmas. He pointed to this photo, that commendation, and explained what all the files and maps were for in the wine cellar that served as his war room. Anna brought a tray down and placed it in the middle of the great table where Blakely and Wafford sat across from one another. On the tray were two lidded beer steins, a bowl of pretzels, crackers, hard cheese, seeded rye bread, mustard, and sliced cold sausage. She placed small plates and napkins in front of them and retreated up the steps.

"Thanks, Anna! Help yerself, Ed. Try the sausage with some mustard"

Wafford went to the door and locked it. "I always keep this locked whether I'm here or not. Hans and Anna are taking Louise shopping soon, so it'll just be us by ourselves down here."

Wafford came to the table and picked up his stein. "Here's to happy holidays and the best new year ever."

"And here's to a safe trip back to see your boys." They clinked steins and lifted the lids with their thumbs. It was dark beer, celebrating the holidays, sweet and icy cold. Blakely took another swig and put the stein down.

"Ah, good beer."

Blakely dipped a piece of sausage into the mustard and bit off a piece. It was quite spicy, yet sweet and tangy. "The sausage is tasty."

"Glad you like it. Hans drives all the way to Berkersheim for that sausage. A butcher there is famous for it." Wafford mopped up some mustard with a large piece of sausage and stuffed it into his mouth, chewing earnestly. "By the way, Ed, I broke one of my own cardinal rules today."

"How so?"

"By inviting you directly here. It's against my better judgment to have anyone working for me–sorta covertly–to come to the house. I'd prefer sticking to protocols and meeting at places like the *Palmengarten* or the *gasthaus* or at Betty's."

Blakely squirmed uneasily. "Then, why did you, sir?"

Wafford looked around wanly. "Oh, I just thought you'd truly appreciate seeing a genuine G-2 war room like we used to have. Not many have an appreciation for such things anymore. You know what I mean?"

Blakely looked softly at Wafford. "Yeah, I know what you mean, Jim. And I thank you for breaking a rule so I could see it."

"Besides," Wafford broke into a grin, "I want to hear directly from the horse's mouth how you knocked an hour off the night compass course record at Fort Riley. You may not be aware of this, Ed, but I was the one who designed that course. Did you know that?"

Blakely took another swig and wiped his hand across his mouth. "No, sir. I didn't."

"Tell me honestly how you did it, Ed. Cecil tole me it had somethin' to do with nighttime sea navigation techniques."

"Yes, sir. That and using the topographic map and a watch. Instead of maintaining a straight line bearing from beginning point to ending point, which would take you through thick underbrush, steep hills and ravines, and two pretty deep streams, I plotted a course using the stars and topo, so's we could stay above the heavy tree line and go around all the obstacles."

"I don't follow how the topographic map worked."

"The topo is just like a sea chart where you are trying to avoid shoals and shallow water. I applied the same principle to charting our course, choosing the widest, flattest, and most obstacle free terrain on the topo map, but still keeping inside the compass course. We were able to literally run the course, once I had plotted distances and directions and yardage, using celestial navigation. It was just like I was racing a sailboat on the sea at night, except it was on land."

"Amazing. I still don't understand it all, but it's amazing." Wafford sipped beer and ran his hand through his hair. "You thought this up yerself?"

"Yes, sir."

"Damned amazing." Wafford stared at Blakely and took another swig. "You do know, Ed, the real intention was to run through the obstacles on the course, not try and go around them. We wanted to see whether our men could make it through dense vegetation and difficult terrain and still arrive at their destination within a reasonable time."

"Yeah," Blakely grinned. He tilted his head to one side. "That's what they told us. But that isn't how things play out in real life—especially when cutting time and obstacles can save lives."

Wafford smirked and took a large swig. "Cecil says they made you repeat your way of doing it several times in front of the generals."

Blakely grinned and looked down at the pastoral scene on the side of the stein. "Yeah. It was pretty funny. They waited until there was no moon before inviting our team to show them how we did it. I guess they thought a lack of moonlight would make us slow down. But that didn't happen. The stars were brighter. Made it easier to keep our bearings."

Wafford stuffed cheese in his mouth and washed it down. "Ole Cec says they changed the rules after you showed 'em how you did it. That true?"

"Yes, sir. They're now teaching some navigation as part of the compass classes."

"Just amazing." Wafford shook his head and looked across the room. "Got somethin' I know you'll wanna see."

Wafford got up and turned. He strode around the table and opened a glass case on the wall. "Wancha to see my special prize," he said, lifting out an open pistol case displaying a pistol, tools, and clips. "This here weapon belonged to Heinrich von Etter. It's a paratrooper's pistol, an automatic *Schmeisser.*"

He laid the case down and gently removed the pistol from its holder and handed it to Blakely.

"Wow! Beautiful. It's in mint condition." The slight scent of gun oil was clean and pleasant.

"Had it professionally restored by a German gunsmith, Ed. It's as fine as can be."

"I can see that." Blakely ran his fingers over the smooth barrel and chased handle. "You must be very proud of it. But how do you know for sure it belonged to von Etter?"

Wafford leaned in and turned the gun around. He pointed to the steel casing. The letters *HvE* were neatly engraved. "No doubt about it, son. As I believe I mentioned to you, I took this weapon off Eugen Horst when we identified him and Beck up in the mountains. I've kept it ever since."

Blakely examined the fine steel maintenance tools, the removable shoulder stock, and clips still filled with live ammo, replacing each of them in their pockets. "Beautiful."

Wafford carefully put the case back in the cabinet and turned the lock. He slumped down in his swivel chair. "Now tell me 'bout the woman down in Heidelberg, Miz Schiller. What'd she have to allow?"

"Not a great deal, sir. She'd already been asked several times whether Estel had packed anything like a Minoan artifact in her cases. *Frau* Schiller reiterated that she hadn't. There was nothing notable except that Joachim Grenz met Estel von Etter at Graz when Estel was on her way down to Trieste. Grenz was on furlough. They met just for the day. She said Professor Storey had asked her questions about the meeting and she had nothing to add. She did not know that Estel was still alive until being arrested in October. She had assumed Estel was killed along with the rest of the family in July. She had no communication with her except for the postcard you already know about."

Wafford sat, elbow on table, head against fist, looking again deflated. "What about Miz Swartzlander down yonder in Trieste?"

"She had no communication with her at all."

Wafford drummed his fingers on the table and half closed his eyes. "So, it is possible that Joachim Grenz gave Estel a piece of the artifact when they met. She takes it with her to Trieste. She puts it in the hands of Miz Swartzlander for safekeeping before going into hiding?"

Blakely shrugged and emptied the stein. "Don't know, sir."

"As I recall, Miz Schiller visited Miz Swartzlander with Estel before the war. And they corresponded some… Did you get her last address?"

Blakely dropped his head momentarily, then looked across the table at Wafford. "I meant to. *Frau* Schiller said she'd have to look it up. She didn't have it with her at the restaurant. I can call her and ask her for it. I have her card where she works at a Catholic social services center."

Wafford tilted his head to one side and continued drumming his fingers. "Naw. That's all right. I have half a mind to go down there myself. Maybe even pay Miz Swartzlander a visit. If she's still alive and living there, I can find her. Trieste isn't all that big."

The two men sat silently. The good cheer of the season had evaporated from the war room. Wafford gazed at the ceiling, poking his mouth with his index finger. "Hear or read anything about the investigation in Berlin?"

Blakely locked eyes with Wafford. It was a dumb question. Hell, Wafford had all these stacks of latest *Berliner Zeitung* editions at his fingertips. How would he know as much about what was going on as Wafford did? "No, sir. I've been checking some newspapers, but haven't seen any articles."

Wafford looked at his watch. "It's still pretty early. Why don'tcha give that woman Justina Schmidt a call. See what she can tell you."

Blakely leaned in. "You mean right now?"

"Sure. Why not?" Wafford picked up one of the two black phones off the roll-top desk and handed it across the table.

"I don't have the number with me for the museum."

"I've got it." Wafford pulled out a drawer and retrieved a folder. He flipped it across the table. It contained Blakely's Berlin report and the packet of instructions with a list of phone numbers. Blakely dialed the number. The lady at the desk put him through to Schmidt's extension.

"I'll put it on speaker phone," Wafford whispered as he pressed a switch and took the receiver from Blakely and hung it on the cradle.

"This is Justina Schmidt."

"Merry Christmas, Dr. Schmidt. This is Edward Blakely calling from Frankfurt."

"Edward. Oh, so glad to hear your voice. Merry Christmas."

"I wanted to see whether any new developments were happening regarding the Krusen murder investigation or the relic?"

"Oh. I was going to call you, Edward. Inspector Krebs has released back to me some of Georg's belongings, including a photo album from before the war. There are clippings also, when he was a paratrooper."

"They could be of interest."

"*Ja*. Oh, before I forget, all the news stories about the Minoan fragment have caused the Greek government to demand that it be returned to Crete. They wish to place it in the museum at Iraklion."

"I see."

"*Ja...*"

"What about Beck? Is he still in custody at *Spandau?*"

"He is there."

"Anyone else been arrested?"

"No. They are looking for another man. Eugen Horst. Also from Paraguay. They think he has escaped to East Germany."

"Anything else?"

"*Nein*. That is all the news I have to report."

"Can I stop by soon and make photostat copies of the photos and clippings?"

"Certainly. Just call me when you arrive in the city so I will be here. I look forward to seeing you again."

"Yeah, me too, Dr. Schmidt."

Blakely nodded at Wafford who shook his head negatively.

"Guess that's it for now. Thanks for the news."

"*Ja*. My pleasure. Goodbye."

"Goodbye."

Wafford pressed the switch and sat back down. "Well done, Ed. I'd like you to go up tomorrow, if you can make it. In fact, I might pay a visit to Mr. Beck at *Spandau* myself soon."

It was strange to think both of them had to make the trip to Berlin, but Blakely knew Wafford could probably pull strings at *Spandau* that he could not possibly pull. "What time can you have orders cut for tomorrow, sir?"

Wafford stood up and scratched his head. "I can have 'em by midnight. You can pick 'em up at Betty's after 1000 hours tomorrow."

"Very good, sir. I've enjoyed our time together today."

"Me, too." Blakely stood before the locked door. Wafford opened it and patted Blakely on the shoulder. "You're my first guest I've had in my war room in over three years, Ed. Glad you could come and visit a spell."

They climbed the stairs and Blakely pulled on his London Fog.

"I'll drive you back to your billets."

"No, no. I can take the *strassenbahn*, sir. I know where I can catch it. No need to make a special trip. Besides, it wouldn't look too hot for us to be seen in the same car together, right?"

Wafford grinned and held out his hand. "Right. Take care not to slip on the ice."

They shook hands and Blakely left the colonel standing at the kitchen door. Blakely turned and looked back. The colonel waved before closing the door. A strange admixture of a man. He seemed so lonely, shy, almost desperate. He could be at once loving and gentle, yet quick to anger and disappointment. He was personal yet aloof, living in a fantasy world of his own making while moving about secretively in a very real world of danger and intrigue.

Chapter 19

A Chase to Rothschild Park

The trolley ride from Eschersheim was pleasant, although the car was too warm and stuffy. He decided to get out and walk the several blocks to downtown, taking time to enjoy the exercise and shop windows. It was an elegant part of Frankfurt, just south of the *I.G. Farben* building, north of the old *Opern Haus* and *Rothschild Park*. He liked the area because of its smart shops with latest fashions displayed. There were furniture stores, fine radio and television stores, fancy lighting and plumbing fixture shops. As he stepped off the *strassenbahn*, his senses were accosted by acrid coal smoke in the heavy, wet air. Yes, everyone was staying warm tonight, stoking their stoves on another freezing, black night.

Two men got off just behind him, following a few paces behind. When he stopped at a window, they stopped at one next to it. When he moved on, they followed. Oh, shit. Steady as you go, Ed, he said to himself, trying to decide what his chances were to take off running or whether it was not better to bide his time. Few people were on the street. Not many cars, either. He figured he could outrun them, but there was no way he could be certain of that, especially with the treacherous patches of ice and snow. God, they were big. And they weren't more than twenty feet away. Maybe it was his imagination. He decided to check them out.

He started walking again, then abruptly jaywalked across the boulevard to where there was a lady's specialty shop. The window displayed handbags of every size, shape and color. One of the men was crossing just to his left rear. Turning, he realized the other was crossing the street to his right. He pulled into himself, coiling his strength, ready to react to whatever might happen. Neither man seemed to be holding a weapon; they didn't have to, he thought.

Their size told him both were powerful. He walked directly to the window and stopped to look at the handbags.

The two men stepped right up next to him on either side, pretending to look at the handbags. They said nothing. Blakely turned slightly to look first at one, then the other. The guy to his right was probably six feet, three inches, dark hair slicked down, wearing a Tyrolean green overcoat. To his left, the guy was heavy-set, slightly shorter. His face was absolutely scary. An ugly pink scar ran in a zigzag pattern from his right ear to the corner of his mouth. Their eyes met for a second before Blakely turned back to the window.

Let the reefs hold, he told himself as he heard voices. He glanced back. A middle-aged couple was approaching. Easy, now, steady as you go. He drew in all his energy to his task. He moved steadily out from between the two men and fell into step with the couple just as they passed by.

The two men stayed at the window for several seconds, then turned and began following the three at some distance behind. What were they? Common thieves? If they had been common thieves, they might have rolled him at any time when the street was empty. Were they some of our people checking him out? If they were, he damn sure would give the CID a full report and tell them to call off the hounds. By the looks of them, they were probably some of Horst's hired hands, which made it all the more dangerous. If only this couple would keep walking.

These guys could be KGB or East German agents. They didn't look intelligent enough to be Intelligence agents. Almost an oxymoron. Ox and moron, he joked, allowing himself the chance to spill some wind from his sail before he would have to determine a new tack. He suddenly realized they were just two blocks from *Rothschild Park*, which was dark and filled with thick evergreens on both sides. What the hell to do?

The dozens of prostitutes in the park wouldn't be of any help. He grinned to himself at the thought of all the women attacking the two guys and protecting him with their bodies. Ludicrous. Without turning, he could hear a *strassenbahn* approaching from behind. There was a stop ahead, but he would have to re-cross the street. It was time to come about. Just as he began formulating a plan, the couple abruptly turned away from him into a side street. He was alone again, except for his two friends. They were walking faster. He could hear their footfalls on the patches of ice.

The *strassenbahn* came down the hill with a rush and then ground to a halt at the corner. A few people were starting to get off. This was it! Without any warning, he came about, and made a dead run across the street toward the rear end of the trolley, making his mark before his pursuers had a chance to follow. He made the turn, disappearing around the trolley, and ran toward the forward-most door of the first car, then stood waiting for the last person to climb down before boarding.

He watched for the goons to see what they would do. Yes, you bastards. Do it. Miss the mark. Turn inside it. Be stupid and do what I hope you'll do. They did. Instead of one of the men coming up behind him, both boarded the *strassenbahn* through the rear door as they saw Blakely step on board through the forward door. He pretended to move further into the car, paused five seconds, then did a 180 in close quarters. At the last split second before the pneumatic doors closed, Blakely bolted out onto the sidewalk just as the *strassenbahn* started moving again.

The driver shouted something. He stood on the curb watching as the trolley moved away. He waved at the two guys who stood helplessly watching him disappear into the night. What if there was a car following? He ran across the boulevard and waited with a crowd that had gathered beneath the marquee of a movie house. No sign of a car following. Re-crossing the street, he boarded another trolley and passed safely through the darkness of *Rothschild Park* and past the opera house, into the brightly lit business section of downtown Frankfurt. He got off at the *Hauptbahnhof* and walked the short distance to *Meir's Bavarian Garten*. He needed a beer. Maybe some of his buddies would be there to walk with him back to the *Gutleut Kaserne*.

His heart was still pounding as he climbed up the wide stairs to the balcony and sat at an empty table and ordered a beer. He took off his trench coat and realized his shirt and jacket were soaked with perspiration. He mopped his face with a handkerchief.

"Have you been in a steam bath, my friend?"

Blakely looked up. It was one of the bouncers. "I had a close call with a couple of hoods. I think they wanted to rob me, even though I don't have anything of value to give them."

"So you got away from them. Sometimes running is the more intelligent decision," the bouncer said in a teasing way. "I'm Viktor Kohl."

"Ed Blakely." They shook hands. He was a giant of a man with long arms and huge hands. Kohl sat down in a chair at the next table, allowing room for him to stretch out. He reached into his shirt pocket and pulled out a pack of Lucky Strikes, offering one to Blakely. "No, thanks."

Kohl had probably never run away from anything in his life. He was likely in his forties. Maybe a former boxer. His nose was bent slightly to the right and flattened so it didn't end in a natural curve. He also had a serious cauliflower left ear.

"I've seen you here before. You're new to Frankfurt, aren't you? With CID?"

"No, sir. I've only been here a couple weeks. You saw me with an old friend, Master Sergeant Sylvester Charon."

Kohl nodded. "That's right. I know him well. He and I often would tell war stories to each other over a beer or two. He just retired, I believe. Went back to the states."

"Yes, sir."

Kohl stood up and patted Blakely on the arm. "I must now go back to work. Any friend of Charon is my friend. You be sure to let me know if you need help anytime. We'll take care of thugs together. Count on me, okay?"

"Thanks, Vicktor. Glad to know that." He watched Kohl disappear down the steps. Damned nice of him.

The waitress brought a blue stein of dark beer. He sipped the sweet, tangy liquid, recalling his afternoon with Jim Wafford, and how much he had enjoyed drinking with him in the war room. No question, the two guys belonged to Horst. They must have been staked out at Wafford's and followed him all the way. He'd have to get word to Jim before leaving for Berlin.

Chapter 20

Revisiting Justina Schmidt

Upon arrival in Berlin, Blakely discovered the city was filled with snow. More was predicted for late afternoon. Not very much traffic except delivery trucks and snow plows. The *strassenbahns* and taxis were running, however.

He called Justina from Berlin Headquarters. She would not be able to see him until 1600 hours. She and Dr. Schaus were in meetings. Blakely checked into Hotel *Grunewald* and spent the afternoon reading the remainder of *A Farewell to Arms*. A helluva thing. Betty was right. It was a most awful and unpredictable ending. It reminded him of the title of a Hemingway short story: *Winner Take Nothing*. Blakely found himself weeping at the *Tenente's* loss. Life wasn't fair. He supposed that the other forty-three possible endings to the story would have been no better. It was inevitable that Catherine and the baby would die, now that he thought about it, and that the *Tenente* would be left by himself, desolate, inconsolable, alone. And that was how it all ends, finally. Winner takes nothing.

By the time he left the hotel and walked along the narrow, shoveled path between knee-deep piles of snow to the Museum of Egyptology, more snow was falling. Silver dollar flakes, making visibility difficult. He tried to shake the gloom he felt as he climbed the steps to the second floor where Justina's office was located.

She looked up from her work as he entered her doorway. "Ah, Edward. I'm so glad to see you. Sorry we couldn't meet any earlier."

"That's fine, Justina. With all the snow, I guess I'm lucky to be here."

"*Ja.*" She stood up and came around the desk and offered her hand. He held it. She looked quite sexy in a dark green wool sweater and skirt.. A silk scarf of lighter green was wrapped loosely about her neck, secured by a gold scarab pin. She, too, seemed subdued, preoccupied, as though she had received bad news. Her eyes had a vacuous quality about them. Her smile was smaller, not lighting her lovely face like it had when they dined together. "I have everything spread out in another room for you. Please leave your coat here and come with me."

"Okay." She was all business as she moved past him. He followed her around a corner and into a paneled room. Spread across the large conference table were pages obviously ripped unceremoniously from a photo album, dozens of loose photos of various sizes, and yellowed, tattered clippings arranged helter-skelter.

"Inspector Krebs gathered these off the floor of Georg's flat. I suppose you will want time to study them and then to make photostat copies of those you feel are important. The copier is just outside the door. May I get you some tea or coffee?"

"No, thanks." Blakely glanced at her as she lingered in the doorway. She was totally aloof. He took off his jacket.

"I will be in my office, if you need anything."

"Thanks."

She left. He had no idea where to begin. He circled the table, examining the black and white photos, some obviously official *Wehrmacht*. You could always tell. They were either of excellent quality with carefully posed subjects or else developed "hot" with too much contrast, a result of quick and sloppy fieldwork. At least that was how they explained it at Army Intelligence School.

He picked up a picture showing four cadet officers in dress uniform with parachutes. He looked on the back. 1937 was written in pencil. No names. Which one was Krusen? He walked back to Justina's office. She was busily writing something using a fountain pen and hadn't heard him approach.

"Sorry to bother you, Justina, but could you identify Georg Krusen in this photo?" She looked up.

"Oh, sure." She took the photo and pointed. "That is Georg. Second from the left."

"Do you know the names of the others?"

"*Nein.*" She handed the photo to him. "Sorry I'm not more help. Georg never shared with me his photo collection except a few childhood pictures. They are in an envelope on the table. I do know a bit about them, if you are interested."

"Thanks. I appreciate you sharing with me." He returned to the conference room. He felt certain the other three guys in the photograph were Heinrich von Etter, Joachim Grenz, and Freddie Braun, but he had no way of knowing for sure.

He fished absently through the photos, shuffling them around, pulling out all the ones with Krusen in them. He came upon a group photo showing an entire unit. There was a caption on the back: *Stendal, 5 April 1937.* Probably graduation from paratrooper training. Yes. It matched the one with the four guys he had just looked at. Standing next to Krusen was a tall, athletic, blond-haired officer, holding the unit guidon. He bet it was either Joachim or Heinrich.

Frau Schiller would know. Yes, I'll make copies and take them down to her. She'll know. Why waste time? Same with the clippings. I can copy them and study them later. He started gathering the photos into one pile and the clippings into another.

There was the envelope Justina mentioned. He opened it and pulled out several pale, sepia colored prints. There were small children, parents, other adults. Some taken in front of what looked like a hardware or dry goods store. A handwritten caption on the back of one said: *Linz, 1921.* Another showing a middle-aged couple in front of the store said: *Jacob and Beth Goldstein, 1927.* So, the Krusens were friends with Jews. Well-dressed. A handsome couple. Jacob held his hand at his vest pocket where a watch chain crossed his middle and the fob dangled at his right side. Prosperous. Confident. Looked like a happy man. She was smiling. Another photo was of the same couple with a young teenaged boy. The boy had a broad smile on his face. He wondered what had happened to them after 1933. He put the photos back in their envelope.

Just as he was copying some of the last photos, Justina appeared next to him. "Are you staying over tonight?"

"I'm on stand-by for a flight out of Tempelhof at 1:30 am. Depends on weather. I also have a room at the *Grunewald* just in case I can't make it."

"Do you have dinner plans," she asked solemnly.

"No."

"May I take you to dinner?"

Blakely scratched his cheek. "Well, sure. But let me treat you. You be my guest. I'm on an expense account."

"*Nein.* It is important I take you to dinner. Can you meet me back here at seven o'clock?"

"Sure." He tried to smile. "I'm looking forward to it."

"*Gut.*" She turned part way and stopped. "Did you find any of the photos useful?"

"Yeah. I'm copying everything. I hope you don't mind me making two copies of each."

"No, not at all."

"Any chance you have some big envelopes or a large paper bag I can put the copies in?"

"*Ja.* I get some for you."

He was dumbfounded as to why she should invite him to dinner. She must have more bad news to share. Perhaps it had to do with the upcoming wedding plans. Maybe Chris had gotten cold feet and called off the proposed engagement. Helluva thing, just before Christmas. But then, Chris seemed the kind of guy who could change his mind on a dime. Maybe his dad had gotten to him after all, bribed him into coming back into the family after his discharge and becoming a lawyer. Who knows?

Chapter 21

The Menderhof Kafe

Justina was waiting inside the door as he instructed the cabbie to pull over. She was wearing a long, dark ankle-length coat with a black felt hat, black leather gloves, leather boots, and shoulder bag. They said little in the cab. An iron sign above the *Menderhof Kafe* said it was founded in 1872. He opened the heavy door. A rush of warm, sweet scents including fried onions enveloped them. The place was elegant, with dark wood paneling, high ceiling, classical paintings, sounds of a string quartet playing in the background amidst the light clatter of plates and whispers coming from the dining room. The *maitre d'* stood before them holding menus.

"*Froliche Weinachten, Fraulein* Schmidt."

"*Froliche Weinachten,* Walter." Walter helped her to remove her coat. Blakely took his off and handed it to Walter. He hung the coats on pegs along the wall. She looked up at Blakely somberly. "Would you mind so much if we went to the bar?"

Blakely shrugged. "Fine by me." She still wore the same green skirt and sweater, but the scarf had been removed and three buttons at the top of her sweater were open, showing the swells of lovely white breasts. He followed her down a wide hallway into a cozy room where the bar stretched along one end and tables and chairs filled the remaining space. Several people sat at the tables. Three men sat on bar stools. A *Grundig* radio at the far end of the bar was playing Christmas carols. Justina pointed to a table in the corner away from everyone. It was next to a window that was heavily frosted with ice. She removed her gloves and hat and placed them with her handbag in the chair next to her. Blakely helped her into her chair, then sat in the chair closest to her.

A waiter appeared.

"Good evening, Dr. Schmidt. What may I bring you and your friend?"

"Ah, Joseph. I would like an American drink, an Old Fashion, please."

"And you, sir?"

"I'll have a scotch and water. Haig is preferable. And maybe some peanuts or something?"

"Very good, sir."

Blakely leaned closer. "So tell me, Justina. What's going on?"

She took a deep breath and looked at him. Tears rimmed her eyes. "I must apologize, Edward. This is not fair that I should be telling you, crying on your shoulder… I do not even know you…" She reached into her bag and retrieved a lacy handkerchief and daubed her eyes. "I have to speak with someone. I don't know what to do. And I thought you'd understand."

Blakely patted her gently on her arm. "It's okay. Tell me what you're not sure about."

The waiter returned with a tray and placed the Old Fashion and scotch and a bowl of filberts before them. Justina raised the Old Fashion glass to her lips and took a good sip. She put the glass down and immediately ate the cherry off its stem.

"Too much is happening so fast, Edward."

Blakely took a swig while watching her shaking her head slowly.

"I have been seeing a man for nearly two years. He's very nice. An American. He is like me, an archeologist. He wants to marry me."

"Yeah? So what's the problem?"

"He tells me because I am *Deutsch*, his parents will disown him if he marries me." She took another healthy swig.

"I can see that would be a problem. But if you both love each other, so what?"

"Edward, you must know better. That is no way to begin a marriage."

"Yeah. I guess you're right. Still, you don't think you can work things out?"

"He is in the Air Force. He has five more months to go. He wants to stay here. He doesn't have any prospects for a position here, even though Dr. Schaus is trying to assist him in finding one... I just don't know, Edward. I love him, but I also have my mother to support. He has no money and no prospects. I do not make sufficient money to support all of us."

She finished off her drink. Blakely tossed his remainder down. He beckoned to the bartender for two more. Hell, why not get drunk. The waiter brought two fresh drinks and removed the empty glasses.

"Are you planning a wedding soon?"

"He intends to propose on Christmas Eve. The wedding we won't have until he is discharged."

"I see. Why not postpone everything for a while? Give both of you some time to work it all out. Give his parents time to come around."

"*Ja.* But he is so insistent. He wants to do it now."

I'm sure he does, Blakely thought, glancing at her pretty neck and breasts. "But if he really loves you, he'll understand. If you need more time, I'd suggest you take it. Let him do what he needs to do. Doesn't that make sense?"

She was weeping again, mopping her eyes. "I guess so. But I feel awful, knowing he would be disappointed if I told him I needed more time."

Blakely swung his chair around so that it was close to hers. They lifted their glasses at the same time. "Here's to you for a better new year, Justina."

"You, too." They clinked glasses and sipped. Justina leaned closer. "Do you know, Edward, I thought about encouraging my fiancee' to make the Air Force a career—do archeology as a side-line—until our talk the other night. You convinced me it is not a wise choice."

"No. It isn't a good choice right now. On the other hand, it would provide steady income until he could locate a position. Wouldn't have to re-up for more than a few years."

"I know Christopher—that is my fiancee's name–would be very unhappy to stay in service. Even more unhappy, if he cannot become a professional archeologist. But... I cannot find a position for him. And I also have my own career. I have my own dreams of making discoveries." She took another swig. "Why does everything you wish for get so complicated?"

"Don't know the answer to that. You call your boyfriend your fianceé. Sounds like you feel committed to going through with the proposal."

She looked down, touching the rim of her glass and circling it with her index finger. "*Ja*. We've talked about it for so long, that is how I see him. Until recently, I've been totally positive in my resolve to marry him. "

Blakely listened patiently as she continued exploring, covering the same issues over and over, through another Old Fashion and scotch. Justina was grasping Blakely's sleeve with her hand, holding it lightly.

"I still don't know what I should do."

"Guess we'd better eat," Blakely said, noting Justina was no longer weeping or teary-eyed.

"Can we stay here? I'd rather not go to the dining room."

"Of course." Blakely waved at the waiter.

"They serve *goulash*. Do you like *Hungarian goulash*?"

"Very much."

The waiter approached. "Joseph, we'll have two cups of *goulash* for a starter and a bottle of *Egri Bikaver*."

"Yes, madam."

That's all we need on a snowy night after four drinks: two *goulashes* and a bottle of wine to go with it. Blakely smirked at his joke, then touched Justina's arm. "I have a confession to make."

"And what is that, Edward?' She leaned closer, nearly bumping heads. Her dark hair had a wonderful sheen and there was a subtle fragrance of lavender.

"I am acquainted with your fianceé, Christopher Cunningham."

"No!" Her mouth dropped. She squeezed his arm.

"Yes. I met him the other time I was up here. Had a nice chat with him over at the Hotel *Grunewald*."

"He didn't tell me."

"Well, there wasn't much to tell. We just talked for half an hour or so. Seems like a terrific fellow. I can see how you'd fall in love with him."

"He is quite bright. A Rhodes scholar at Oxford."

A funny answer. "Yeah. He told me. He's kept his English accent pretty well."

"*Ja.*" She looked down at her glass, hoisted it to her lips, and swallowed the last drops. "*Ja.* That is so."

The waiter brought two steaming cups of *goulash* and the wine. He opened the bottle and poured a small amount into one of the two fat wine glasses. Blakely moved it in front of Justina.

She smiled and leaned against his shoulder before picking up the glass and tasting. She nodded to Joseph. He poured two healthy servings of wine into the glasses.

"Will that be all, madam?"

She turned to Blakely. "Would you like a small beefsteak with potatoes? I feel quite famished tonight."

Blakely glanced at the goulash and shrugged. "Sure. Why not?"

Joseph nodded and left.

Blakely picked up the bottle and read the label. "How'd you come upon *Egri Bikaver?*"

"*Emigres'.* We have many in our midst due to the uprising. One of the chefs here is Hungarian. That explains also the wonderful *goulash.* Do you like it?"

Blakely swirled his fork and raised it to his mouth. "Quite nice. Been a long time since I had *goulash.* And the wine is superb."

"*Ja.* There is a saying about Hungarian wines. They are like Gypsies. They can be very light on their feet or very sturdy in their legs."

"Never heard that one before. I do recall this is a famous wine because of a battle some years ago. The Magyars drank it the night before going into battle and fought so fiercely the enemy believed they had drunk bulls' blood. Am I correct?"

"True. A Hungarian friend once told me that story. Sixteenth century. They were fighting the Turks. Ah, Edward, how do you know so many things for being so young?"

"For being a naive American, you mean?"

"No. Christopher is also American. But he doesn't know wines like you. He doesn't know how to sail. He doesn't know how to enjoy a dinner like you do. You seem so comfortable, so mature with perfect strangers."

Blakely smiled. "Maybe Chris just doesn't show off like I do. He maintains that English reserve he learned at Oxford and from his family back in Philadelphia."

"Can I share a secret wish with you?" Her hand was on his arm again and she was leaning her breast into his shoulder, even as she continued eating the goulash with her left hand.

"Sure."

"My secret wish—before I met Christopher—was to save all my money and, when my mother died, go to Cairo or Athens to live."

"Really. Sounds exciting."

"*Ja.* My wish was to join digging expeditions and work with the best archeologists in the world. I would stay there my whole life, devoting myself to my passion."

"What's to stop you from doing it?"

"Reality. The reality is I have no real standing as an archeologist. Only as museum employee. One who studies what others have already discovered. To become more, one has to be bold and go where there is plenty of real archeology to do. Make discoveries. Make a name for yourself, just like you do in boat racing."

"Yeah, well, you could take your mom with you and find a job in Egypt, couldn't you?"

"Perhaps. I wish I were more like you, Edward."

"In what way?"

"You told me you want to return to sailing. That is your passion. Not any sailing. Sailing for yourself, doing it your way. I like that very much about you. I've been thinking I'd love to sail with you sometime when it is very windy and I could learn from you sailing skills."

Blakely grinned and touched her arm. "You'd probably be very disappointed when I flipped us over and we had to swim for our lives."

They laughed and bumped heads lightly. "You see, Edward, that is our difference. I am equally passionate about archeology as you are about sailing, but I don't have what it takes to just go out on my own and take risks."

"You take risks every day. Why not take a little bigger one and fulfill a secret wish?"

She looked away and then finished off her wine. The waiter appeared and poured their glasses half full again. She had put her fork down.

"Are you finished, madam?"

"*Ja.* Thank you, Joseph."

"And you, sir."

"Yes."

"Would you like more wine with your steaks?"

Justina and Blakely looked at one another, grinning. "As you say, Edward, why not? It's Christmas!"

The waiter removed their bowls, silverware, and the empty bottle.

Justina grasped Blakely's hand in hers and squeezed. "Oh, to be brave and just do it," she said under her breath. She looked away toward the window. Candlelight played upon her face and breasts, making her skin soft and inviting. Her left hand moved up. Her index finger scraped upward on the frosted window, collecting a growing pile of ice on her fingernail. She moved her finger and the ice to her mouth and sucked the ice off. *Oh, Holy Night* was being sung by a choir on the *Grundig.* Blakely felt a tingling sensation as he watched her sit back. Patrons were saying good night and merry Christmas to the bartender.

Justina was looking closely at Blakely as though she were about to close the distance and kiss him. He shifted slightly, feeling the tingling sensation returning. She pulled away and glanced at her handbag in the chair, then lifted her hands to her hair and pulled it back from her face. It was a lovely gesture, sensual in the half-light, her sweater pulling her breasts upward, expanding the swells momentarily.

Joseph and another waiter returned with the steaks, wine, a fresh loaf of bread, butter, and French fried potatoes. Joseph poured wine into the glasses.

"I shouldn't be eating so much," Justina whispered, putting her hand on Blakely's arm.

"It's fun now and then, isn't it?"

"Ja! And tonight I want you to have a special treat."

"Yeah? And what is that?"

"A holiday surprise. It's very special. You will see."

Blakely felt more tingling. Was she taking him home with her? Certainly, she'd had enough to drink… He half-heartedly cut bite-sized pieces of steak and ate them with the salted French fries. Too much food. He poured more wine. They clicked glasses and drank. It was all too much. Here he was, sitting next to a beautiful woman who was about to become engaged to the wrong guy and they both knew it. What to do about it? He gazed at her cleft and knew she was watching him closely. She reached for his hand and gently squeezed it before letting it go.

"Thank you for listening to me. I needed someone to be with me tonight."

"Glad I was here for you."

Joseph returned. "Would there be anything else? Some *schnapps* or dessert, perhaps?"

"Ja, Joseph. Could we have two small glasses of *Barhonich* with coffee?"

"Yes, madam."

"That is my surprise, Edward. Something special from my child-hood."

Blakely hid his disappointment. "And what is *Barhonish*?"

"Cognac with honey. It is enjoyed during the holidays in the north of Germany. When I was very young, my uncle would give me a small taste of it on Christmas Eve."

It arrived in small shot glasses along with cups of dark coffee. Blakely touched his shot glass to hers, looked at the golden liquid and drank it down. Heat exploded in his chest and stomach. Must be 150 proof. He reached for the coffee and took a large sip.

Justina was laughing. "Gut, ja?"

"Gut and hot!"

She looked wistfully at Blakely while sipping her coffee. "I hate for this evening to end. The music, the food, everything brings back good memories suddenly."

Blakely glanced at his watch. "Yeah. Me, too. Guess we'd better make it a night though. I've got to call Tempelhof and cancel my flight. I'll stay over at the hotel."

"Ja. I've got to look in on mother. She'll be worried."

"Would you like anything more, madam?"

No, thank you Joseph. Would you put the bill on my account? I'll take care of it later."

"Yes, madam. *Froliche Weinachten* to you both."

"*Ja.* And to you also." Justina arose and gathered her hat, hand-bag and gloves.

"I should like to walk in the snow with you, Edward. Would that be all right?"

"Of course."

"We can walk across to the park. There is a cabstand on the other side. I can take a cab from there."

He held her coat as she slipped it on. They left the *Menderhof Kafe.* The street was empty and snow was still falling. A church bell was tolling mournfully in the distance, a deep, repeated, sonorous tone.

"The snow is too deep. Let's walk in the *strasse*," she said, clutch-ing his arm. They walked arm in arm down the deserted street between darkened apartments for three blocks or so, without a car disturbing the quiet. He could hear the sounds of snowflakes landing on his shoulders. Her hat was turning white. She tugged him lightly, turning toward what looked like a park where billows of snow had turned a fountain into a grotesque monster in the half-light.

"I don't mind getting my feet wet, do you?"

"No." Of course, she was wearing high boots. They entered the park, trudging through foot-high snow that creaked beneath their footfalls. His pant legs were getting wet. Snow was filling his shoes. There was a gazebo in the middle of the park, heaped with snow, but fairly dry beneath the round roof. They stepped into it. She turned and put her arms around him. He pulled her tight. She looked up at him. He could barely see her face, but knew she was weeping again.

"Thank you for tonight, Edward. Please hold me."

She reached up and kissed him, holding his head between her gloved hands. She released him. He leaned down and kissed her back warmly, tasting a combination of cognac and coffee. Her hands came round his neck in a close embrace. The kiss lasted longer than it should have, but he didn't care. He pulled her to him in a close embrace and kissed her again for what seemed like minutes. They released one another and she rested her head against his chest.

Without words, they turned and plodded through the thick snow to the boulevard where a few cars passed by, making sizzling sounds on the frozen ice and snow. They stood next to the taxi stand. She turned again and hugged him. He pulled her close and kissed her forehead. She raised her head and kissed him on the lips, holding him closer this time, until the sound of slapping windshield wipers and crunching tires broke their reverie, the dark suddenly erased by the glare of headlights.

"*Froliche Weinachten*, Edward."

"*Froliche Weinachten*. And good luck with those secret wishes."

"Thank you. Will I see you again?"

"No. I don't think so. Give my best to Chris when you see him. I wish you both a happy marriage."

"Goodbye."

He closed the door as she pulled out her handkerchief and daubed her eyes. He looked at his watch. He turned and hustled across the snow, realizing that his feet and legs were sopping wet and his toes were freezing. Damndest Christmas he'd ever experienced. And it wasn't over yet.

Chapter 22

Second Guessing

The *gasthaus* and bakery on *Ginnheimer Strasse* were decorated for Christmas. Green and red lights twinkled around the plate glass windows. Wafford was already there, sitting in his preferred corner with his back against the wall. They shook hands and Blakely put a large paper bag on the chair and took off his overcoat and sat down. The colonel looked tired like he hadn't gotten any sleep. He was slouched in the chair with legs sprawled.

"Well, watcha got?"

Blakely pointed to the bag. "Those are copies of old photographs and clippings that belonged to Georg Krusen. There are lots of group photos of Krusen and his army buddies. If you'd like, I can take them down to show *Frau* Schiller. I'm sure she could identify several of the people."

"I'll take a look at them, myself. Miz Schmidt couldn't confirm IDs?"

"No. All the photos were taken long before she knew Krusen, same with the clippings. Krusen never discussed the pictures and articles with her."

The colonel leaned his head on one elbow, almost like he was suffering from a hangover. He took a sip of coffee as he stared vacantly at Blakely.

"What'd CID say about my run-in with the two thugs the other night?"

Wafford dropped his arm to the table. "Never contacted CID. I don't want them involved. I 'spect Horst is here. My plan is to flush him out first, then have the whole bunch arrested."

"But sir... At this point, I don't see why you wouldn't let CID take over. They've got the resources. You haven't..."

Wafford's face reddened. "Don't second guess me, Sergeant. I know what I'm doing."

Blakely put both hands on the table and studied them. The guy'd officially crossed the line. "Sorry, Jim. I didn't mean to second-guess you. Any more sign of them?"

"You mean the two men who followed you?"

"Yeah."

"No." Wafford brought his fist up to his chin. "But Anna thought there'd been a suspicious vehicle passing by the house now and then. Easy to spot. One of those tri-wheels. Yellow. A coal delivery truck."

"Any ID?"

"Not yet. Hans followed it yesterday morning nearly to Saxonhausen."

"What if you reported it to civil police, Jim? Or maybe Anna could report it."

"How many times do I have to tell you not to second guess me?" Wafford's voice was becoming weak and shrill. "And by the way, I want you to lay low a coupla days."

"You don't want me to go down to Heidelberg? I could get *Frau* Swartzlander's address from *Frau* Schiller and she could go through the photographs and clippings with me at the same time."

"What'd I just say?"

Blakely nodded and looked down at his hands again. "Sorry, sir. I'm just trying to help."

"You can help best by staying out of the way until I inform you otherwise. Is that clear?"

"Yes."

"Have a report and expense statement for me?"

"They're in the bag."

"Very good." Wafford avoided eye contact. "Oh, by the way, Ed. I'd stay away from the English Bookstore 'til after the holidays. No need us compromising Betty."

So it was a matter of compromise. Sounded deadly serious. "No, sir. Is that all?"

"Guess so. Sorry, Ed, but I gotta do this my way."

"I understand." He didn't, but what the hell could he do about it? Blakely got up and reached out. Wafford shook his hand half-heartedly without getting up. Blakely grabbed his trench coat and, without putting it on, strode out the door.

Chapter 23

Decision Time

"Check."

Lester grimaced and took a puff on his cigarette. He moved the rook between Blakely's queen and his own king. Blakely pounced with his bishop, taking the rook.

"Shit. You got me three in a row. I don't want to play anymore," grumbled Lester. "How 'bout some cards?"

Nash appeared in the doorway. "Blakely, you got a call."

"Thanks." He followed Nash to the orderly room. "Blakely here."

"It's Christopher, Edward. Can I meet you some place?"

Blakely thought a moment. "How about the waiting room at the *Hauptbahnhof*?"

"All right."

"What time?"

"Twenty minutes?"

"See you."

* * *

Chris seemed undone, shifting on the bench, toying with his pipe. "He wants me to spy on a coal yard in Saxonhausen. Frankly, Edward, I don't want anything more to do with this. He's gone too far."

"Yeah, you're right. I was with him this morning. He looked shot out and desperate. What's the point of the stakeout?"

"Says Horst is likely there or will arrive there shortly. I'm supposed to identify Horst, then report back. James says Horst should be easy to recognize because he has red and purple burn scars about his face. It sounds simple enough, but with my luck I'd be spotted in a minute."

Blakely felt the smooth bench with his hand, running it back and forth. Everything was out of bounds. Why not disobey Jim just this once? "Would you consider doing the stakeout with me?"

"Why in blazes would you want to, Edward? We've both done more than enough. Why risk it?"

"Just four days before the colonel leaves for New York. If we spot Horst, you can report back to Jim. If we don't, we're off the hook for the holidays. How 'bout it?"

"I've never tried to spy on someone before."

"We'll stay out of harm's way, Chris. Count on it. If there's any danger, we quit. Okay?"

Chris eyed Blakely over his pipe. He sucked in smoke, making the pipe sizzle. "I'll have to think about it."

Chapter 24

Stakeout in Saxonhausen

The *strasse* along the Main River was filled with parked, nondescript cars, trucks, motorcycles and bicycles. Men in grimy work clothes bustled about under sheds and open garages, their breaths showing in the cold, bending pipes, fitting glass, sawing boards, building crates. Trucks filled with coal, lumber, cement, Christmas trees, poultry, and scrap metal roared by in both directions.

The docks were also a flurry of activity. Barges were being loaded and unloaded by small cranes and stevedores. Other barges moved steadily up and down the river, occasionally blowing their whistles in the gray light.

A wooden sign with peeling white and black paint announced *HALDERMANN* on the side of a ramshackle, two story warehouse. Along one side and behind the old building were black piles of various-sized anthracite and bituminous coal ranging from pea to chunk. A beat-up yellow, tri-wheel truck with canvas bags of pea coal stacked in its bed was parked in front. No signs of activity. At the rear, behind the coal, a small, blue and white barge with rusted stack and rails sat light in the water, shifting uneasily in the current, bumpers nudging against a rotting dock.

The barge had a low, forward cabin in the bow and a tall pilothouse at the stern. Between them were three flat hatches beneath which Blakely assumed were coal containers. Since it was riding so high in the water, Blakely judged the bins were empty. Not the most prosperous operation, he thought, as he and Chris walked past at a brisk pace. The vacant lot surrounded by a low wooden fence next to the coal yard was filled with knee-high brown weeds and every sort of nautical debris from old boilers to carcasses of rotting boats. In the very middle of the lot was a large, gutted pilothouse without windows or hatch, tilting to starboard like it was about to topple into the weeds.

There were two possible stakeout locations: a *gasthaus* almost directly across the street and a bakery-deli a few doors further away. Neither could be considered safe from detection.

"What do you think?" Chris puffed nervously on his pipe.

"Let's check out the bakery," Blakely replied. "Sepp Halder and his buddies are probably regular customers of the *gasthaus*."

"I agree."

They crossed the street. The bakery and deli had a stone front with three large windows behind which there were a few empty tables and chairs. Along the back of the shop stretched dairy and pastry cases and a counter with stools. They entered. An old man with a cane leaning against his stool was eating at the counter. He turned and glanced up as Blakely closed the door. A young girl with red hair behind the counter greeted them. They ordered coffee and tea and sat down at a window table. A slight curve in the street afforded them a decent view of the warehouse, the empty lot, the coal yard, as well as the dock and the barge.

Chris tapped the ashes from his pipe into a metal ashtray. "I don't like this a'tall. If we can see them, they can see us."

"You're right about that." Blakely grinned sardonically, turning serious. A man had come out of the building wearing blackened coveralls and a dark skullcap. He climbed into the tri-wheel truck. He started the motor and backed out of the lot and onto the street. He roared up the street in a cloud of black smoke toward the bridge.

"I say, is that one you recognize?"

Blakely could not be certain. "I'm not sure whether he was with the blond haired guy or not. He did have about the same build."

Cunningham nervously pinched the tea ball against the inside of his cup with a spoon, watching the liquid darken in the cup. "How are we going to do this? We can't stay here all day. The young woman will likely call the police to us."

Chris was right. Not only was this surveillance a stupid idea, it was close to being impossible. "What if we did it randomly?"

"I don't follow you."

"We don't stay here all the time. Maybe one of us should walk down the street and stop here or there at various shops, then leave. Come back in two or three hours and walk the opposite direction or stop by here for a snack."

"I suppose." Chris took a quick sip of tea. "But how would we coordinate it?"

"We wouldn't, except in a general way. Every now and then, we might meet up at the bridge or maybe at that bar just this side of the bridge. There might be other meeting places on down the street."

Cunningham nodded absently. "How about you starting us off?"

"Sure. Why don't you take a break for a couple hours? There's a USO canteen about two blocks on the other side of the bridge. They've got a nice lounge."

"I may see you in two hours or so?"

"Yeah. After I finish this coffee, I'm going to take a walk further down the street and see what is there."

"Alright." Chris pushed his chair back and stood up. He patted Blakely on the back. "Be careful, old boy."

"I will."

"Cheerio."

He watched Cunningham walk past the coal yard and up the incline toward the bridge. It started raining. Chris turned the corner at the cross street. Blakely paid for the drinks and headed out. He pulled the hood of his jacket over his head and walked five blocks. There was a bus terminal with a waiting room. He crossed over and entered the waiting area. It was a large room with a space heater. Men and women sat bundled on wooden benches, some eating food, others whispering. One old man was sleeping. The black slate schedule board above the ticket counter indicated bus service to and from many surrounding towns and cities, including Mainz, Giessen, Hanau, Offenbach, and Darmstadt.

It was a good place to take a break. He stretched and sat down, pulling his hood off as he did so. He glanced at his watch. 1100 hours. He'd stay half an hour and then check out the coal yard.

* * *

The rain was turning to sleet. Blakely hunched over with the gray hood covering most of his face. No activity except the yellow truck was parked in front of the small porch. The bed was empty. He checked his watch. It was 1430 hours. Coming down the other side of the *strasse* from the bridge was Cunningham, braving the sleet in a checked tweed cap and brown overcoat. Really, thought Blakely, the guy was too obvious. It was clear he didn't belong on a back street in a working section of Frankfurt. Cunningham crossed the street and changed direction, walking slowly until Blakely caught up.

"Have you seen him?"

"Only the chap driving the lorry. He turned the corner just as I was walking opposite about fifteen minutes ago. I presumed he had made his delivery and was returning."

"Yeah. The truck's parked in front, empty. Did he see you?"

"No. I turned away and watched him out of the corner of my eye. He never looked in my direction."

"Good." Blakely hunched his shoulders. "Getting too damn cold out here."

"I should say. How long must we continue this farce?"

"Let's stay until dark. That'd be an hour from now. There's a bus terminal down the street on the left. It's got benches and it's warm. I'll stay nearby for a while. We can meet back at the end of the bridge and grab a *strassenbahn*."

"Alright. See you soon."

Blakely walked to the bridge and waited fifteen minutes before heading down to the bakery. Sleet covered the pavement. It was slightly mushy and not that slippery. In another hour or so, it would be treacherous. He ordered coffee and a ham sandwich and sat down at the window table. The outside light was fading. He realized he was on display. He picked up his sandwich plate and coffee and sat down at the counter with his back to the window, glancing only now and then toward the coal yard. Eventually, he walked toward the bus terminal, intercepting Cunningham half way there. Surveillance was over for the day.

Chapter 25

A Rescue in Ice

"If we don't see him today, I must tell the colonel I can no longer work for him. I have duty tomorrow. Then, I plan to be in Berlin for Christmas. After that, I am on duty again for four days."

Blakely glanced at him. "We do what we have to do."

"Quite right. Quite right."

They walked gingerly on the sleet-covered sidewalk. Salt and sand had been sprinkled on the surfaces, but it was still difficult to maintain traction. 0800 hours. They split up and followed the routine of the previous day. At 1000 hours, Blakely was sitting in the bus terminal reading a *Life* magazine.

"Taking a trip somewhere, fella?"

Blakely looked up. It was Kentop, the courier he'd gone to Berlin with. He was buried in a blue nylon parka with hood. Blakey closed the magazine and stood up and shook Kentop's hand, figuring quickly how to cover.

"Nah. Just taking a break. I've been exploring the area around the *Kaserne* this morning. That's all."

Kentop nodded at the window from which you could see ice formed on all the wires and lampposts. "Kinda weird to be exploring on a day like this, ain't it?"

"Yeah, I suppose so. I just get antsy sitting around the barracks. I've got to get out and walk off some of my excess energy no matter what the weather. Know what I mean?"

"Yeah. Same here. If you're finished exploring, I'll walk back to the *Kaserne* with you. That is, if you want."

Blakely drew a deep breath. "That'd be great. I was ready to turn around."

They were approaching the bakery when the door opened and Cunningham stepped onto the sidewalk in front of them. Blakely tucked his head down, praying Chris would not acknowledge him. He didn't. He walked in the opposite direction.

The two men crossed the bridge and plodded the ten or so blocks to the *Kaserne*. Kentop was explaining what had happened during his last two trips to Berlin while Blakely mostly listened, putting in a word here or there when necessary. They parted ways at the Orderly Room. Blakely went to his room. Lester was lying on his bunk reading a *Reader's Digest*. He glanced at Blakely.

"Kinda hard walking out there."

"Yeah. Not too bad, though."

Blakely pulled off his coat and sweater. He lay down on his bunk and closed his eyes. Poor Cunningham. Out in the cold by himself. He'd rest for an hour, then go back, using a different route so he wouldn't run into Kentop again. Talk about weird. What the hell was Kentop doing at the bus terminal at 1005 hours, if he wasn't going on a trip? Didn't make sense. Blakely felt himself drifting off to sleep.

* * *

Blakely suddenly awoke and glanced at the alarm clock. "Damn!" Well, Flakely Blakely, you've done it again," he muttered. Slept three hours. He arose and threw on his sweater and coat. Chris will be mad as hell or else worried that I've been picked up. It was 1331 hours when he turned the corner into Saxonhausen and approached the coal yard. Uh, oh. Looks like a convention. Son of a bitch! I missed it all. Blakely's chest sunk as he glanced quickly at the vehicles parked in front of the warehouse: two old Mercedes sedans, the tri-wheel truck, a motorcycle, and one of those English Mayflower cars that look like a miniature Bentley. Hell. Chris is going to be furious with me.

He crossed the *strasse* and glanced in the window of the bakery. No Cunningham. He made the long walk to the bus terminal. Chris was sitting on a bench in the corner eating a cinnamon bun out of a napkin. When he spotted Blakely, he gave a sigh with his eyes raised to the sky.

Blakely sat down next to him.

"Where in God's name have you been? Who was that chap in the parka? I thought you'd been caught. I've been waiting for you all this time, hoping you would know to come here. I was just now on the verge of contacting James for instructions as to what I should do."

"Sorry, Chris. The guy I was with is from my barrack. He and I did courier duty to Berlin together. He saw me here in the terminal and insisted I walk back to the *Gutleut Kaserne* with him. I didn't want to raise any suspicions, so I went along. After trudging through the ice, I decided to take a little nap and overslept. I do apologize."

"Promise me you'll stay in better touch, Edward."

"Yeah. I promise."

"Would you like part of my cinnamon bun?"

"No thanks. Did you get to see any of the people entering the coal yard?"

"I was here. How could I?"

"Damn. I really screwed things up. We missed our best opportunity to spot Horst. There's a bunch of cars and a motorcycle parked in front of the warehouse. Probably some sort of meeting."

"You don't say."

"Yeah. I'm going to watch a while from the bakery. Maybe you can come along in half an hour."

"Alright. Let's plan to meet every two hours back here."

"Agreed."

It was near dusk when Blakely figured he would check out the coal yard one last time before meeting Chris back at the terminal and calling it a day. It had turned colder. He entered the bakery and ordered a hot chocolate. He peered out the window just as Cunningham came into view on the other side of the *strasse*. Suddenly, three men rushed out of the warehouse and surrounded Chris, grabbing at his arms and shoulders. He tried pushing them away, but he was no match for them. They moved him quickly into the building and closed the door. No question, two of them were the same guys who had scared hell out of him the other night: one dark haired, the other blond and built like a wrestler.

"Holy shit," muttered Blakely under his breath. "We're both toast." He took one sip of the hot chocolate and rushed out the door. He walked briskly toward the terminal for half a block, then crossed the *strasse* and retraced his steps toward the coal yard. I must get to the vacant lot, he whispered. He jogged the last few yards and turned into the lot and bent over, shuffling through the high weeds and ice amongst old boilers and wood hulls. He ducked into the open hatch of a rotted pilothouse that listed precariously among the weeds. A rat scampered into a hole in the floor. From his vantage point, he could see everything from the *strasse* to the river. Lights were on upstairs in the warehouse. Dark figures moved behind tattered lace curtains.

About fifteen minutes later, lights came on downstairs and three men burst out the door and separated in both directions, one going across to the bakery, another proceeding toward the bus terminal and the blond guy heading up towards the bridge. Yes, you sons-a-bitches, you are looking for me, but you won't catch me. He immediately admonished himself for his bravado. Hell, they'll be coming here when they don't find me on the street. Now that I'm here, I have nowhere else to go. So be it. I am trapped. There's no escape.

After many minutes, during which it had gotten totally dark, the three men returned to the warehouse without searching the vacant lot. Blakely gave a sigh of relief. A light came on at the rear of the building. A door opened. Cunningham was pushed through the opening into the light. His arms were bound and he was gagged. Two men walked him toward the barge. A third jumped aboard, slipping down on the icy deck. He got up slowly and opened the hatch to the forward cabin, A light came on inside, visible through small port windows. A forth man stood in the light, seemingly directing the men. His face was a blotch of pink, purple and white. No question. It was Eugen Horst.

"Be sure the hasp is locked," Horst said in a low voice.

The men lifted Cunningham onto the barge and shoved him roughly into the cabin and closed the hatch. What sounded like a padlock was snapped into place. The four returned inside the building, slamming the door. A bolt turned.

Blakely weighed his chances. Run for it and call the authorities? Rescue Chris by breaking the lock? Neither seemed a reasonable choice. He watched the warehouse. The lights downstairs went out. He waited for them to come out the front door. No one. More lights went on upstairs. Ah, he thought, they're all gathered upstairs. Maybe there's a chance. He studied the barge. Bow and stern hawsers. Plenty of leeway between the bow and the small packet boat tied below it. Why the hell not? He removed his coat and ducked down, quickly crossing the open area to the fence. He climbed over and made for the dock.

He threw his coat aboard and wrestled the frozen stern hawser off the cleat. He scurried to the bow and removed the second hawser, then pushed with all his might against the dock. The barge shifted slowly under his weight as he jumped aboard. He slipped down on the icy deck, crashing into the starboard rail. He got up, hoping the noise hadn't alerted the *Nazis* and entered the rear pilothouse. No downstairs lights came on. He unlocked the wheel and turned it over and over until it stopped when the rudder was fully to starboard. Slowly, the bow came round and into the current and moved forward. The windshield was a glaze of ice. He peered around the hatch to get his bearings.

Blakely felt along the forward wall of the cabin as well as the control panel for a light switch. None. He continued feeling the panel while holding the barge on a sharp turn to starboard. She slowly picked up speed in the growing current. He spun the wheel back as the tub fell well away from shore.

His fingers touched a key. Must be the ignition. He turned it. Next to it was a button. He pushed it. The starter groaned and turned the engine. She fired and began chugging. He punched a toggle. Running lights flashed on. He could see the panel now. Another toggle. The pilothouse's dome light came on. Just next to the wheel was a brass gearshift. He pushed it forward and the barge burst into life. Yes, damn it. She was under power. Now where do we go? He pulled back on the throttle, slowing the engine to a crawl because now the current was taking them swiftly down river.

Locking the wheel in place, he searched around the cabin for a tool to break the padlock. Behind him, a fire ax was strapped to the aft wall. He unfastened the straps and rushed to the forward cabin. "Stand away from the hatch, Chris. I'm breaking it down."

He slashed at the hasp, cutting it off its hinge. The second blow stove in the hatch. He tore it away and removed the gag from Cunningham's mouth.

"Oh, God, thank you, Edward. You saved my life!"

"Not quite yet. Come back to the pilothouse so I can keep this tub in the river while I untie your hands."

They moved slowly on the iced deck to the cabin. The barge had slipped well across the river and needed to be turned back into the middle. Blakely unlocked the wheel and came to port while Chris stood there shaking. His teeth were chattering. Blakely untied the ropes. Chris rubbed his wrists as Blakely pushed the throttle forward.

"Get my coat from the deck and put it on," cried Blakely over the roar of the diesel. "Don't want you freezing to death."

"Thank you, Edward. Don't know how to repay you." Chris took a step and his feet went out from under him. He fell hard on the deck. He retrieved the coat and put it on, including the hood.

"I want you to take the wheel."

"But I've never done it before. Why should I?"

"I can't see where we're going because of the ice on the windshield. I'll stand in the hatchway and tell you when to turn. Now grab the wheel and hold it steady."

Chris was still shaking as he took over the wheel. "What do we do now?"

"Get this barge back to shore. We want to avoid the river patrol."

"Why? We've done nothing wrong. Those men must be reported and arrested."

"Want to lose your courier job?"

"For God's sake, no."

"Turn more to port."

"What?"

"Turn left a little is what I mean… I don't want to lose my intelligence analyst job either. Getting involved with the river patrol will mean we're into deep shit with civil police as well as the military. Neither of us wants that, right?"

"Quite right, old boy. But how do we avoid it?"

"Now back to the right a bit. That's good… We cross over, find an empty slip, ditch the boat, and run like hell, that's what we do."

It was easier said than done, he thought, as he surveyed the shore. Most of the docks were full of barges and small container ships. Fences and locked buildings protected the docks. Eventually, however, they came upon what looked like a public access ramp with no gates or fences. Behind the ramp area stood huge black factories with great chimneys billowing sparks and smoke.

"Let me take over, Chris."

They switched places. "See that light to our left? There's a boat ramp. We're going to beach this baby on the ramp and run for it. I've got to come about so we can hit it head-on. Okay?"

Blakely swung the bow to starboard and pushed the throttle forward. The boat came about and slowed as it fought the current. "Tell me when we're pointing toward the ramp."

"You are slightly above the ramp."

"Good." Blakely shut the running lights off, gunned the engine, and turned to port. "Hold on, Chris."

The barge struck the concrete ramp with a dull crunch, throwing Chris against the starboard rail. Blakely stalled the engine and threw the key into the river before helping Cunningham across the deck and onto the slippery ramp. Lights flashed from across the water. A patrol boat had started its engine and turned in their direction. A searchlight beam covered them. Blakely grabbed Cunningham's arm and they both slowly crawled up the iced concrete and gained their footing on the frozen gravel entry path.

"Let's run, Chris. Come on, man. We can't get caught."

It appeared they were in a public park. There were benches here and there. Blakely turned off the gravel path and onto the frozen grass. It was easier running. He headed toward a cluster of trees beyond which, there were lights and a boulevard with trolley tracks. The boulevard ran between windowless industrial plants. A gated lot was filled with cars. The stench of hot steel and coal told him it was probably a foundry. They continued running until Chris, lagging behind, begged Blakely to slow down.

"Please, Edward. I cannot run any further. Let them arrest me, if they must."

"We've got to keep moving. The river patrol has alerted city police by now. Let's separate at the next cross streets. If there is a trolley line, you take the first trolley you can get, no matter where it goes. I'll do the same. Okay?"

"I have no money. They took my billfold. And why shouldn't we stay together? Either we make it or we don't."

"The cops will be looking for two men, not one. Trust me, it's better this way." Blakely pulled several coins and two five *mark* notes from his pocket and handed them to Cunningham.

"I'd rather we kept together." Chris was huffing and puffing. He put the money in his pocket.

"This is no time for discussion. Tomorrow, leave a message for me at the *Kaserne* with a time. We'll meet at the *Neuer Wall Kafe* again and sort all this out."

The next intersection had trolley tracks running in both directions. "You walk that direction and I'll cross the street and walk in the opposite direction. Good luck. Hope to hell we see one another outside a jail sometime tomorrow."

"Me, too."

Blakely watched Cunningham walking slowly down the dark street. The guy was out of gas. Blakely turned and began jogging slowly on the iced sidewalk, spotting a trolley stop at the end of the block next to another factory. The familiar sounds of *strassenbahn* wheels grating on steel compelled him to pick up the pace.

Chapter 26

Debriefing at the Neuer Wall Kafe

Blakely hunched over his coffee mug, gripping it with both hands. The warmth of the ceramic felt good. He tried for the hundredth time to make sense out of what had happened. It all seemed like a nightmare, even this morning. He took another sip, going over last night's string of events once again as they unfolded. They weren't pretty. Chris appeared in the doorway looking gaunt and disheveled. Blakely waved him over.

"You're twenty minutes late." He grinned. "I thought maybe you were in the hoosegow."

"Not funny, Sergeant." Chris sat down without shaking Blakely's extended hand. "I was awake the entire night, worrying that I would be arrested. I am ready to turn myself in."

"That's the last thing you need to do. Why are you so worried about being arrested?"

"Why? You know damn well why. They know all about me, thanks to you."

"Thanks to me? Who are you talking about? Horst?"

"Yes, dammit. You know bloody well who I'm talking about. They have my wallet with all my cards, ID, driver's license, money. Either they or the police will be coming after me. I'm late because I had to report my billfold was stolen. I also had to take the *strassenbahn*. I don't dare drive without my license and military ID."

"Sorry I got you into this, Chris. What did you tell them?"

"Who?"

"Horst. Did they rough you up? Interrogate you?"

"They threatened me. I had no choice but to tell them all I know."

"Like what?"

"That James had one fragment of the relic. That you and I were working for him. That we have no idea where the remaining pieces of the relic are. Naturally, they didn't believe me."

"What did you say about me?"

"I gave them your name, where you were billeted, your rank. That's pretty much all I know about you."

Blakely took a deep breath and looked at Cunningham. He was unglued, sweating. His hands were shaking.

"How 'bout a cup of coffee? You look shot-out."

"Tea," he whispered, "I'll have a cup of tea."

Blakely got up and carried his mug to the counter where an elderly woman held court with three old male customers and ordered the tea and got a refill of coffee. He sat down next to Chris.

"Listen, Chris, I don't think we have anything to worry about. Horst and his buddies have probably left Frankfurt for the time being."

"Why?"

"I'm sure the police have traced the barge back to Sepp Halder. They will pay Halder a call, if they haven't already done so. Horst has to be scared they'll find out he's a war criminal. Same with Halder."

"How are you so sure Halder is wanted?"

"Jim said so. Inspector Krebs in Berlin knew Horst was wanted. I feel certain he's put out an all points bulletin on Horst. I'm pretty sure Heinz Beck told Krebs by now that Horst was the guy behind the murder. Probably said Horst was really the one who murdered Krusen. Krebs knew about Horst and his relationship with Beck when I interviewed him."

"None of that matters. Say Haldermann or Halder, as you call him, is not a criminal. What would prevent him from reporting his boat missing and saying he found my wallet on the dock?"

"Everything. It wouldn't add up. Halder knows that. Come on. What would a first lieutenant in the U.S. Air Force, who is also an Oxford Ph.D. in archeology, be doing stealing a rusted out, empty coal barge on a cold, icy night and grounding it a mile down river, then running away? It doesn't make any sense. The police would immediately suspect Halder of some kind of funny business. Especially since Halder isn't the most prosperous coal dealer in the world. If they looked much beyond Halder's legal papers, they'd discover he's a former *Gestapo* thug wanted by a war tribunal. Halder wants none of that."

The old woman waddled over and placed a tray with a mug of hot water, a tea ball, sugar, milk, a napkin and a spoon in front of Cunningham.

"*Danke.* I dunno." Chris fiddled over his tea paraphernalia, then tasted the result. He looked up. He was close to tears. "I can't think straight. My inclination is to go over to CID immediately and fess up. Tell them everything. Get it off my chest. As a superior officer, I am advising you to do the same."

Blakely felt the absurdity of what Chris was saying. Superior indeed. He set his mug down. "What we've done is bought Jim Wafford some time. By the time Horst comes out of hiding, Jim and his wife will be back in the states with their kids."

"But what about us? We'll still be here—at the mercy of these thugs. The only way we can be safe is to tell what we know and let our superiors decide how they will protect us."

Blakely nearly laughed at the lieutenant's naivete'. "Protection? What's the military way of handling problem personnel, Chris? How would they protect you? Think about it. What normally happens?"

Chris sipped his tea and avoided eye contact. "To use the colonel's favorite expression, I wouldn't have one iota."

"Yeah, well, it's been my experience that they immediately transfer you. If you need protection, they send you to some god-awful place. Guam? Alaska? Okinawa? How'd you like to go to Guam and be a desk jockey? Say goodbye to your cushy courier job."

Chris shrugged and looked down at his tea.

"Besides, I know you are in line for promotion. Do you want to pass that up? I thought you needed the money. A captain's pay isn't too bad. Not only that, just think how disappointed Justina would be, knowing you fucked up somehow just before you two were getting engaged."

"Don't try cajoling me, Sergeant. And watch your language. I'd also appreciate it if you didn't bring Justina's name into this. My relationship with her is none of your business. And for that matter,

I wish to God I'd never met you. You are the one responsible for getting me into this mess, after all. I had already told James I was through, but no, you had to convince me otherwise. You and your damned Good Samaritan rubbish."

Blakely pulled back and took another swig of coffee. "Guess there's nothing more we have to say to one another. I can't stop you from going to CID. I just don't think it's justified. Why self-indict yourself and lose everything you've worked towards?"

"You are quite correct. We have nothing more to say to one another."

Blakely got up and paid the bill at the counter. He was about to leave when he had an idea. He returned to his chair and slumped down. Chris gave him an angry glance.

"Tell you what. Let's take a taxi past the coal yard and see what's going on. I'll betcha ten to one you won't see any cars, trucks or motorcycles. You won't see any activity at all."

"What would that prove?"

"They've split. Gone. Hiding out. Let's go. I'll prove it to you."

"I'm not going."

"Aw hell, Chris. It'll only take a few minutes. The taxi can drop me back to the *Kaserne* and take you to your base. Nobody'll see us. Won't be any reason to be afraid."

Chris reluctantly got up from his chair and followed Blakely out of the *Kafe* and down to the intersection with *Dreieich Strasse*. Blakely hailed a taxi and gave the driver directions.

Neither Chris nor Blakely spoke the whole way to the coal yard. As they approached, Chris slid down in the seat. Two police cars were the only vehicles parked in front of the warehouse. A cop leaned against the first car, smoking.

"See? I told you. Cops already got the place under security. Horst and his gang might already be arrested and in jail. Now do you believe me?"

Cunningham straightened himself and pulled on the sleeve of his coat. "What do you suggest we do," he asked in a whisper.

"Go about our business like nothing's happened. Do our courier work. Check in with Wafford as soon as we can. You've gotta let him know what's happened."

"You do understand I'm wiping my hands of all this business."

"Yes, sir. I take it you've decided not to inform CID?"

"You know I can't afford it, as much as my better judgment tells me that is what I ought to do." He drew out his pipe and tobacco and lit up, filling the middle of the cab with blue smoke. "I want to be discharged with a clean record, make captain if I can. Guam or Alaska has no appeal to me. I do want to be discharged here in Germany hopefully as a captain."

Blakely grinned. "Good thinking. When will you meet with Jim?"

"You know, it might seem a bit awkward, but why don't we see him together? Get the whole business out in the open. No more secretively getting about. Would you agree?"

"Fine by me. You tell me when, Lieutenant."

"I'd like to get it over."

"How 'bout this afternoon? You set it up and have Betty call me with instructions."

The taxi pulled up in front of the gate at the *Gutleut Kaserne.*

Blakely paid the fare to Rhein-Main Air Force Base, got out, and smiled at the lieutenant. "Thanks for reconsidering, Chris. Look forward to seeing you later today."

Cunningham nodded grimly. "Cheerio."

Chapter 27

Double Exposure

The two men sat shivering on the park bench, stamping their feet on the iced pavement. The animals were less noisy except for what sounded like three parrots squawking at one another. Blakely wanted to say something, but there was nothing left to say. Chris was still angry with him, even as—as Chris put it—he had saved the lieutenant's life. He guessed that in Chris's mind, it was wrong for an enlisted guy to save an officer's skin. That didn't happen in the movies. It was always the other way around. The *Tenente* was supposed to save the enlisted guy's sorry ass. So be it. He couldn't wait to see how Jim Wafford would react when he saw the two of them together. But that was also the *Tenente's* decision. He was, after all, the officer in charge in this charade.

Blakely watched the ducks huddled together near a bush at the edge of the pond. Everything was bleak, leaden, still. Chris drew on his pipe, making a bubbling sound. Spit, thought Blakely. It was spit bubbling at the bottom of the bowl of the pipe and along the stem each time he pulled smoke into his mouth. God almighty. How could he stand it? Sucking warmed spit along with the smoke, a wonderful combination. Something Justina would have to get used to. Nice tobacco spit kisses.

Two elderly women appeared across the pond. They sat down. One pulled a paper sack from her shopping bag and shook it gently. The ducks came alive, some scurrying on foot, others flying, until they surrounded the two women. They started throwing grain or something. The ducks quacked and chased each other, competing for the food. The goddesses of plenty had arrived. They were being beneficent, munificent, kind, mostly feeding the strongest few, the lucky ones who were the quickest of the multitude. The weaker got nothing. Blakely felt scornful and ugly for some reason he couldn't put his finger on. He guessed he was angry because he'd had a bellyful of game playing where nobody was going to win.

A camel colored coat and hat ducked around the kiosk and gained speed. Even from this distance, Blakely could see Wafford was really pissed. His face was already livid, growing purple. He took a shortcut by leaving the curved sidewalk and striding across the iced grass, swinging his arms as though on a forced march. Blakely and Cunningham stood up at his approach.

Before he had gotten within twenty yards, the colonel was yelling in his shrill, whiny voice. "What the hell you boys doing out here together? God dammit! Don't you listen?"

He turned to Chris. "What's he doing here, Lieutenant? You didn't tell me Blakely would be here, too."

"Well, James, we thought it best if we both explained..."

"You have violated my contracts with you. Both of you! Not only that, you've compromised the whole mission. What in hell's name were you thinking?" He looked from one to the other of us. "In the first place, how'd you even discover each other? I've taken greatest precautions to keep you separated—for your own good..."

"Sir," Blakely said softly, putting his hand on Wafford's shoulder. "It's no good any more. Horst knows all about you, me, Chris."

Wafford pulled away from Blakely and turned on Cunningham. "Lieutenant, I hold you responsible for compromising this mission. Explain to me what happened on stakeout. Tell me how you made contact with Sergeant Blakely."

Chris shrugged. "I wasn't at fault, sir. Edward, here, contacted me first. And insofar as compromising the mission, Colonel, it was already compromised. Apparently, this Horst chap knows your every move. He was here in Frankfurt with several of his men until last night."

"Last night? What happened last night?"

"Three bloody goons abducted me off the street. Were it not for Blakely here, I might not be alive."

"I don't understand. You were supposed to observe the coal yard and leave immediately, if you spotted Horst. Your instructions were to inform me immediately after you positively identified him"

"Well, James, that was the problem. I did not see Horst 'til these hooligans grabbed me and took me inside the warehouse. That's when I recognized Horst."

Wafford's face was purple. The veins in his neck protruded. He took off his hat and crumpled it in his large hand. "I don't understand what yer tell'n me, Lieutenant. Not one iota... And you say Blakely here was on stakeout with you? That was unauthorized. Explain how you got him into this? I ordered Blakely to stay out of sight until I gave him new orders."

"I can explain," said Blakely. "It was my idea. I felt like Chris needed help just in case something happened. And as it turned out, it was good I was there."

"You had no orders to do so, Sergeant. It was entirely out of line...I distinctly ordered you not..."

"But Colonel, don't you see? Had it not been for Blakely here, I would probably have been tortured and murdered by now..."

Wafford shook his head. "You both are insubordinate. You disobeyed my orders. I don't want to hear anymore about it. Clearly, the mission's compromised. Kaput! You both are finished, dismissed. I want you two to turn in final reports and expense statements by 1200 hours tomorrow at the English Bookstore. You are to disassociate yourselves. And if you share one iota about my mission to anyone, I will personally see that you have hell to pay. Is all that clear?"

"Yes, sir," said Blakely. "But could I..."

"Not one iota, Sergeant. It's too late for any explanations. And I would have expected better performance and loyalty from a trained intelligence NCO like yourself."

Wafford turned away and walked a few steps. He turned back. "Give me five minutes. Then you leave next, Lieutenant. I forbid you from discussing any of this with one another after I leave."

They nodded at the colonel and glanced at one another. Both watched the colonel stride across the frozen grass toward the exit. As he disappeared, Chris gave a sigh. "Well, old boy, I blew it."

"How so?"

"It was, after all, my idea that we should meet together."

"Yeah, well, it doesn't matter. Had we told him everything that happened last night, he'd likely have had apoplexy. I'm just glad all three of us are still alive. Aren't you?"

"I feel as though I can breathe again. Now I can take leave to Berlin, enjoy Christmas with Justina. Not worrying whether someone is following me. I purchased her ring a few days ago. Plan to give it to her Christmas Eve."

"I wish you the best, Chris. Maybe we can keep in touch after all this blows over. I think once Jim goes stateside and spends time with his boys, he'll come back with a more balanced perspective, don't you?"

Chris pulled on his pipe and blew smoke. "No, Edward. I think not. The man's daft—as you said yourself in Berlin. My perception is he's beyond helping."

"Yeah. maybe you're right. We did the best we could under the circumstances."

Chris nodded and held out his hand. "Can't say I enjoyed our relationship, Edward, but thank you again. You are a brave man."

"Thank you, Lieutenant. So are you."

"Hardly. Well, Cheerio."

"See you."

Blakely sat down on the cold bench and watched Chris disappear through the exit between the hedges. Such an abortive ending with two men he had come to like in very different ways. All three had been ill-suited for the challenges facing them. The so-called mission had been a total disaster from the very beginning, if one really looked objectively at it.

The two old women got up from the bench on the far side of the pond. One of them turned the paper bag upside down, causing the mallards to scurry about their feet, competing for the last crumbs. The high, whiny voice of Jim Wafford still rang in his ears. Where would his rage take him this afternoon? He hoped Jim wouldn't do something stupid, but you never could tell... He got up slowly, shoved his hands into his pockets, and ambled slowly toward the gate.

Chapter 28

The Gift

Wafford shut the kitchen door and hung his overcoat on a peg. "Louise? Anna? Where is everyone?"

"Up here, Jim," cried Louise. She came down the open stairs, carrying a spool of red ribbon. "Anna and I were wrapping presents. Is something wrong?"

Wafford smiled sheepishly and kissed her on the cheek. "I decided today you deserve something special this Christmas." He handed her an envelope.

"What can this be?"

She opened the envelope to find an airline ticket on Pan American to New York in her name.

"What is this? I thought we were going back together. You said we were leaving on the twenty-seventh."

"I know, Louise. But something's come up. So I thought I'd surprise you and arrange for you to fly out early so you could be with the boys for Christmas."

She looked closer. "Oh my God. This is for tomorrow morning. I can't possibly be ready in time."

"No problem, Louise. Not one iota. Anna and Hans can help you pack. There's nothing to worry about."

"This is all so unexpected. But I wanted us to go together."

"Yeah, well, I have some things to take care of. I'll join you later as we planned. I've already called stateside. The boys have arranged to meet your plane. Ya'll have reservations through New Year's at the Embassy Hotel."

"Well, I don't know what to say. It's such a drastic change. You do remember I invited friends over for drinks and dinner tomorrow night. Anna was planning to serve turkey with your favorite dressing. Will you still be here to enjoy it?"

"No. You'll hafta cancel it. I will be doing some traveling. Unfortunately, Louise, these things have priority. They can't wait any longer. I'm running a close timeline now."

She put her hand on his shoulder. "Will you be all right?"

"Of course I'll be all right. I'll just miss you is all. It's some business I must do, so I thought, why spoil Louise's holiday when she could be with the boys?"

"That's so sweet of you. You are so thoughtful."

"Yeah, well… Hans can drive you to the airport tomorrow morning. Your flight leaves, what time?"

"9:05 a.m."

"Fine. I have another little gift for you. Would you like it now, or shall I give it to you at dinner?"

"Let's wait until dinner. That will give me time to get my little presents together for you. Gosh, this is such a surprise. I just wish I had purchased more gifts to take along. I won't have time."

"You've already sent them plenty of presents. I sent them some money. You being there is the best present they can have."

"Is this something to do with Harry's operation or is it your 'mission' thing?"

"Now, Louise, don't disparage my little project by calling it my 'mission thing.' This has nothing to do with Harry, and I can assure you it isn't dangerous."

"You say that, but I never really know."

"Never you mind." Wafford pulled her to him and kissed her forehead. "Don't you worry your mind one iota."

He pulled away slowly, dropping his hands. "I'm going down to the war room to finish up a little work there. See you at supper. He turned and went down the steps to the wine cellar. He unlocked the door, turned on the lights, and locked the door behind him. He slumped into his swivel chair. He loosened his tie. A bead of sweat formed on his forehead. He pulled out a fresh handkerchief and blotted the perspiration and threw the folded cloth onto the table.

What have I done? You've done what you had to do, he answered himself in a whisper. I didn't let the boys finish… I still

have no earthly idea what happened, 'cept the lieutenant identified Horst. And something 'bout him being captured and Blakely
saving his life? I was out of line, losing my temper like that. So
were they. The whole mission is kaput. Only one thing to do: go
into salvage mode. See if ole Beck will negotiate. Then see the
Schiller woman down in Heidelberg. Maybe even have a talk with
that widow woman down yonder in Trieste...

He picked up the receiver and dialed.

"English Bookstore. Happy Holidays. How can I help you?"

"Even'n, Betty. This is Jim Wafford."

"Merry Christmas, James."

"Yeah. You, too, Betty. Say, listen, Ed Blakely—you remember
him?"

"Most certainly. Nice chap."

"Yeah, well, he's 'sposed to leave a package for me tomorrow
around noon. Could you tell him I apologize for what I said to him
today?"

"Yes. Anything more?"

"Tell him I'll be in Berlin and Heidelberg the next couple days,
but I hope to see him when I get back. Can you tell him that?"

"Yes, James. I'll be sure to tell him."

"Thanks, Betty. See you soon."

"Cheerio."

Chapter 29

Croft is Informed

Louise waited until her husband had opened the war room door and locked it behind him. She quickly climbed the stairs to their upstairs den, sat at the mahogany secretary, and dialed a number.

"Hi, Susan. This is Louise. Is Harry there by chance? Good. May I speak to him a moment? Thank you. Harry? Yes. Thank you, Harry. I just wanted to tell you that Jim has made plans for me to fly by myself to New York tomorrow rather than flying out together as we originally planned. Yes. That's right. No, I don't need transportation. Hans will take me. Harry, why I called was to let you know Jim is going to be working on his 'mission' while I'm gone. I just wanted to let you know. Yes. Would you look after him for me? He won't tell me, but I know he's been anxious the past several days. You will? That's wonderful, Harry. Give Susan my love. And oh, I just remembered. Our dinner party for tomorrow night is off until we get back. All right? Thanks. I hope ya'll have a merry Christmas, too. I will. Thanks. Bye-bye now."

Chapter 30

The Stag is Hunted

It was with a heavy heart that Wafford climbed aboard the BOAC commercial airliner bound for Frankfurt. Like an old stag that had attracted the attention of first the wolves and now the human hunters, he knew he could not find a suitable place where he could stop and face his pursuers. Not only had he misjudged his own abilities, he had miscalculated the numbers and kinds of players involved in the game. Moreover, he had nearly gotten two innocent young men killed.

He had been followed from his home to the airport. He had been followed to Berlin. He recognized two of the men from CID as he approached *Spandau Prison* in a cab. He had assumed that with his specially printed orders—signed yesterday at SHAFE Headquarters—that he would have immediate access to Beck.

It was a final insult that the British guards at *Spandau* refused to allow him to see Beck. Calls to Inspector Krebs and to his close friends at Berlin Headquarters Command were for naught. He was outside the wall, so to speak, without friends, influence or choices.

As he rode back on the plane, he looked closely at the swagger stick with the .50 caliber machine gun shell casing for a handle, a shaft of lemon wood from an English golf stick, and the copper clad bullet at the pointy end. He recalled how he strode around Salzburg in 1945 like a peacock, carrying it proudly because it had been a gift to him from the men in his CIC unit. He recalled how he looked in his Ike jacket, wearing cavalry boots, his father's Colt .45 with its handsome leather holster and leather strings tied to the bottom part of the holster around his leg. Now, examining the nicks and burrs in the shiny copper point, the scratches and scars in the varnished yellow wood, and the dulled finish of the brass casing, he realized the stick was an anomaly, just as he was, and he laid the stick across his lap and looked out the window and watched the propellers turning and felt suddenly very old, out of date, and tired.

He anticipated there would be a large, formal delegation that would meet him at Rhein-Main to take him into custody. Or, they might have just two men there, who would quietly join him on the tarmac and walk with him to an awaiting car. That was how he always liked to conduct those sorts of final ceremonies—quietly, politely, orderly, and with dignity all the way around, so nobody got hurt or too embarrassed. And in all likelihood, the two would be former friends, colleagues, whom he would immediately recognize. That was always an ironic touch that temporarily softened the blow to one's ego.

To his bewilderment, there seemed to be no hounds, wolves or huntsmen standing at the bottom of the steps as he ducked his head through the open door of the aircraft and felt the sting of icy cold on his face and neck. His eyes began to water and his nose began to run. It was difficult to see clearly as he carefully stepped down the steep, moveable stairs to the black tarmac below. Perhaps they're waiting inside where it is warm, he thought, thinking that was the only sensible thing on such a night. It was 1930 hours. He walked in a file with the other passengers across the tarmac to the light of an open doorway where people were gathered, waiting for friends and relatives returning from Berlin.

He stepped into the lighted room, moving through the crowd toward the long corridor leading to the baggage claim area beyond, expecting some hounds to begin nipping his heels or a hunter to step out of the shadows to confront him head-on. Neither occurred. He claimed his B-4 bag and carried it slowly toward the parking lot, feeling his Beretta .25 pressing against his ribs. The capture is always filled with suspense, he considered. It was never when you expected it; most of the time it was on the other fellow's turf.

He pushed through the set of double doors and then through the second set and stepped out to the curb. Hans had the Mercedes running. It was parked in the favored spot, usually reserved for generals. No sign of any pursuers. Maybe they'll let me go home and have a shower first, a bite to eat.

"Evenin' Hans. Thanks fer meetin' me." You could always count on Hans, he thought, as Hans shook his hand and opened the rear door for him. Hans closed it and placed the B-4 bag in the trunk.

Wafford sat back in the soft cushions, allowing himself to settle into the seat and relax. He was sweating again. He took off his favorite *Class A* hat and placed it on the seat next to the swagger stick and reached for a handkerchief with which to wipe his brow, face and neck.

"Is it too warm for you, Colonel?"

"Feels good, Hans. Anything happening while I was away?"

Hans coughed into his hand. "Well, sir, there were a few phone calls from your old colleagues."

"Oh? And who may they be?"

"Sergeant Charon called from Boston, wishing you a merry Christmas. Major Booker at SHAFE wished you well. Harry Croft"

"What did Harry want?"

"Anna took the call. Asked whether you had gone to Berlin or Heidelberg? She told him she wasn't sure."

"Good answer." Well, well, he thought. Old Harry was behind this. I wonder who tipped him off? "How was your holiday, Hans? See your grandchildren?"

"*Jawoll.* We drove to Mainz to see them and have dinner with my daughter and husband. Very nice. My grandchildren are no longer little babies, so they want less to do with old Hans anymore."

"That's what happens, isn't it?" Wafford thought about his own boys and how they had reached a certain age when they didn't want to play the old games or have much to do with Dad or Mom. They needed to find their own way. He looked through the windows at the passing cars and watched absently as the lights of Frankfurt's taller buildings appeared in the distance. He imagined how it was in New York. Louise and the boys must be having a swell time. He missed his boys and his wife terribly at that moment. He wiped his eyes as the car sped toward Eschersheim. It was useless to try talking anymore to Hans. They were both old and could only talk now about the past.

The colonel felt and heard the gravel under the wheels and awoke. He pulled himself alert again. The headlights showed no activity save for the electric Christmas candles in the front windows and the porch light was lit.

"Hans, what is your schedule tonight?"

"I have none, Colonel."

"I have one more favor to ask. Would you mind driving me to the *Hauptbahnhof* after we have something to eat? I have a train to catch at 2230 hours."

"That will be fine, sir."

Wafford opened the kitchen door. Anna was at the refrigerator, sorting through its contents.

"Hi, Anna. How's everything?"

"Mrs. Wafford called you from New York. She said she would try again each day until she reaches you. The number is on the secretary, if you would like to call her."

"Good. Anna, I'm going to take a shower. Would you give Hans something to drink and prepare a little supper for all of us? I'll only be a few minutes. After we eat, Hans is taking me to the train station. I need to catch a train tonight."

"*Ja?* May I ask where you are going?"

"Heidelberg first, then maybe I'll go on down to Trieste. I should be back in a few days."

He turned away and picked up a large package of newspapers Hans had placed near the door to the wine cellar. He opened the door and descended. He dialed the combination and opened the steel door, turned on the light, and looked around. He put the stack of papers and swagger stick on the table. Pulling off his military overcoat and placing it on the chair next to the table, he moved about from one area to another, looking over his many activities and projects. He realized that, like himself, his beloved war room was another relic which had outlasted its usefulness. Everything was becoming electronic now.

There was nothing more to be done by anyone in this room. There was no time, no energy, no reason to come here to solve puzzles or to anticipate the movements of the enemy. He gathered together the photographs and papers from Berlin and placed them in a large manila envelope. He planned to review them on the train.

He moved to the display case, opened it, and removed the green velvet bundle from its place on the top shelf. Untying the brown shoestring, he removed the soft wrapping from the polished wooden relic. He reached into the cabinet again and withdrew a fourteen-inch length of leather boot string, ran it through the leather thong of the relic and tied it securely using a special knot he had learned as a youngster in the Boys Brigade.

Loosening his tie and shirt collar, he placed the leather loop around his neck, inserted the relic inside his shirt, closed the door of the cabinet, and turned away. Glancing at the swagger stick, he opened the cabinet again to put the swagger stick in its place on the shelf, then thought better of it. He closed the cabinet. Taking his coat, the manila envelope and swagger stick, he turned out the light, locked the door, and returned upstairs. Hans and Anna were talking in low voices at the kitchen table.

"Hans, I have a little present for you. Maybe some day, one of your grandchildren would like to have it. I've carried this swagger stick around with me for too many years. Would you like to have it?"

Hans looked up from the kitchen table at the colonel and then at the swagger stick. "*Jawoll*. I would like to have it if you don't want it anymore, Colonel."

"I want you to have it. You have been very good to me."

He gave Hans the swagger stick and turned toward the stairwell. "That is the least I can do to thank you, Hans," he said in that quiet voice he used when he had to maintain control. "I'm going to get my shower. When I come down to dinner, I'd like some hot tea, Anna."

* * *

Wafford felt better for his shower. He shaved and slapped Old Spice on his jowls and ran a comb through his thinning hair. He stood before the mirror and watched as he stretched the boot string over his head and felt the smooth wooden relic against his chest. He chose dark brown trousers, a white shirt, solid green tie, and a beige and brown wool jacket, his brown slouch hat, and brown overcoat. He placed the manila envelope, his toilet articles, two handkerchiefs, two sets of underwear, two dress shirts, two ties, and two pairs of socks in a small, black leather overnight bag. He took one last look in the mirror and went downstairs.

The three sat together at one end of the long dining table. Anna had prepared turkey, cranberry sauce, chestnut stuffing, mashed potatoes, Brussels sprouts, applesauce, and coleslaw, part of the meal Louise had originally planned for Christmas Day.

"Very good, Anna," Wafford said almost in a whisper, not looking up from his plate. "You always make the best chestnut dressing."

"*Danke.*"

They said very little to one another. Wafford glanced at his watch. It had been a long day. He stabbed at his food and chewed half a Brussels sprout before giving up.

"Sorry, Anna. But I'm not that hungry right now."

"*Ja.* I understand, Colonel. Suppose I make you some turkey sandwiches to take with you on the train. Would that be *gut?*"

"That'd be real nice of you. Maybe I can have them before I nap on the train." Wafford glanced at Hans. The old man leaned over his plate, knife and fork in hand, concentrating on eating his food. "How much time before we hafta go, Hans?"

Anna left the table and started preparing the sandwiches. Hans reached into his coat and pulled out a gold pocket watch. "Ten minutes. Plenty of time." He replaced the watch.

Wafford hunched over his plate and picked up his teacup. He sipped the hot, sweet tea slowly, watching Anna wrap two sandwiches in waxed paper. He emptied the cup and sighed. Anna turned. "Would you like more tea, Colonel?"

"No more, thank you."

Wafford watched Anna place the sandwiches and four Tollhouse cookies in a brown bag. She went to the doorway and unzipped his overnight bag and placed the bag in the case. Hans got up from the table. "I'll start the car so it will be warm."

Anna began to clear the plates. "Appreciate all you do, Anna. You, too, Hans." Wafford got up slowly and put on his overcoat and hat.

"Have a safe journey, Colonel," Anna said as Wafford left the house.

Hans timed their arrival at the *Hauptbahnhof* perfectly. Wafford stepped out of the Mercedes. Hans came around and handed him his overnight bag.

"Can you tell me when I should meet you back here?"

"I don't know how long I'll be, Hans. My schedule is sorta open ended." Wafford grinned at the old man and shook his hand. "Have a good New Year, my friend."

Chapter 31

The Defenestration

Wafford turned and left Hans standing there watching him as he walked across the cobblestones to the station entrance. They are here, he sensed, just letting me run. Well, I'll give the bastards a good run for their money. He pretended not to see some of the Americans and nationals sitting in the waiting room watching him from behind newspapers and magazines, some leaning against the great concrete pillars nonchalantly. The cavernous *Hauptbahnhof*, which miniaturized its occupants by its immense dome and marble floor, rang out with voices and echoes of people and trains arriving and departing. He always liked the sound of the train announcers' voices and the echoes of them, much like the sounds at Mammoth Cave or some of the grottoes he had visited in Spain.

The prospects of riding in a train to any destination always filled him with excitement and anticipation. When he spotted one of Croft's men, however, his heart sank. The stag was being brought to bay; the hunters were all within range. Yet he kept walking, out through the swinging double doors to the cold, semi-dark platform with its high, domed roof of iron frames, glass panels, soot and pigeons. Half a dozen long trains waited their turn to be pulled out of the station by noisy steam engines, diesels and the quiet electrics.

He remembered the many times when he would come here just to see and hear the steam engines with their great power and plumes of steam and smoke, watching them huff and puff their way out of the station, tugging and pulling the heavy cars until they picked up speed and moved along on shiny, stainless steel wheels which sometimes screeched and howled against the rails.

But now, he had to use all his energy just to keep walking without seeming to be aware of all the eyes upon him. He moved through the gate and out along the gray cars with their dirty windows, where hot, smelly steam hissed beneath them as they were being prepared for departure.

A conductor helped him as he lifted himself up the steep metal steps, holding onto the cold bar-rail and moving through the passenger car door that was always stiff and hard to open. He was out of breath and sweating profusely as he moved down the narrow aisle to his compartment. Number eight. It was just what he needed, to be by himself, he thought. If they wanted to follow him to Heidelberg, that was okay with him. He opened the compartment, threw his bag on the long seat, locked the door, and took off his overcoat, jacket and hat.

He washed his face at the little sink. Just give me time to talk to this woman Schiller and maybe Miz Swartzlander. That's all I ask. I'll go on to Munich and down to Trieste, if they are curious enough to let me do it. That's it. That's why they aren't taking me in. He dried his face on the hand towel and replaced it on the rack. The idea gave him new energy. They know I'm close to solving the puzzle, and they won't take me until I solve it for them. Then, they'll arrest me on a bunch of charges. At least they are keeping Horst off my back.

A whistle sounded. The train jerked into movement almost at the same instant. Right on time, as usual. He was on his way. He shifted over to the window and opened the shade. The lights above the brick wall came from the *Gutleut Kaserne.* Blakely was probably there in one of the rooms, fast asleep. He realized he had been too tough on the boy. Lights of factories and train yards flashed intermittently until everything went black. The train had entered a cut and then a tunnel.

He pulled the curtain down, turned on the small reading light in the wall, and got out his little book of names, addresses, and telephone numbers. In the back of the book was the address and telephone number of Katrin von Rosenheim Schiller. He hadn't warned her of his impending visit, but planned to call her in the morning from his hotel.

As he sat back and rested, he touched the outside of his shirt and stroked the outline of the fragment, which hung from the leather string around his neck. The light pressure of the boot string now felt uncomfortable on the back of his neck. The wood felt smooth and cool against his chest, however, and he took comfort in its smoothness and remembrance of all the times and places and operations of the past when he had worn it beneath his uniform as a good luck charm. Strange to say, but he realized it had become more a part of him than either his dog tags or his wedding ring.

He pulled the overnight bag closer and began unzipping it. He stopped. No. He wouldn't try to go through Blakely's reports tonight. He was too exhausted to look at anything or think about his day in Heidelberg tomorrow or his plans after that. Instead, he reached down and removed the brown paper sack. Good Anna, he thought, as he opened it and unwrapped a turkey sandwich with cranberry jelly, salt and pepper, lettuce and mayonnaise. He unfolded the waxed paper and spread it on his lap, placed one half on the paper, and lifted the other half of sandwich to his mouth. He bit off a large mouthful. It was good. He looked across at the sink to be sure there were paper cups in the brass rack. He would have the water later. He wanted to concentrate on the taste of turkey with just the right amounts of salt and pepper. He dropped his head back on the cushioned seat and felt himself dozing off, feeling the small portion of sandwich in his left hand. He allowed himself to sink back in the cushioned seat, dropping his hand onto the remaining half of the sandwich on the waxed paper on his lap.

He barely heard the click. There was no chance to scream or shout or swear. An arm went around his head. He couldn't see. He punched at the body above him to no avail. Something was stuffed into his mouth. Hands gripped his ankles and jerked him to the floor. His head thumped against the carpet. A heavy weight upon his stomach took his breath away. He couldn't move his arms. He gasped for air. The weight shifted. It was easier to breathe, but hands were tearing his shirt and undershirt away, a tug at his neck, then a snap. His body was turned slightly. Another hand was removing his wallet from his back pocket. Something struck the side of his head with a plop, numbing the left side of his face. Searing pain engulfed his head and left arm. There was a sensation of being lifted, shifted, pushed into freezing wind. His face burned with cold. A rushing noise, the rancid smell of burning coal. He felt a push, floating weightless in the wind, then slammed against something hard, cold, his tangled body cracking into pieces of sharp pain. He lay there realizing the sensation of slipping away, his senses clouding, his legs and arms growing colder, not able to move, not really caring to move, not...

Chapter 32

Worst News

Blakely walked out of the theater, adjusted his eyes to bright neon lights and the sounds of the boulevard. *The Man in the Gray Flannel Suit* had been enjoyable. They had found the perfect German voice for Gregory Peck. He pulled his collar up. The walk back to the *Gutleut Kaserne* was invigorating after spending nearly two hours in the stuffy movie house where half the people smoked. He entered the barrack and was about to climb the stairs when Nash called to him.

"Hey, Blakely?"

"Yes?"

"Got a message for you. You're 'sposed to report to CID, Room 100, at 0730 hours tomorrow morning in *Class B* uniform."

His face warmed. "Did they say what it's about?"

"No. Sergeant Kentop told me to make certain you received his message. He also cautioned not to be late."

Oh, shit. So Kentop is CID. It makes sense. He climbed the steps with a weight settling in his chest. Kentop checked me out on courier duty. He was at the bus terminal when Chris and I were on stakeout. He would have been my partner, had I agreed to do courier duty the other day. Maybe that invitation was intended to keep me out of trouble. And I turned them down. Yeah. It all fit. CID must have known every move we made.

He glanced at his watch. 2200 hours. He considered calling Betty and arranging a meeting with Chris and Jim, but he presumed they were also contacted. Maybe, in Jim's case, Kentop and his superiors had actually driven to Eschersheim and arrested him. No. They couldn't have done that. What am I thinking? Wafford is in Heidelberg, or possibly on his way to Trieste by now. He wished he could contact Jim, let him know the jig was up, but there was no way. Besides, Jim knew what he was getting into when he started his damned mission. Now, they were all in trouble. And it was his fault that Chris was caught up in it. Hell, Chris had wanted out and he convinced him to stay involved to help him to protect Jim. Well, that was a laugh and a half. Protect a retired lieutenant colonel? Who had he been kidding?

He showered and climbed into his bunk. Lester was gone for the night. No doubt spending the night with his fiancée. Poor bastard. He had to face his family back in Tennessee in a few weeks. He's been worrying for days what they'd think of his future bride. Why am I saying Lester's the poor bastard? Hell, I'm in deeper shit than he'll ever be in, and I'm talking like I don't have problems. My success in the military is ending in disgrace. I'll probably be demoted to private and given a dishonorable discharge for all my shenanigans. Maybe sentenced to a stockade cell for six months. And I thought at the time that I was doing the right thing. I was helping Jim by keeping him from going off the deep end. Playing Holden Caulfield. Yeah. Sure. *Frau* Schiller was right about human nature. It's all about ego. Easy Ed Blakely was doing all this shit to show off how good he was. How he's better than Cunningham or all those other guys will ever be.

He tried to calm himself and not to think about all that had happened during the past three weeks. He rolled and tossed. Images of *Nazis* appeared. He was being chased. They would almost catch him and he would come awake. Sweat bathed his face and neck. He sat up and pulled his T-shirt off, wiped his face and neck with it, and threw it on the floor. He dozed intermittently, chased by thugs until he awakened again with a start. Around 0400 hours, he drifted off.

* * *

The clerk ushered Blakely into a conference room where four officers and one enlisted—Kentop—sat stiffly along one side of a long, wooden table. Blakely came to attention and saluted. The officer in the center returned the salute and said "At ease." He motioned with his arm for Blakely to sit on one of two leather chairs across from him. He sat down and placed both arms on the table, folding his hands together.

"Sergeant Blakely, let me introduce myself. I am Colonel Charles McVey, chief of CID. On my left is Colonel Harry Croft, G-2, ASA Europe, Lieutenant Tom McCloud, on his left, Colonel Croft's liaison with CID. On my right is Major Elliot Thrasher, my deputy, and to my far right is Sergeant Thomas Kentop, a CID investigator, who, I believe, you've met before."

"Yes, sir. More than once." Blakely tried to smile as he leaned in, making eye contact with each man. He felt quite calm under the pressure. They were all gazing at him with serious expressions.

McVey pulled a sheaf of papers closer and opened a black eyeglass case. He took out a pair of silver wire glasses and adjusted them. The guy was probably in his late forties, graying hair, big shouldered, wearing his tie slightly askew as though he'd been up working very early. He cleared his throat. "I have very bad news for you, Sergeant Blakely."

Blakely feared the worst. Yes, they were going to court martial him. He knew it. This was the end of the line for Easy Ed Blakely in the military. The rest of his life would be tainted with disgrace. Christ! How could this happen after doing so well at Army Intelligence School, at Language School, at Mac?

"Your friend Colonel James Wafford is dead."

"What?" Blakely could hardly breathe. "Excuse me, sir, but did you say Colonel Wafford is dead?"

"That is correct, Sergeant. I am deeply sorry. I know the two of you became friends."

"But how, sir? Last I knew, he went to Berlin and was going from there to Heidelberg?"

"True. It happened on the Heidelberg train."

"Yes, sir?"

"Two of Eugen Horst's men—I believe you've encountered them before–broke into his compartment, stole a Minoan artifact from around his neck, and threw him out the train window. What is known as a *defenestration*. He was found in a corn field near Morfelden by a farmer yesterday afternoon."

"Oh, my god." Tears welled. Blakely clenched his hands together. "I bear some responsibility for that, sir."

"How's that, Sergeant?" The Colonel removed his glasses. "Explain what you mean."

Blakely steadied himself, taking a deep breath before attempting to answer. "I failed to obtain certain information for Colonel Wafford from a woman in Heidelberg, sir. Had I gotten what he needed, Jim Wafford would not have been on that train."

McVey and Croft shook their heads negatively. Croft said, "No, son. You had nothing to do with the Colonel's death. It could've happened any time, anywhere. Unfortunately, none of us could prevent it from happening. And believe me, we tried our best to protect Jim Wafford from harm."

McVey replaced his glasses and removed the top sheet of paper and glanced at the next one. "We're not here this morning to assign blame, Sergeant. This is merely a preliminary hearing to develop a chronology of events leading up to the Colonel's murder. A formal inquiry into this whole matter will be conducted sometime later. I can assure you that we are not in any way accusing you of violating military rules of conduct. We'd like to take a deposition telling us about every communication and event relative to your relationship with Colonel Wafford. Are you willing to do that?"

Blakely rubbed his chin momentarily. "Yes, sir."

"Very good, Sergeant. Major Thrasher and Sergeant Kentop will guide you through the process. Shouldn't take a long time, since we'll be recording your statements on tape."

"Yes, sir." Blakely touched his mouth with his hand, considering. "There's one more thing I'd like to say."

"Yes?"

"It's about First Lieutenant Cunningham, sir."

"What about him."

"I hope you won't find him in violation of military conduct either, sir. I hafta tell you I convinced him to keep working for Jim Wafford. Chris wanted to quit when it appeared to him that the Colonel was getting into dangerous territory. In all honesty, Lieutenant Cunningham is innocent of any wrongdoing, sir. All he did until the stakeout that night was to conduct interviews. He was trying to earn some extra money for his wedding is all. He wouldn't have done the stakeout without my encouragement and support. Besides that, he's just before getting promoted to captain. I beg you to consider these things when you make your report about his involvement, sir."

McVey's frown softened into a weak smile. "You seem overly protective, Sergeant, especially for someone who just arrived on assignment from stateside. First, you say it was your fault that the Colonel was murdered. You also contend that it was your fault that Lieutenant Cunningham got in over his head working for the colonel." McVey turned and grinned at Croft before looking back at Blakely. "How do you explain why you feel so guilty?"

Blakely pulled himself ramrod straight in the chair. "Guess if I'd done my job better, I could've kept both of them out of trouble, sir. I'd hate to see Lieutenant Cunningham's career ruined because of all this."

McVey turned toward Croft "Harry, do you have anything to ask Sergeant Blakely?"

Croft gave Blakely a soft smile. "No, Colonel. I look forward to having Sergeant Blakely in our shop. He's obviously a team player."

"That's what I'm thinking," said McVey. "Sergeant, do you have any further questions we can answer before your deposition is taken?"

"Yes, sir. I don't understand, sir. I assume you had some men on that train. How'd it happen that Colonel Wafford could be killed?"

McVey nodded his head while looking down at the table. He raised his head. "Hindsight being what it is, we should have placed one of our men outside the Colonel's locked compartment once he was inside. We didn't. We had a man at either end of the train, thinking that Horst's men would make a move at some point after the Colonel arrived in Heidelberg. We were wrong. The two men who killed Wafford had a compartment in the same car. They jimmied the lock, overpowered the Colonel, and threw his body out the window after ripping the Minoan fragment from his neck. They cleaned out his compartment, returned to their own, and tried to debark the train at Weinheim. We knew Weinheim was not their destination, so we arrested them. One of them had the fragment and Jim Wafford's wallet in his pocket.

"When our people had the conductor unlock Colonel Wafford's compartment, they were shocked to find nothing there. No body, no signs of any struggle, no suitcase. Not even his hat or coat. We made a search of all the compartments on the train. Nothing. It was hours later—that afternoon—when Morfelden police reported an unidentified body was found in a field near the railroad. A preliminary report shows the Colonel must have died upon impact. His coat, hat, toilet articles, and leather case were found by our people scattered down the tracks."

Blakely shook his head, tears welling. "Wow." All of it was so unreal, so unbelievable.

"Do you have any other questions?"

"Yes, sir. What about Horst?"

"Eugen Horst was arrested yesterday morning at the Heidelberg train station. Seems he drove down, expecting to meet his cronies when the train arrived. We found maps and ID papers in his car that suggest the plan was to head to the East German border. He's now in custody at Rhein-Main Air Force Base. Do you have any other questions?

Blakely hung his head down. "Guess not, sir."

"Anyone have anything to add?" McVey looked in both directions, then turned back to Blakely. "We'll give you a ten minute break to collect your thoughts before you meet with Major Thrasher. There's coffee and doughnuts and a restroom through that door." He pointed at a door behind Blakely. "Gentlemen, you're dismissed."

Blakely stood at attention as everyone filed out of the room except Croft "At ease, Sergeant," Croft said softly, placing a hand on Blakely's shoulder. "I'm awfully sorry for the bad news... Jim was at heart a good man. I worked with him close to seven years. I'll miss him and I know you will, too."

"Yes, sir. Just wish he'd gone stateside with his wife like he was supposed to."

"Yeah. That was the plan we hoped he'd follow. We knew something was up when he changed his mind. It all unraveled so quickly, though."

"Yes, sir. Has Mrs. Wafford been notified?"

Croft glanced away. "I spoke with Louise last evening. Twice. She was quite devastated, as you can imagine."

"I'm sure, sir." There was something about Croft he didn't like. Perhaps he was only imagining it, but Croft seemed too smooth somehow. Suave? More than suave. There was something artificial about him. Like, he really wasn't feeling as badly over Jim Wafford's death as he said he did. He tried to dismiss the thought, thinking his mind was too mixed up with so many emotions to consider such things. This was no time to judge others...

Croft looked up and patted Blakely on the shoulder. "Yeah, well... At least she has the two boys with her. That's some consolation."

Croft dropped his arm, tried to smile, and offered his hand. "I'm looking forward to having you on our team, young man." They shook hands.

"Me, too, sir."

"After you finish your deposition, I suggest you pack a bag and go off to the mountains someplace. Schruns, maybe. Go somewhere where there's not a lot of people. Go skiing. Do some cross-country. There's good snow right now. Put what's happened out of your mind for a while. You've got plenty of time. Clearances won't be granted for at least another month."

"Thank you, sir. I just might do that."

"You should. It'll do you good. See you in February."

"Yes, sir."

Croft walked across the room and closed the door quietly behind him. Blakely sank into the chair and dropped his head into his hands. Stay easy, stay easy, he whispered to himself. Heave to, but don't break. The image of Jim Wafford lying in a heap, dead, in a snowy cornfield was impossible to shake. And no matter what CID said about it, he felt to blame down to his very soul.

Chapter 33

Reflection

Blakely peered into the mirror as he formed a Windsor knot in the black and red regimental tie. Only three weeks ago, he had stood for the first time before this very mirror, dressing himself in the same clothes: the Oxford button down, the gray flannels, the *Florsheims*, the tweed jacket, and the *London Fog*. He recalled his high hopes for meeting some *frauleins* and working with Sylvester Charon and Jim Wafford.

What a difference three weeks could make. The world he had known was changed forever. He cinched the knot and drew it tighter beneath the collar, pulling on the two ends and making sure the dimple in the tie was centered. He was not sure why he was getting so dressed up because he had no particular place to go, no plans. Yet he felt it important that he not hang around the barrack room moping. Everyone else had split.

He thought back over the disastrous morning. The process of giving a deposition was not in any way like McVey had described. Instead of an hour, it had taken all morning. Instead of just Kentop and Thatcher, there had been two lawyers from the Judge Advocate Section sitting in and listening to every word. A court reporter had been there taking notes beside the technician operating the tape recorder. He had been compelled to turn over the key to the storage locker at the *Hauptbahnhof* to Thatcher so the documents there could support his testimony. It was serious shit. And he did not know whether he wouldn't come under indictment in the future, despite McVey's assurances that he would not. He had gone over and over the events of the morning without any resolve.

And after the sadness of Jim's death had lifted, it was replaced by growing anger. Wafford had deceived him, taken advantage of his naivety, and put him in harm's way. How could he do such a thing? The very thought of Jim Wafford brought a wave of contempt.

He threw the trench coat over his shoulder and descended the stairs and fled out the door. Barracks lights in the quadrangle cast a dull sheen on the wet cobbles. It was warmer. A fog was closing in, enveloping him in moist air. He put on the trench coat and buttoned it. Most of the ice from the sleet storm had melted. He turned in one street and then another, not caring where he was heading. What was that Chinese proverb? You must change direction, unless you intend to arrive at the direction in which you are headed? It went something like that. No matter.

Eventually, he realized he was approaching the bridge that crossed the Main River to Saxonhausen just below Haldermann's Coal Yard. He walked to the center of the span and leaned against the metal rails. The condensation coming off the water had the scent of diesel fuel. Christmas lights blinked here and there in the fog. No boat traffic, hardly any cars on the streets. He glanced toward the darkness of the coal yard. Some night that was. Flakely Blakely Rescues Air Force Officer from *Nazi* Thugs. Yea!

Bells began to toll. It's strange how you can tell the rich churches from the poor ones. The rich have deep, sonorous bell tones while the poor ones sound tinny, cheap by comparison. Christmas Eve. That's why they're ringing. The *Tenente* might be down on one knee this very moment, proposing his eternal love to Justina. He imagined her in tears as Chris asked her to be his lawful, wedded wife. Were they tears of joy or sadness? Probably both, he surmised. Yes, she would save Chris from himself one way or another, make him a respected archeologist at least in the minds of the local populace. But she would know better, that he would be just another keeper of mostly stolen artifacts like she was, while the real archeologists were out there digging up new graves and looting old treasures for their own fame and fortune.

They were to hold a special memorial service after Christmas for Jim. Croft was in charge of arrangements. He was still debating whether to attend. He tried to disregard the anger he felt boiling around in his chest. Jim Wafford knew better than to get everybody in over their heads. Right now, he hated Jim Wafford for what he did to Chris, to himself, to his wife, to his children, to his reputation. All for nothing. Winner take nothing.

He reached back, remembering the last time he went sailing just before coming to Germany. It was an especially windy day with whitecaps, thirty-five knot gusts, and he had taken extra precautions by checking sheets, sails, grommets, knots, cables, tiller, stays and turnbuckles. He wanted to extend himself beyond where he normally allowed himself to reach, as he felt an immense energy and spirit welling up from within, which he hoped would match the strength of the westerly winds. He could feel the boat strain and knew something could snap at any time. But he had faith in himself and understood that his boat was the result of thousands of years of experiment and design. It was the best man could build—with all the extraneous and incorrect elements discarded. His boat was the essence of man's belief in his own creation.

He remembered how grand was the feeling of that last sail as his boat lifted silently on the wind and he hiked out to the max and flew across the water toward Mission Point. Waves slapped the bow; foam splashed his face. Two small porpoises dove and came up to glisten momentarily before diving again before the prowl. They seemed to take such delight in leading him across the bay through the whitecaps, just the three of them together sharing a moment in time before going their separate ways. He wished he were back there, now, doing what he was supposed to be doing in life, rather than playing military games that he knew in his heart he could never fathom.

He leaned over the rail and spat into the roiling water surrounding the bridge support. No, he thought. I can't hate Wafford any more than I can hate anybody. He suddenly felt terribly sad. Tears flowed and dropped off his cheeks. *Father No Name* would be in his forties by now. Perhaps he was a merchant marine working this very river tonight. Christmas. Jim Wafford. *Father No Name.* If you don't know *your father*, how can you know *the Father.* He wanted to pray, but he couldn't. He had tried often from the time he was a kid. It didn't work. He wiped his eyes with a handkerchief and wondered how his grandparents—his legal parents—were preparing to celebrate Christmas. Mom was probably making chestnut dressing. Dad was likely splitting wood for a nice fire.

He pushed away from the rail and turned back. There was no way to resolve what he felt. All his resources, all his skills, all his talents had been taken from him, leaving him empty and without hopes. And he supposed that if he could think of forty-four different solutions to his problem, none of them would have a happy ending.

Chapter 34

A Decent Ending

The call was so unexpected. Cunningham said he would like to meet him at the English Bookstore at 1700 hours to say good-bye before leaving in the morning for Fort Hamilton. Blakely had called ahead and asked Betty whether he and Chris could use her office behind the store. It was her idea to make the occasion a sort of going away party. She planned to serve tea and scones. Blakely encouraged her to join them.

Blakely swung down from the trolley onto the sidewalk. His Ike jacket was too hot. He was sweating, but knew better than to take it off while on duty. Flowers were blooming along the island between the tracks and the boulevard, an abundance of colors. *May-time, the only pretty ring time* came into Blakely's head unbidden. One of the English lyric poets, he thought, trying to recall the period. Renaissance? Had to be Renaissance. Senior English. Yeah. He entered the bookstore to the tinkling bell over the door. Betty appeared in the doorway to her office and smiled at his entrance. Her bright yellow dress, white apron, lipstick and touches of rouge made her look younger and less spinsterish, he thought.

"Hi, Betty. Thanks for going to the trouble of making tea." She held out her hand and Blakely took it and gave it a squeeze.

"My pleasure, Edward. It was quite a surprise, really. I never expected to hear from Lieutenant Cunningham again."

"Me neither."

"Come on back. I'm just now putting the cozy on the teapot."

He followed her behind the counter and into a large back room that served as a combination kitchen, office, book packing and shipping station, and storage area for additional books. In the center of the room was an oblong wooden table where Betty had placed lace doilies, white napkins, white cups and saucers. A record was playing on the phonograph in the corner. He didn't recognize the music. "Unusual tune, Betty. What is it?"

"Shubert's *Nocturne in D for Strings*. Yes. It is quite different from his other trios and quartets. I only play it on special occasions."

"Never heard it before."

"You don't hear it played often. Do make yourself comfortable." She motioned toward one of four wood and leather chairs at the dining table. She went about tending to a double burner hot plate upon which a metal teakettle was letting off steam. She removed it and poured the tea into a pretty green tea pot. She took a red-flowered, insulated tea cozy and placed it over the pot.

"We finally get to have our tea," Blakely said, smiling. He tucked his overseas cap into his belt.

"Your rain check."

"You have a great memory."

Betty turned and smiled. "I knew from the beginning that you and I would become good friends. And we have, haven't we? You, me, and Mr. Hemingway."

"True."

Betty strode over to a closet next to a tiny refrigerator on the counter and pulled out a baker's box and opened it. She carefully arranged several scones on a large white plate and brought it to the table. She went back to the closet and retrieved three smaller plates, a green cream pitcher and green sugar bowl that matched the green teapot and arranged them on the table. She pulled out silver spoons from a drawer and placed them around. She reminded Blakely of Wanda Landovska hovering over her harpsichord with those talons of fingers, making sure she struck the right keys in proper sequence in a difficult section of a Bach concerto, yet she at the same time did it so effortlessly. "Do I have everything," she muttered.

It was rhetorical, but Blakely felt some response was in order. "I think you've done it perfectly, Betty. Chris, being the anglophile that he is, will be totally delighted."

"Do you really think so?"

"Absolutely."

"Oh, the sugar." She filled the sugar bowl from a bag in the closet.

The bell tinkled. Blakely stood while Betty went out front. "Welcome, Christopher," she announced. "And you are now a captain! My congratulations."

"Thank you, Betty. Has Edward arrived yet?"

"He's here. Come." They appeared in the doorway. Blakely stood up. He had to admit that Chris Cunningham looked much more military than how he remembered him. Sharply creased trousers, spit-shined shoes, the proper dimple in his tie, and two silver bars on each shoulder. His brown hair was freshly trimmed. They shook hands.

"Well, old boy, I didn't expect I'd want to see you again, but after five months, I felt it only right that I say a proper good-bye and tell you once again how grateful I am for what you did that night on the river."

"Yeah, well, thanks for the phone call. It meant a lot, Chris. The way we left it just wasn't right."

"I totally agree." Chris placed his *Class A* officer's hat on the counter. He seemed to scrutinize Blakely in military fashion as only a ninety day wonder officer would do. "I see you haven't changed, Edward. Still the maverick…"

Blakely smirked. "What is it this time?"

Chris shook his head from side to side while grinning. "How do they let you get away with it?"

"With what?"

"Your shoes, Edward. They haven't been shined probably in a year."

Blakely looked down at his shoes. True. They were scuffed and unpolished. He looked back at Chris. "Not high on my priority list, Captain."

"I should say not." They all sat down, Betty between them. Chris pulled out his pipe and began loading it. He looked around. Blakely supposed he was looking for an ashtray. Finding none, he put his pipe back in his jacket pocket. "You are one of a kind."

Blakely pushed back in his chair. "Yeah. I like it that way."

"You two boys have more to talk about than scruffy shoes," said Betty, holding her hands together in an appeal for peace. "Now, who would like tea and a scone?"

Blakely and Cunningham grinned at each other while reaching at the same time for the same scone. Betty poured tea.

Same priggish Cunningham, thought Blakely. Can't leave well enough alone. "So what are your plans?"

"Glad you asked. Justina and I are getting married next month. I've obtained a faculty position at the university, thanks to Dr. Schaus."

"It's all working out, then."

"I'm so happy for you," said Betty.

"Yes. I'll be returning from Fort Hamilton within the week. I begin my teaching duties starting in August. That will give Justina and I ample time to settle in. And what about you, Edward? You enjoying your work?"

Chris lifted a scone to his mouth and bit off a chunk, leaving a few crumbs around his mouth.

"Yeah. It's quite interesting. Doing plenty of monitoring. Can't tell you more than that, but, yeah, it's fun to see the bigger picture."

"Have you changed your mind about staying in?"

"No. I'm looking forward to going back to California. I belong on my own boat."

"I would agree. I take it you are working under James's old boss, Colonel Croft?"

Blakely took a swig of tea. "At first I was. I guess you heard about the Senate investigation into Jim's death. Seems they were concerned about breaches of security. Scuttlebutt has it that Croft allowed Jim to use certain military resources he shouldn't have had access to after he retired."

"But why would he have done that," asked Betty.

"One scenario says Croft and Professor Storey were using Jim in hopes that he would discover where the Habsburg gold and jewels were hidden. Anyway, soon after the Senate investigation, Croft was ordered stateside. I heard from a friend at Mac that he was forced to retire. As for the professor, he's still here in Germany writing and publishing."

Chris wiped the crumbs away with a napkin. "What would they have stood to gain out of it?"

"There was some talk that Harry Croft intended to make a deal with Jim. He would let Jim use some resources and protect him for a share of the booty. Of course, that is only a rumor. How Professor Storey fits in is anybody's guess. Anyway, it was all hushed up by last month. Have you heard anymore about it, Betty?"

"Nothing. I find it difficult to believe Professor Storey would involve himself in such sordid affairs. After all, he is quite successful, a Fullbright scholar and all."

Blakely sipped and held the cup in both hands. "After seeing how the agencies operate over the last few months, I really don't believe Jim needed to depend on Croft for resources in his operations."

"How's that," asked Cunningham.

"With all the agencies competing for dollars, they work against each other. The Air Force doesn't communicate with the Army. The Navy does its own thing. Then you have several intelligence agencies that don't talk to each other: FBI, ASA, CIC, NSA, CIA, and a bunch more. They all withhold their data until they can put on a show for Arlington or the White House. I guess what I'm saying is that Jim Wafford saw all this separateness developing as the cold war changed the way we did things.

"Jim was clever enough to take full advantage. He moved along the seams between agencies, using whatever agency he needed. He could get orders printed in one agency and apply them to another. It was simple. He could get whatever he wanted because he knew people in all the agencies. That's how you and I got involved, Chris. You were Air Force. I was Army. Jim chose us from two different branches so there would be no communication between us—or so he thought.

"And that is where Harry Croft comes in. Jim trusted Harry as an old colleague. But Harry knew Jim was onto something big, so he began to monitor Jim's activities, which ended up with us being monitored as well. Unfortunately, even Harry Croft couldn't predict what would happen when Horst and his guys returned to Germany. It got out of Croft's control as well as Jim's. And Harry didn't seek help from CID until it was too late."

Chris reached across and took another scone. "I can't agree with you more. By the way, Betty, these cherry scones are delicious."

"Thank you, Christopher."

He set the scone on his plate. "Justina and I have talked about the two fragments of the relic. Given that two murders were committed because of them, I've convinced her that they do hold the key as to where Heinrich von Etter hid the treasure. We also believe James knew more than what he ever shared with you and me. Would you agree, Edward?"

"For sure. You mentioned one time that you located Freddie Braun, but that he was ill and you couldn't interview him."

"Yes."

"You also said Jim followed up and actually spoke with him before Braun died. Is it possible that Braun also had a piece of the relic?"

"Now that you mention it, that's most plausible."

"More tea," asked Betty.

"Please," said Blakely. "Ever been down in Jim's war room in the wine cellar?"

Both Betty and Chris shook their heads negatively.

"Well, it was quite something: an authentic World War II war room, replete with maps, telephones, files, orders of battle. I suspect he had all sorts of stuff hidden down there. Ironically, I understand it was Harry Croft who assisted CID in sifting through all of Jim's files in preparation for the official investigation. No telling what he may have copied or stolen."

"Ah, well. Perhaps, Edward, some things will come to light in the future. Justina and I would love nothing more than to do an archeological expedition on Crete to determine the origin of the relic. We suspect that our search could lead us directly to the treasure… But right now, there is insufficient evidence to even consider such an adventure."

"Yeah. It is intriguing to think about, isn't it?"

Chris pushed back his chair and stood up. "Yes. Well, old boy, I must be going. Betty, thank you for the wonderful tea and delicious scones. Edward, I wish you luck."

"I wish you and Justina all the best."

"Thank you. I hope to make one last plea to my father before we marry… His blessing would mean so much to both of us."

Blakely patted him on the back. They shook hands. Chris looked once more down at Blakely's shoes before turning and walking toward the door. "Cheerio!"

"Cheerio"

"See you," said Blakely, watching as Betty waved and Chris went out the door.

Betty turned and smiled wanly at Blakely. "Good of him to stop by."

"Yeah. A decent ending to the nightmare after all."

"And where are you in the short stories?"

"I finished *The Faithful Bull* and just started *Fathers and Sons.*

Betty smiled. "Very good. You're making progress."

Blakely studied her for a moment. "Just out of curiosity, Betty, are you with one of the agencies?"

Betty looked directly at him, lowering her hand from her mouth. "You should know better by now, Edward. You do not ask such questions."